THE HUNT FOR THE HOLY GRAIL

A James Acton Thriller

Also by J. Robert Kennedy

James Acton Thrillers

The Protocol
Brass Monkey
Broken Dove
The Templar's Relic
Flags of Sin
The Arab Fall
The Circle of Eight
The Venice Code
Pompeii's Ghosts
Amazon Burning
The Riddle
Blood Relics
Sins of the Titanic

Saint Peter's Soldiers
The Thirteenth Legion
Raging Sun
Wages of Sin
Wrath of the Gods
The Templar's Revenge
The Nazi's Engineer
Atlantis Lost
The Cylon Curse
The Viking Deception
Keepers of the Lost Ark
The Tomb of Genghis Khan
The Manila Deception
The Fourth Bible

Embassy of the Empire
Armageddon
No Good Deed
The Last Soviet
Lake of Bones
Fatal Reunion
The Resurrection Tablet
The Antarctica Incident
The Ghosts of Paris
No More Secrets
The Curse of Imhotep
The Heretics Bible
The Hunt for the Holy Grail

Dylan Kane Thrillers

Rogue Operator
Containment Failure
Cold Warriors
Death to America
Black Widow

The Agenda
Retribution
State Sanctioned
Extraordinary Rendition
Red Eagle

The Messenger
The Defector
The Mole
The Arsenal
The Betrayal

Just Jack Thrillers

You Don't Know Jack

Jack Be Nimble

Templar Detective Thrillers

The Templar Detective
The Parisian Adulteress
The Sergeant's Secret

The Unholy Exorcist
The Code Breaker

The Black Scourge
The Lost Children
The Satanic Whisper

Kriminalinspektor Wolfgang Vogel Mysteries

The Colonel's Wife

Sins of the Child

Delta Force Unleashed Thrillers

Payback
Infidels
The Lazarus Moment
Kill Chain

Forgotten
The Cuban Incident
Rampage

Inside the Wire
Charlie Foxtrot
A Price Too High
Righteous Hell

Detective Shakespeare Mysteries

Depraved Difference

Tick Tock

The Redeemer

Zander Varga, Vampire Detective

The Turned

THE
HUNT
FOR THE
HOLY GRAIL

A James Acton Thriller

J. ROBERT KENNEDY

For James Earl Jones, who both terrified and delighted us.

May the Force be with you.

Always.

THE
HUNT
FOR THE
HOLY GRAIL

A James Acton Thriller

"Then Jesus said unto them, Verily, verily, I say unto you, Except ye eat the flesh of the Son of man, and drink his blood, ye have no life in you. Whoso eateth my flesh, and drinketh my blood, hath eternal life; and I will raise him up at the last day."

John 6:53-54
King James Version

"We do not worship, we do not adore, for fear that we should bow down to the creature rather than to the creator, but we venerate the relics of the martyrs in order the better to adore Him (God) whose martyrs they are."

Words of St. Jerome
A.D. 420

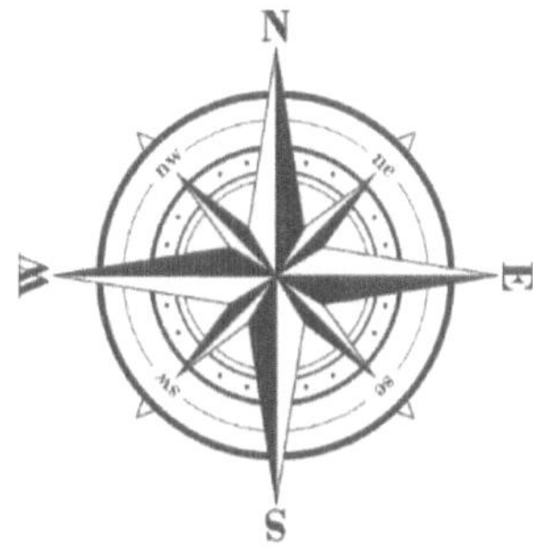

PREFACE

Is the Holy Grail real? Many believe it is because it is in the Bible, however they would be wrong. No mention of it is made in the New Testament. It was a fiction created by medieval writers, first in *Le Conte du Graal* (The Story of the Grail), written around 1180 by Chrétien de Troyes, a French poet. Later writers expanded the lore, linking it to the Arthurian legend, and to Joseph of Arimathea, claiming he had collected the blood of Jesus after the crucifixion using the Holy Grail. Again, there is no mention of this in the Bible.

What is in the Bible are multiple descriptions of the Last Supper. There are specific references to Jesus raising His cup and referring to its contents as His blood. This entire interaction led to what Catholics now recognize as Communion. If we believe there was a Last Supper, then there had to be a cup. Jesus and his apostles had to drink out of something.

So, what if this cup, used by Jesus at the Last Supper, had been recognized at the time for what it might represent? And if the words He spoke were taken literally, someone could believe this cup indeed contained His power.

What would happen if that cup were found thousands of years later?

Would it be treated as an incredible archaeological find?

Or would it become an object sought for its power, by those who would stop at nothing to possess it, including murder?

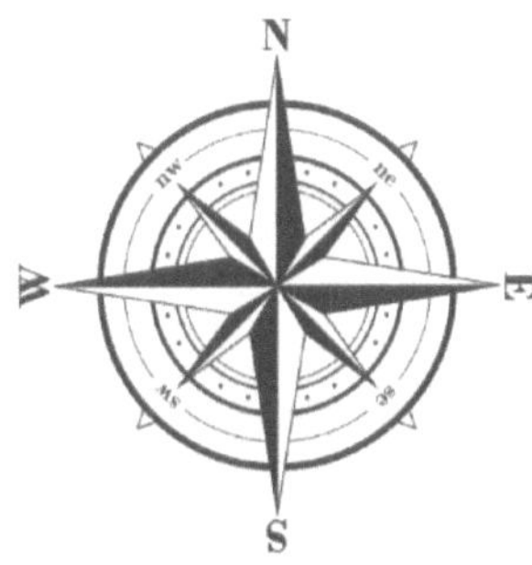

Operations Center 2, CIA Headquarters

Langley, Virginia

One day from now

CIA Analyst Supervisor Chris Leroux stood gripping the back of his chair, his eyes glued to the satellite feed shown on the massive display arcing across the front of the state-of-the-art operations center buried deep below CIA headquarters in Langley, Virginia. This was an operation like no other. He had long ago lost track of how many missions he had run, but he could honestly say this one was unique. Only a handful of people on the planet were aware of what was really going on, and even though he was privy to all the intel, he still couldn't believe what was happening.

Their subjects were on the run, pursued by an ever-growing mob, and if they didn't get out of the area soon, they might be cut off. Elements of Delta Force's Bravo Team were inbound, but they wouldn't make it in time. They were at least ten minutes out, and this could be over in a matter of minutes. This failed mission could turn into a bloodbath.

"Anything from the Brazilians?" he asked his second-in-command, Sonya Tong.

She shook her head. "Negative. They're refusing to enter the zone. They said if our people can reach them, then they'll protect them, but they won't go in."

"Cowards," spat Senior Analyst Marc Therrien from the back of the room. "Isn't it their damn job?"

Leroux didn't bother responding. Entire swaths of Rio de Janeiro were controlled by gangs, no-go zones, at least when it came to the police.

Randy Child, the team's tech whiz and youngest member, hammered at his keyboard then pointed at the display. "We've got trouble."

Leroux cursed at what Child had found. He grabbed his phone and dialed. It was answered moments later.

"Hello?"

He recognized the voice and the panic in it. "Professor Acton, this is Chris Leroux. Listen to me carefully. In fifty meters, turn left, or you're going to die."

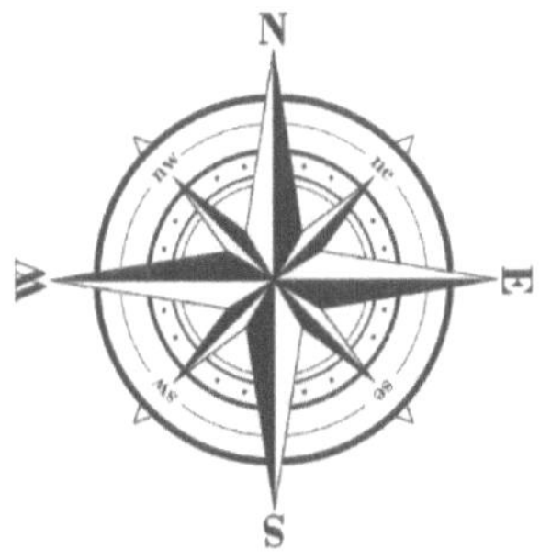

Jerusalem

AD 33

"But father, I was supposed to meet up with my friends for the festival!"

Hannah recognized the whine in her own voice, a tone that never worked with her father. But she was desperate. Everyone would be there, including David. He was so handsome and sweet. He was quiet, unlike the other boys always putting on a show. David preferred to sit to the side and draw. He was an incredible artist, and she was fascinated by him. Yet he barely noticed her, though perhaps that was not entirely true. If she caught his eye, he always smiled, but returned to whatever he was doing. And if she did manage to coax a conversation out of him, she always went home with a smile.

If she were to marry, he was the type of man she would want.

"We have guests. They won't be here all night. When they're gone, you can join your friends." Her father smirked at her. "You can join David."

Her eyes shot wide and her mouth fell open, but no words came out.

Her father chuckled. "You think I don't see the way you two look at each other?"

Her heart fluttered, her stomach queasy. "What do you mean? He doesn't look at me in any…I don't know…special way."

"Ha! You forget I was a boy once. I looked at your mother the exact same way he looks at you."

She couldn't help but smile, her eyes now wide with excitement. "What are you saying?"

"What do you think I'm saying?"

"Are you saying he likes me?"

"Obviously."

She hopped on her toes.

"And I take it that means you like him?"

She nodded vigorously. "Yes. Isn't he the sweetest boy?"

"He seems friendly, handsome. Your children would certainly be beautiful, and with your brains, smart."

Her cheeks flushed, and she turned away. "Children?"

"It is what you want, isn't it?"

"Of course, I want children! A whole bunch of them!"

Her father stopped what he was doing and sighed wistfully. "To have the sound of children around here again would be nice."

She reached out and squeezed his arm. She was the only child in the house, her mother never bearing any more children, and now dying in the next room, a slow, painful, horrible death. She prayed to God every night to bring relief to her mother, but her prayers always went unanswered. It sometimes made her question her faith. If God were real, why did he allow such suffering? How could that ever be part of some grand plan?

Her cousin Berenice rushed into the kitchen. "They're here!"

"Then show them in, show *him* in."

Berenice gave Hannah's father a look. "What a great idea! Much better than me just leaving them outside."

Her father stuck out his tongue at his niece. "Aren't we the smart one?" He slapped his hands together. "Now, show them in. And make sure their cups are full. Hannah, help her."

Hannah wiped away a tear that threatened to escape, family troubles pushed aside for the moment. "Who are these people?"

"Our guest of honor is called the Teacher. Treat him and his friends with respect."

Her eyes narrowed. "Teacher? Teacher of what?"

"Of life. The way."

"The way?"

"What God expects of us, of how to live better lives in peace and harmony."

Berenice bounced. "I'm so excited to meet him. I've heard so much about him."

Hannah shrugged. "I've never heard of him."

"You must have heard of him. Everyone around here has heard of him. He and his followers have been all over these parts for years. His sermons are apparently inspiring. I've heard he's even healed people of their ailments, even brought people back to life."

"Nonsense. Only God can do that." She glanced over her shoulder at the room where her mother lay. "And he never does."

Her father reached out and squeezed her shoulder. "Now, now, dear, God works in mysterious ways."

She sighed, picking up a carafe of wine from the counter. "Well, whoever he is, I hope he eats fast. I want to meet up with my friends before the festival ends." She headed for the door, then turned. "What do I call him?"

"You call him, sir, but his friends call him Jesus."

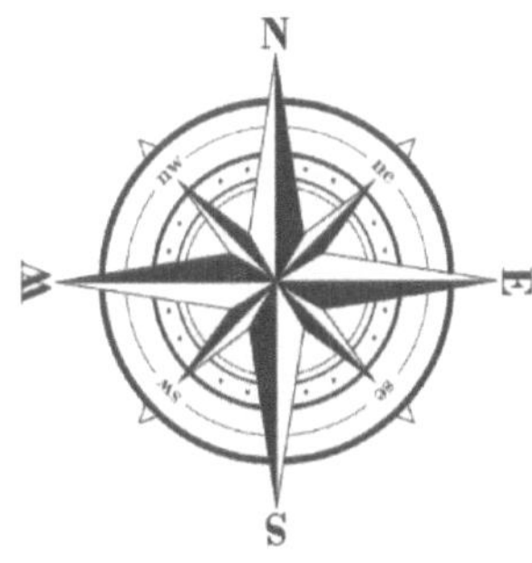

Water Tunnel No. 3 Project Utility Corridor

New York City, New York

Present Day

"Whoa, whoa, whoa, whoa, whoa!" Frank Marconi held up a hand as he shouted, the massive drilling machine grounding to a halt. "Back it up! Back it up!"

It was a simple order, though not so simply executed. It took several minutes to back it out ten yards, most of it wasted on safety protocols, though he agreed with them. He hadn't lost anyone on his crew yet to any sort of injury, and didn't intend to start now.

They had been digging a new maintenance tunnel under the streets of New York City for days. The massive drill rig was computer-guided, their route meticulously plotted by the eggheads above ground at City Hall. New York City was almost 400 years old, and they were digging under one of the oldest spots. Most of the public didn't realize that much of what they now called home was built atop the homes of their forefathers.

It made his life a headache sometimes.

On the job for over thirty years, he had seen incredible things—historical things that often had them diverting their route so other eggheads could get in and explore what had been discovered by accident.

Like, perhaps, today.

The dust settled, the fine mist sprayed from the machine binding with the particles, allowing them to fall to the ground. He inched forward, clicking on his flashlight, peering through the wall that had just collapsed in front of them. Others joined him.

"What do ya think we've got?" asked Johnny Russo, one of the younger men on his crew.

"I'm not sure. Let's check it out. Just be careful. None of this is stabilized." He stepped through the crumbled stone wall, playing his flashlight around. The dust inside was still heavy, the beam interrupted by millions upon millions of particles gently floating in front of them.

"Holy shit!"

He turned to see where Russo was directing his flashlight and gasped. A white flag hung on the far wall, bearing a red Maltese cross that instantly revealed what couldn't be possible. Where they stood couldn't have seen the light of day for over 150 years. He wasn't much of a historian, but he knew enough to be aware the Templars had been wiped out long before, and there was no possible way they could have been in New York City.

He sighed.

There was no way this project was getting completed on time.

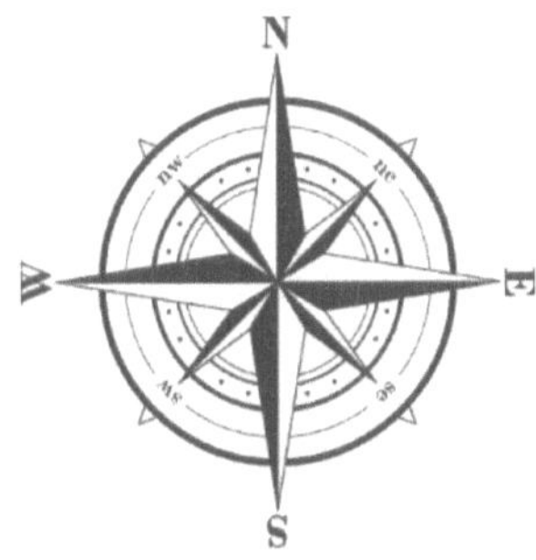

Jerusalem

AD 33

"But you are not to be like that. Instead, the greatest among you should be like the youngest, and the one who rules like the one who serves. For who is greater, the one who is at the table or the one who serves? Is it not the one who is at the table? But I am among you as one who serves."

Hannah's cheeks flushed as the charismatic man acknowledged her with a smile as he spoke. There was something about him. Something irresistible. It had nothing to do with whether he was attractive. He was, but he was over twice her age. It had nothing to do with that. It was his words, his manner. He was enthralling. Everything that came from his mouth sounded profound to her, and his friends, his followers, appeared to hang on his every word.

She continued to round the table, refilling their cups, as this man named Jesus raised his bread, giving thanks. He began breaking off pieces and handing them to his friends. "Take it. This is my body."

She stared at him. It was such a curious thing to say. What did he mean, this was his body? Who was this man? He spoke with such confidence, as if he understood how everything in life worked.

She filled his cup, and he smiled up at her.

"Thank you, sister."

She curtsied, saying nothing as she moved on.

He held up his now-filled cup. "This cup is the new covenant in my blood, which is poured out for you." He passed it around, each taking a sip. "Very truly I tell you, unless you eat the flesh of the Son of Man and drink his blood, you have no life in you. Whoever eats my flesh and drinks my blood has eternal life, and I will raise them up at the last day."

She headed for the kitchen. Eternal life? What was he talking about? Who is this man? She entered the kitchen, her father still busy. She refilled the carafe then leaned closer to her father, whispering. "Who is he?"

"I told you, he's a teacher."

"No, that's not what he is. At least, that's not all he is. Have you heard what he's been saying in there?"

Her father appeared disappointed. "No. I have been busy in here."

"He's talking about the bread being his flesh, the wine being his blood, and that if you drink of his blood, you can have eternal life, or something like that."

Her father smiled. "What do you make of it?"

"I know what I should make of it."

"And what's that?"

"That he's crazy. He's insane. He's talking about his friends eating his flesh and drinking his blood. That's sick. Twisted." She frowned. "Yet there's something about him. I can't stop listening to him. I can't stop looking at him. I'm like his friends, whom I'm not sure are friends at all. It's like they're more his followers, as if they worship him."

"An interesting choice of words. Worship might be the right way to describe it."

"What do you mean?"

"I mean, he's the son of God."

Her mouth fell agape. "What?" She scoffed. "Now who's crazy?"

"You heard your cousin. He's rumored to have healed the sick, brought the dead back to life, turned water to wine, and even walked on water. He gave a sermon at Mount of Beatitudes that I was fortunate enough to have attended, and it was the most inspiring thing I've ever heard. And then when he performed his miracles, I knew he was telling the truth, that he was indeed the son of God sent to save us all." Her father clasped his chest. "The peace he brings is just…" He hesitated. "Joyful. When I heard him, I felt joy for the first time in a very long time."

"So, you believe he is who he claims to be?"

"I do."

She lowered her voice further. "What do the rabbis think? To claim you're the son of God?"

"Not just that, my child, the King of the Jews."

"They'll kill him for sure," she hissed.

"That may be, but I don't think he fears that. In fact, I'm sure he doesn't." He jerked his chin toward the carafe. "Go in there, serve our guests, but listen and learn. Everyone who gets to hear him speak should take advantage. What you hear may change the way you see everything, because if he is who he claims to be, then tonight, in our home, we host the Messiah."

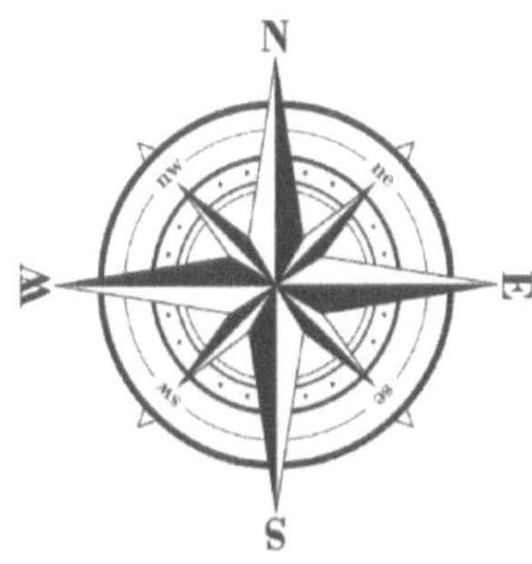

Discovery Site, Water Tunnel No. 3 Project Utility Corridor

New York City, New York

Present Day

Detective Justin Shakespeare cursed as he climbed through the opening in a stone wall, stumbling over a rock lying on the ground, knocked out of place by the impressive piece of machinery he had just passed. His portly frame, a curse of his diabetes, wasn't designed for this type of environment, but he had a job to do.

He was homicide, and someone had reported a murder.

He shone his flashlight, his eyebrows jumping at what appeared to be Templar memorabilia. "What the hell am I looking at?"

Frank Marconi, the site supervisor, threw up his hands. "I have no idea. I've never seen anything like it before."

Shakespeare played his light across the floor, making sure he wasn't stepping on anything important, but other than rocks, stone, and bits of masonry, he found nothing of significance. He wasn't much for history, though he found the Templars fascinating. He carefully took in the surroundings. "Some sort of collector? A Templar groupie?"

"From the mid-nineteenth century?"

Shakespeare paused, turning toward Marconi. "What do you mean?"

"Well, this room. We're pretty sure it's almost a couple of hundred years since somebody's been in here."

"How could you possibly know that?"

Marconi indicated the door. "It's sealed from the inside. There's no other way in or out. And the buildings overhead were built about a hundred years ago on top of an old neighborhood that had burned down. As far as we can tell, there's no way to get in here from up there."

"Wait a minute. I thought I was here because of a murder."

"You are." Marconi gestured toward the center of the room at a large stone box, what Shakespeare would best describe as a coffin, that had gone unnoticed so far. He stepped over to it, his mouth slightly agape at the sight of a body dressed in full Templar regalia.

"This is why I was called in?"

"Yes. When I called 9-1-1, I told them we had found a dead body."

Shakespeare rolled his eyes. "You called 9-1-1 for this?"

"Who else was I supposed to call?"

Shakespeare shone his flashlight on the dead man's face, remarkably well preserved for someone supposedly dead for almost 200 years. "I'd call an archaeologist."

Marconi's eyes shot wide. "Really?"

"This isn't a crime scene. This is a historical site. Call whoever deals with that shit, not me, not the NYPD. We have corpses a hell of a lot fresher than this to deal with."

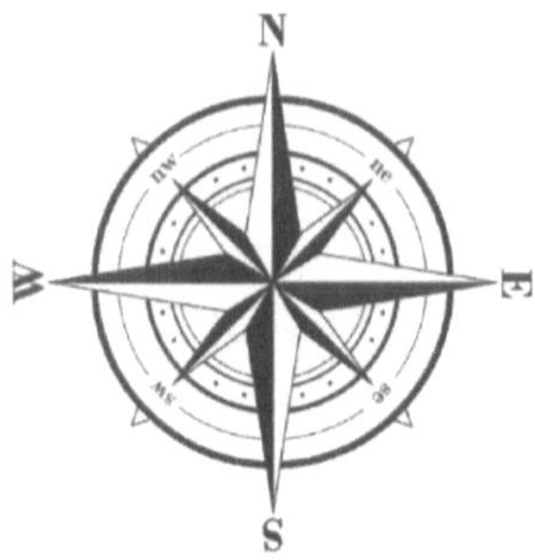

Jerusalem

AD 33

"But the hand of him who is going to betray me is with mine on the table. The Son of Man will go as it has been decreed. But woe to that man who betrays him!"

Hannah's eyebrows rose as those gathered fell silent with Jesus' statement. It was clear everyone was shocked. She stood frozen, uncertain as to what to do, the carafe of wine still gripped in her hand. She did not dare move. It would draw too much attention.

Suddenly, those gathered burst into protest, assuring their leader they would not betray him. Yet this inspirational man appeared certain, and for some reason, she believed him. It was as if he knew the future, as if it was all laid out before him.

Betray. It was a word fraught with numerous connotations, many fairly benign. Betrayed in what way? The way in which it was said suggested grave consequences, and from the bits and pieces of conversation she had overheard during their meal, it appeared everyone here was nervous about the authorities, both Roman and Jewish.

Though perhaps she was wrong. Jesus certainly did not appear concerned. While at various times the others had displayed fear, this man never had, not once.

She refilled the cups until the carafe was empty then scurried toward the kitchen as Jesus proclaimed that one of them would deny knowing him three times before the night was out. The door closed behind her, cutting off the reply, but if the denial was to happen tonight, then so must the betrayal.

Her cousin rushed in after her. "Who do you think is going to betray him?"

"I have no idea."

"I think it's that nervous one. He's always shifting in his seat. His denial seemed a little too earnest, if you ask me."

Hannah refilled her carafe as Berenice placed the plates she had cleared on the counter. Hannah thought of the man her cousin had referred to—at least whom she assumed Berenice was referring to. He had appeared out of sorts the entire time. Did Jesus know who it was? He had to, yet he still allowed the man at his table. It made no sense to her.

She turned to her father. "Who would want to do this man harm?"

Her father grunted. "Too many to count. Many think he's an agitator, a blasphemer, a threat to good order."

"So, the Romans?"

"The Romans, the clergy, ne'er-do-wells. Many people see him as a threat. Many people see him as a liar."

"How do you see him?"

Her father paused, as if searching for the right words. "Dangerous."

Her eyebrows rose. "Dangerous? Him? I don't think he would hurt a fly."

"No, not dangerous in that way. Dangerous in that he's the type of man who brings about change, and people fear change. They get comfortable in their old ways, the ways of their parents, of their grandparents. They like the way things are, even if they aren't good, because they understand them. The Teacher tells us that things don't have to be the way they are, that they can be better, and all we have to do is give ourselves to God and care for our fellow man, rather than exploit them for personal gain.

"You've seen how things are, how corrupt things are. Even our religious leaders are driven by power and greed. Markets in our temples? Seriously? Is this what God would want? I can't believe it. Remember, our leaders are human. Only God is perfect. Our institutions, religious and government, are all creations of man, a man that is deeply flawed. The fact that the Teacher dares to point this out makes him a threat to those in power. If he is indeed to be betrayed tonight, I fear he may not live to see the morning."

Hannah's hand darted to her mouth. "Oh no! Is there any way we can help him?"

Her father smiled. "No, but it warms my heart that you would try. If the Teacher says he'll be betrayed, he will be betrayed, and there's nothing anyone can do to stop it. But fear not, for all is not lost."

"How so, Father?"

"The Teacher has already delivered his message. He's already had his effect on people. As word spreads of his teachings, I suspect those who would do him harm today will find themselves relics of the past as a new way of thinking spreads across the land."

"I pray you're right, Father."

"As do I, my child, as do I."

The door swung open and Peter, one of the two men sent ahead to prepare for the meal, poked his head inside. "We'll be leaving now, sir. My master would like to thank you in person for your hospitality."

"It would be my honor," replied her father, heading for the door as he beckoned the two of them to follow, and though she was about to go spend the rest of the day with her friends, she felt no joy, for even Peter was subdued, and she didn't blame him.

How would you feel if someone you had devoted your life to was about to die, and there was nothing you could do about it?

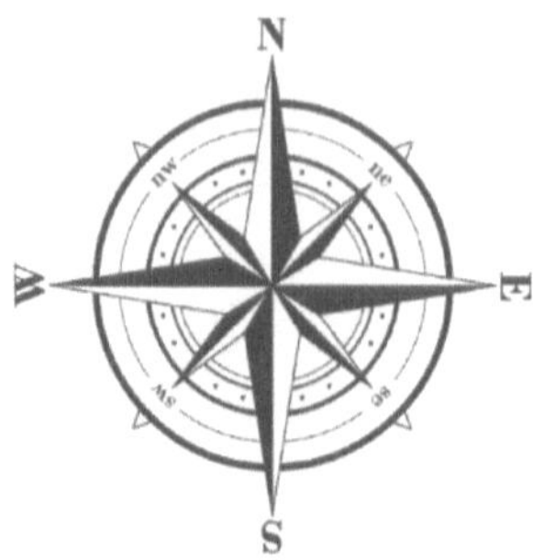

The Vatican

Present Day

A gentle tap at his office door had Inspector General of the Corps of Gendarmerie of Vatican City State, Mario Giasson, looking up from his computer and through the glass wall that allowed him to monitor the activity of his security personnel, but also had him feeling like he was the star of the Aquarium Channel. He was surprised to see Father Esposito, one of the Vatican's lead archaeologists, on the other side of the door. Giasson beckoned him in and Esposito stepped inside, quickly closing the door behind him.

"Do you have a moment?"

"Of course, Father. What can I do for you?"

The man held up a memory card. "May I?"

Giasson nodded, and Esposito inserted it into the slot on the side of the television mounted to the wall. A slideshow began. A shot of a Templar flag piqued Giasson's interest. He rose, rounding his desk, and stood in front of the monitor with Esposito as photographs flipped past showing Templar regalia along with a stone sarcophagus with the remains of a proud member of the Order inside.

"What am I looking at?"

"A recent discovery."

"Something your people are working on?"

"No. This was accidental. Under New York City."

"New York City? How's that possible?"

"We're not sure. It doesn't make any sense. They were digging a new utility tunnel for the subway. There shouldn't have been anything here. Not this deep."

"How old is it?"

"Well, that's just it. We're not exactly sure. However, evidence suggests mid-nineteenth century."

Giasson paused, regarding the man. "Forgive me for saying this again, Father, but that makes no sense. Even I know that in mid-nineteenth century America, few people, if any, knew of the Templars. Who's in the sarcophagus?"

"We don't know. There are journals, but they're all written in Templar code. We can crack it, of course, quite easily. We just haven't had the time."

"When was this discovered?"

"Earlier today. They stopped construction immediately, then called the archdiocese. They sent someone, though they're not equipped for this. Archaeological finds in America related to the Church are few and far between."

Giasson returned to his chair, motioning toward one in front of his desk. Esposito sat. "This is hardly my department. What do you need from me?"

"Like I was saying, we don't have the proper personnel in America. I'm organizing a team to head there, but we can't get there until tomorrow evening at best. We need an expert to go in now and see what we're dealing with, whether this is a hoax or if there's something serious to it."

Giasson leaned back and folded his arms. "You want me to see if the professors will go in?"

"Could you? They don't live far from there. They could be there in a matter of hours. If they say it's legit, then we'll send in a full team. But if it turns out to be a hoax, we could save a lot of time and money."

"Send me the details. I'll pass them on to the professors. Though, knowing them, there's no guarantee they're only a few hours away. They could be on the other side of the world for all we know."

Esposito muttered a curse. "I never thought of that. Please let me know as soon as you hear from them."

"I will."

Esposito retrieved his phone from under his robes then tapped away at it. An email appeared in Giasson's inbox. "You now know as much as I do. I'm sure they're going to want to see those pictures. They're already on our server. The email contains the link and log-in information. Everything they'll need." He rose. "Please ask them to hurry. If it is legitimate, we have no idea how badly the scene is being contaminated as we speak, and I'm sure I don't need to tell you what the implications could be."

Giasson eyed the man. "Implications?"

Esposito glanced over each shoulder as if to make sure they were alone, then leaned closer, lowering his voice. "A Templar in full regalia, buried in a sarcophagus, surrounded by relics of his order in mid-nineteenth century New York City, deep underground. The Order had been wiped out more than five hundred years before. There have long been rumors that the Templars fled to America with their treasure, which is why it was never found."

Giasson wagged a finger. "You and I both know what the professors found in France."

"Yes, but it wasn't the entire treasure." Esposito pointed at the screen. "There's the possibility that this man is a descendant of those who escaped. There could be a vast wealth buried with him."

"I see no evidence of piles of gold and jewels."

Esposito tossed up his hands. "Exactly! But if anyone knows the rumors, they're going to be descending upon that place and tearing it apart looking for the treasure. It'll destroy everything. Please contact the professors immediately before treasure hunters ruin everything."

Giasson rose. "I'll take care of it, Father."

Esposito bowed. "Thank you." He left, hurrying across the security office and out of sight.

Giasson brought up the email, quickly scanning the contents. There was little to go on, but that was the entire point. He forwarded the email to the two professors, then looked up their number, a smile spreading at the opportunity to speak to two people he now considered friends.

He was about to dial the number when he stopped, staring at the images still cycling on his television. Could this be real? Could there be Templars to this day in America? And if there were, why were they still in hiding? None of it made sense. It had to be a hoax, though what the purpose of such a hoax would be, he had no idea. He sighed. There was only one way to find out.

He leaned forward and dialed the number, clearing his throat as the phone rang and rang.

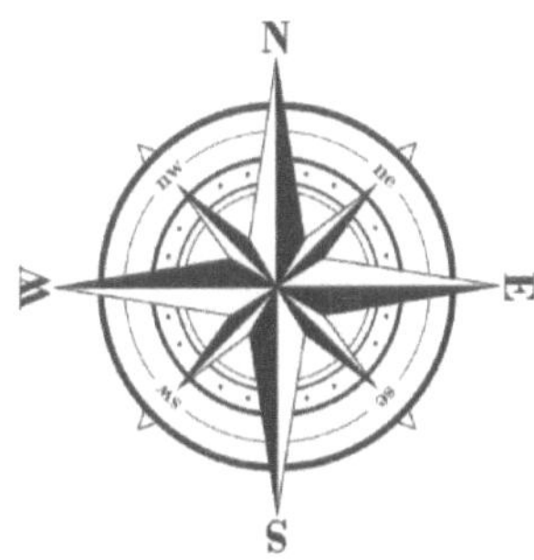

Acton/Palmer Residence, Overlook Village Gated Community

St. Paul, Maryland

"Who wants their buns toasted?"

Hands shot up around the patio, and Archaeology Professor James Acton chuckled. "I think we need a bigger barbecue."

His wife, Archaeology Professor Laura Palmer, gave him a look. "You've been saying that since the day we moved in."

"And I've been right since the day we moved in. This house is huge, and all it has is a four-burner barbecue. Somebody cheaped out."

"What are you talking about? Look at this landscaping. It's unbelievable."

"Yeah, so whoever designed it must have been a vegetarian." He spat.

"Vegetarians barbecue."

"Nothing worthwhile."

She jerked her chin toward a side burner. "And just what do you have grilling there?"

He eyed the onions and peppers. "Meat garnish."

"Uh-huh. If you want a bigger barbecue, get a bigger barbecue."

Interpol Agent Hugh Reading grunted at both of them from his chair under a large, colorful patio umbrella. "I hope this little discussion isn't delaying my lunch."

Mai Trinh, a young woman Acton and Laura had come to think of as their daughter after her exile to America from her native Vietnam, giggled. "I think someone's hungry."

Reading patted his stomach. "Someone is. Very."

Acton twisted his head to address the growing discontent. "Hey, hey, hey. Perfection takes time." He began placing buns on the precious real estate, freeing up more as he removed the sausages. "Anyone who didn't want their buns toasted can get theirs now."

Tommy Granger, a tech guru and Mai's fiancé, shot to his feet. "I'm starving. I couldn't care less whether my bun is toasted."

Mai patted his backside. "Your buns are toasty enough already, hot stuff."

His cheeks flushed.

Laura grinned at Mai, then jerked her chin toward her husband. "Please tell me you're not developing his sense of humor."

"Hey, what's wrong with my sense of humor?" protested Acton.

"It's usually rooted in sexual innuendo or flatulence."

Acton smirked. "I see nothing wrong with that. And besides, it seemed to win your heart."

Laura scratched her chin. "I'm not sure what that says about me, but it can't be good."

"I'll tell you what, the day you stop giggling every time you fart, I'll stop telling fart jokes."

"James!"

Acton grinned. "Yes, ladies and gentlemen, she, like every other woman on this planet, farts."

Tommy jerked a thumb over his shoulder at Mai. "So does she. She's a Howitzer."

"Thomas!"

He darted away. "I'm in trouble now. The only time she ever uses 'Thomas' is if she's really mad at me."

Reading batted the air with his hand. "Bah, a little wind never killed anybody. Hurt somebody, sure."

Acton made up a sausage with roasted peppers for Tommy. "Hurt?"

Reading sat up. "I remember once, Martin and I were heading to a crime scene. He had been out the night before, drank a little too much. He launched what Jim would call an air biscuit that literally watered my eyes. I almost rear-ended the car in front of us. I kicked him out of the car and made him walk the rest of the way. Took him twenty minutes. He never did that again, I tell you."

Laura eyed him. "You made the poor man walk twenty minutes?"

"In the rain."

"Your farts don't exactly smell like spring lilies, now do they, Rose?"

Rose, their domestic whom Laura had had to order to sit in her chair rather than scurry around helping on her day off, waved her hand in front of her nose. "Oh, Mr. Reading. Some days when I open the door to your room, I have to stand back for a moment."

Reading's cheeks, already suffering from a hint of rosacea, went full alarm red. "I'm sure it's not that bad."

Everyone nodded at him, even those who couldn't know.

"Is it?"

Acton roared with laughter, the others joining in as he checked the buns, several he had already had in place nicely toasted. He began dressing the first as his phone rang inside. Rose darted to her feet before Acton could stop her.

"I'll get it," she said as she rushed inside, her son shrugging.

"That woman's always on."

Rose quickly returned, the phone about to go to voicemail. Acton took it, his eyebrows jumping at Mario Giasson's name on the call display. He swiped his thumb. "Mario!" Everybody's eyebrows shot up. "To what do I owe the pleasure?"

"Bonjour, mon ami. I hope I'm not interrupting anything."

"Nothing that can't be interrupted. I'm here with Laura, Hugh, Tommy, and Mai, as well as our housekeeper, Rose, and her son. Is it okay if I put you on speaker?"

"I don't see why not. The moment you hang up, you'll be telling everybody everything I said, regardless."

Acton snorted. "You're right about that. Just a sec." He switched the phone to speaker, then placed it on the patio table. "So, what can I do for you?"

"I've just sent you an email with details about an archaeological find underneath New York City that, if possible, I'd like you and Laura to check out for us."

Laura approached the phone. "Hi, Mario. What could possibly be found underneath New York City that the Vatican would be interested in?"

Acton turned to Tommy. "Can you grab my tablet? It's on the kitchen counter." Rose moved to fetch it when Acton stopped her with a pointed finger. "You sit. You're our guest."

Mai rose, waving off Tommy. "I'll get it."

Tommy held up his sausage, his mouth full. "Thank you," he mumbled through filled cheeks.

Acton eyeballed him. "Smaller bites, dude, or you're going to give yourself gas."

"I'll take that risk."

"Doesn't the Church have people in New York City that can look at it for you?" asked Laura.

"Our people already have, but they're not experts. We don't have an archaeology team in the United States. Father Esposito is preparing a team now, but they won't be there until tomorrow. He's extremely concerned that if the site is genuine, it might be disturbed or looted."

Mai returned with the tablet, handing it over to Acton.

"Just what did you find?" asked Acton.

"We're not sure. And we have no idea if it's a hoax, but I think it has to be, don't you?"

Acton logged in and brought up the email from Giasson. He quickly read it, his eyes widening, then tapped the link to log in. He brought up the photos, Laura and Mai peering over his shoulders, Reading sitting impatiently.

"Well, what the bloody hell is it?"

Acton chewed his cheek for a moment. "I'm not sure, but if I'm to believe my eyes, then it's some sort of chamber filled with Templar memorabilia, with a Templar buried in a sarcophagus in full uniform."

Reading struggled out of his chair, Tommy extending a hand and hauling the man up. "Thank you." He joined the gaggle. "Even I know enough about my history to know that doesn't make any sense."

Giasson agreed. "That's exactly what I said to Father Esposito, which is why we need an expert, namely you two, to go in and take a look. See if this is a hoax and we're just wasting our time, or if it's the real thing."

Acton turned to Laura. "What do you think?"

"I don't know. It has to be a hoax. I can't see how Templars could have been in New York City in the mid-nineteenth century when they were wiped out in the early fourteenth century."

"Mostly wiped out."

"True."

Tommy resumed attacking his lunch. "Could it just be some fanboy? A huge fan of the Templars? Decides to bury himself in his own tiny Comiccon."

Reading groaned. "English, lad, English."

Acton ignored his friend's protest. "Highly unlikely, though I suppose anything's possible. That's certainly more likely than an actual Templar being buried under New York City almost two hundred years ago."

Laura grabbed a hotdog bun and slapped a sausage inside. "There's only one way to find out."

Acton grinned. "Road trip!"

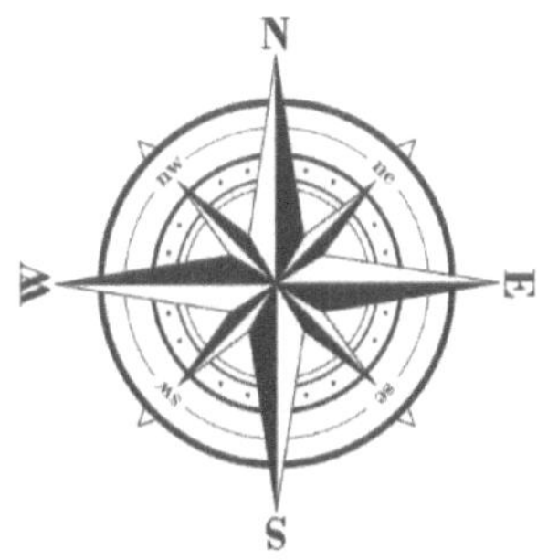

Jerusalem

AD 33

Hannah and Berenice stood respectfully against the wall as their guests left, each thanking her father for his hospitality. The man whom her father called Jesus—a name she hadn't heard once uttered by those gathered—shook her father's hand.

"It was a wonderful meal. Apologies again for the short notice."

Her father smiled and bowed deeply. "It was an honor and no trouble at all."

Jesus patted her father's hand then approached her and her cousin, a broad smile on his face. He extended his hand, and she took it hesitatingly. None of the others had said goodbye in this manner, though all but one—the one called Judas—had smiled politely. He took her hand, enveloping it in both of his, squeezing it gently.

"Thank you so much. Without the two of you, this supper couldn't have been the success it was."

"Thank you, sir." She curtsied as he released her hand and moved on to Berenice.

She didn't hear what Berenice said. She was lost. The moment he had touched her, she had felt something. What, she wasn't sure. A warmth, a tingling sensation, peace, calmness—yet this was a man who expected to be betrayed tonight by one of his own friends. He appeared unconcerned. What was it about him she was so drawn to? She could understand why the others hung on his every word. There was a charisma here she had never encountered before. Was he who her father claimed to be? Was he the Messiah spoken of?

She dismissed the thought. The Messiah, in their home? Folly. But why not? They were a good family. They weren't rich, but they weren't destitute either. Her father was respected in the community, well-liked. Who better than him to host the Messiah? But wasn't the Messiah a god? Why would a god need to eat?

She sighed, and Jesus turned toward her as he released Berenice's hand.

"Something troubles you?"

Hannah rapidly shook her head. "No, sir."

He smiled, facing her. "You wonder who I am."

She gulped, her heart racing, but she nodded.

"Do you trust your father?"

Her eyes darted toward him, standing by the kitchen door. "Of course."

"Then continue to do so."

The man bowed then left, joining his friends outside, and she couldn't help but feel she had been in the presence of someone special, of someone unique. Was he the Messiah? There was no way to know. But if he was, and if the words he had spoken to his friends were true...

She eyed the cup he had drunk from and darted forward as the door shut.

Whoever eats my flesh and drinks my blood has eternal life...

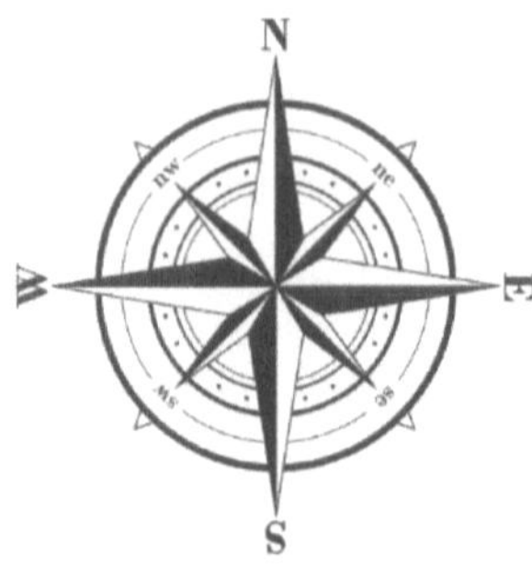

Discovery Site, Water Tunnel No. 3 Project Utility Corridor

New York City, New York

Present Day

"Are you okay?" asked James Acton, concerned for his friend who huffed and puffed behind him.

"A little winded. Don't worry about me."

Acton flashed Reading a smile, but he couldn't help but be concerned. The man had suffered a heart attack and a cardiac event that had his heart rate over 200 beats a minute. Both recently. Though Acton hardly considered the man old, perhaps he was too old for this. At least today. They were in New York City, where they were safe. The only danger here was if the roof came down on them, though the engineer guiding them toward the site had reassured them there was little risk of that.

"Little?" It was Tommy who had picked up on the word.

They were all here as part of the Vatican delegation, with the exception of Rose and her son. She had insisted on staying behind and cleaning up the aborted barbecue, also pointing out that her son had school the next day. Her son hadn't been too happy about it, eager to see what they were about to discover, though his mother had the final word.

"It's just up here," said Frank Marconi, pointing ahead.

They walked past an enormous machine designed to bore holes underground, and Acton was momentarily distracted by the impressive piece of construction equipment. He whistled appreciatively, then glanced over at Laura with a grin. "I want one."

She rolled her eyes. "I know you do. And I'd say, 'Let's get one,' but there's no room in our driveway for it."

He faked a pout. "Awww!" He groaned like a little child might when denied a cookie.

"Maybe you could just rent it for a couple of weeks," suggested Tommy. "Dig an escape tunnel from your new home. It could certainly come in handy."

Acton grinned at Laura.

"Don't even think about it."

His shoulders slumped. "You're no fun."

"Uh-huh."

"Right through here." Marconi beckoned them through a hole, light shining from within.

Laura led the way, Acton following as they stepped across the threshold, each step slightly shaky as they bounced over plywood and through the hole made by the machine before it had been halted just in time. If the crew hadn't been paying attention, they would have sliced right through whatever had been discovered. Acton extended a hand and helped Reading, concerned once again at his friend's heaving chest and pale, clammy skin.

"Thanks. Perhaps this wasn't wise."

"Perhaps. I think you're going to have to take it easy for a while."

Reading scowled. "I hate it when you're right."

Acton snickered. "Well then, you must hate it a lot, because—"

Reading interrupted him. "You're always right. Yeah, yeah."

Acton scanned their surroundings, spotting a chair sitting nearby—ornate and sturdy. He stepped over and put his weight on it. It held. He sat, confirming what he suspected—that like most things, they didn't make 'em like they used to. He stood, addressing his friend. "Have a seat. Tommy, get him a bottle of water."

Reading clearly wasn't feeling good, sitting without protest. Tommy pulled a bottle of water from the duffel bag slung over his shoulder and cracked the top, handing it to their ailing friend.

Laura placed an arm on Reading's shoulder. "Do you want us to call for help?"

Reading batted away the suggestion. "Just let me catch my breath. I'll be all right." He leaned over so he could see past her and cursed. "Would you look at that?"

Acton turned and finally took in their surroundings, allowing himself to be swept away in the moment. His first assessment had been reserved for finding his friend a place to rest, but now he could finally appreciate why they were here. They were in a room, fifty feet underground if their briefing was accurate, though when it was constructed, it wasn't this deep. The walls were thick stone, masonry work evident. This had been dug out and constructed.

A lot of work.

He glanced up at the ceiling—stone as well, with heavy timbers holding up the ground overhead.

Marconi noticed him eying the centuries-old beams. "Don't worry. The wood is in good condition." He indicated several jacks. "We've also put in our own temporary supports, just in case."

"Good thinking." Acton continued to analyze the construction, ignoring what his eyes hungered to focus on. The floor was stone as well. "Any signs of ventilation?"

"None that we found." Marconi directed their attention to the wall behind Reading. "There's a metal door there. We didn't touch it, so we're not sure where it leads, though I suspect up."

Both Acton and Laura stepped over, examining the door.

"Looks like a pretty good seal." Laura ran her finger along the frame. "This is solid. They must have had a hell of a time getting it down here."

Acton rapped his knuckles on the stone wall. "This was made by professionals. And even if it was only thirty feet underground in the mid-nineteenth century, this is one hell of a construction job. A lot of time, effort, and money went into this."

"Maybe they paid for it with some of this."

They both turned to see Tommy pointing at an open wooden chest filled with gold, silver, and precious gems.

"Good bet."

"These must be the journals they referred to." Mai stood in front of a bookshelf in the far corner, half a dozen large tomes lined up, one opened.

"So, what do you think?" asked Marconi. "Hoax?"

Laura dismissed the suggestion. "Not with construction like this. Everything points to something built well over a century ago, exactly as you suspected. There's no evidence to suggest anyone's been in here since this door was sealed." She tapped the locking mechanism. "And this is inside like you said."

Marconi's shoulders slumped. "So then, this is of historical importance?"

"It is." Acton stepped over to the sarcophagus. "The question is whether it's a curiosity or an actual find needing to be properly examined. It's certainly not a modern hoax, but we can't rule out that it wasn't a pre-Civil War hoax."

Marconi's face brightened. "So then, this might be nothing."

"Might be, though I doubt it." Acton gestured at the body. "Tommy, make sure you get lots of photos of him. Get lots of photos and video of everything."

"Yes, sir." Tommy was way ahead of him, already documenting the scene.

Acton gestured toward the proud figure, well-preserved in the near vacuum. "Interesting."

Laura agreed. "His tunic suggests a misunderstanding of the Templar Order, or he was all that was left."

Acton chewed his cheek as he slowly spun, taking in the surroundings once again. "Interesting idea." He jerked his chin toward the journals. "I suspect all our answers are in those."

Mai leaned in, reading the open pages. "It's in some sort of code."

"It'll be the Templar code. Unbreakable at the time, but easy enough now that we know the cipher."

"What *is* the cipher?" asked Tommy. The eagerness in his voice brought a smile to Acton's face.

"I could tell you, but then I'd have to kill you."

Tommy flipped him the bird, and Mai swatted her fiancé. "Thomas!"

Acton tossed back his head and laughed. "Don't worry, Mai. It's all in good fun." He gestured toward a Templar flag on the rear wall. "Each point on the Maltese cross represents a letter. All you had to know was which point to start on."

Tommy perked up. "I could write a program!"

"Do it."

Tommy pulled out his phone, and Acton chuckled.

"Not now."

Tommy frowned. "Right, it can wait."

Acton leaned back over the sarcophagus. "Just who the hell were you? And how the hell did you end up in nineteenth century New York City, five hundred years after the last of your brothers were believed to have died?"

Laura leaned in from the other side. "If this is a hoax, whoever perpetrated it had access to their armor and uniforms."

"Agreed. He might not be a Templar, but everything in this room certainly belonged to them." He paused. "Wait a minute."

"What?"

"Something's missing."

Laura regarded him. "How would you know?"

Acton pulled out his phone, bringing up the Vatican website. He logged in, flipping through the photos until he found one showing the proud warrior in his final resting place. He held out the photo triumphantly. "See?"

Laura squinted, then her jaw dropped. "You're right!" She spun toward Marconi. "Did any of your people take anything from here?"

Marconi held up both hands. "Absolutely not. As far as I know, the only people that have been in here since we discovered it were your people. I mean, church people."

Reading rose, his old police instincts kicking in. "Something's been taken?"

Acton held out his phone. "See what's clutched in his hands?" He gestured toward the body as Reading took the phone. "His hands are still clasped over his chest, but empty. That was there this morning, but now it's gone."

Reading turned to Marconi. "I'm going to need a list of every single person who might have had access to this room."

"Like I said, we sealed it as soon as we found it. Your people came in. That's it."

"Are you one hundred percent positive?"

"Yes."

Reading regarded him. "Really? You were here every moment?"

Marconi shuffled, staring at his feet. "No, I wasn't."

"Then you can't be positive now, can you?"

"No, I suppose not."

"Then let's get working on that list."

Marconi drew a deep breath. "Fine, I'll get right on it."

"Good." Reading stared at the picture, using his thumb and forefinger to zoom in. "Why would anyone steal this when *that* is in the room?" he said, pointing at the chest filled with immeasurable wealth.

Acton exchanged an excited glance with Laura. He could think of only one reason. He turned to Tommy. "Start writing your program. We need to translate those journals. Fast."

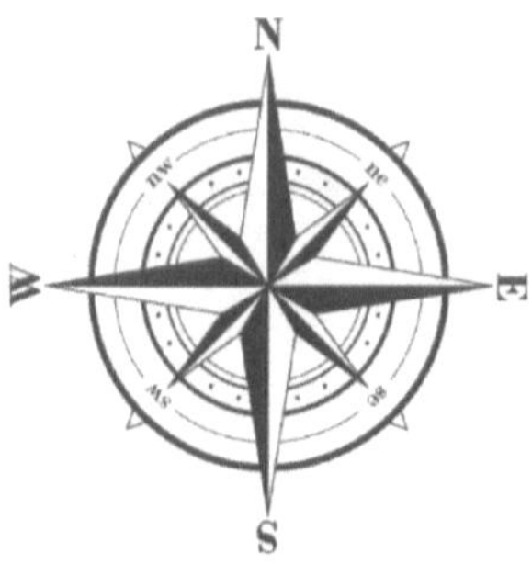

Street Level, Water Tunnel No. 3 Project
New York City, New York

Hugh Reading was back in his element. Sort of. As a DCI at Scotland Yard, he had ended his career dealing with murders. This was a theft—of some trinket about which Acton had refused to tell him why he was so excited.

"Just in case I'm wrong. I'd hate to tarnish my reputation," Acton had said without his customary smirk when delivering lines like that.

Reading had eyed his friend. "You're not being very helpful. I need leverage."

Acton grunted. "If I told you what I think it could be, and you repeated it, you'd be laughed out of Interpol."

"Ever helpful."

Reading leaned against the SUV they had arrived in, taking in his surroundings. New York City was bustling with activity, unaware of what was going on fifty feet below them. That was probably a good thing. If word got around about the gold and jewels below their feet, who knew what might happen?

Acton and Laura were still below, documenting the find with Mai. Tommy was in the back seat of the SUV, a broad smile revealing his delight at coding something helpful.

Reading envied the young man. He remembered when he started his career in the Met Police. It was exciting, new. Every day, he went home with a sense of accomplishment. As he had moved his way up the ranks, the excitement had waned, but that sense of satisfaction was always there. He was serving the public, solving crimes, bringing justice to those who deserved it. It was good, honest work. When forced to leave and join Interpol, mostly manning a desk, it had been such a disappointment. Yet at least he was still in law enforcement.

A loud whining sound startled him, and he spun to see a tow truck hoisting an infamous sports car from his homeland onto the back. He chuckled. Its tires were flat, and it was covered with several weeks of detritus. The windshield was clogged with tickets. Had it been abandoned after a joyride, or by the owner, tired of the mounting repair bills?

He pressed his phone tighter against his ear as the hold music finally stopped and his call picked up, a tired voice answering.

"Giasson."

"Mario, it's Hugh."

"Hugh, mon ami. The fact that you're calling and not one of the professors makes me think something's gone wrong."

"You could say that. For the moment, for a change, I don't think anyone's in actual danger."

"Thank God for that. What's going on?"

"It looks like something was stolen between the time your team took photographs and we arrived."

"Really? What?"

"I'm not sure. Something the Templar was holding in his hands. Jim and Laura seem pretty excited, but they're refusing to say what it was—what they think it is."

"Because?"

"To paraphrase Jim, 'I'd sound like a fool if I told anyone.'"

Giasson grunted. "Scientists."

"Tell me about it."

"What do you need from me?"

"Grease."

"Excuse me?"

"I need you to grease some wheels, like these Americans would say. I'm here unofficially. I need to be official."

"What do you need?"

"Call my boss at Interpol. Make a request that I be assigned to this case. Then call the police commissioner here and request his cooperation with a case very important to the Vatican."

"Consider it done. Anything else?"

"Hopefully that's it, but not a lot of people knew about what was here. You might want to start looking at things from your end to see who knew. No matter what was stolen, something *was* stolen, and my gut's telling me it was an inside job."

"I don't like the sound of that."

"Experience has told me that even if you work for the Vatican, it doesn't mean you're immune from temptation. If they knew what it was that has the professors so excited, they might not have been able to help themselves."

"True. I'll get on it from this end after I make those calls for you."

"I appreciate it, Mario."

"Anytime. Keep me posted."

"Will do." Reading ended the call as Tommy let out a jubilant hoot. Reading opened the passenger side door. "Problem?"

Tommy grinned. "It works!" He held up the laptop, an image of a page from the journal displayed along with the text beside it.

"What's it say?"

Tommy's jaw dropped. "I forgot to read it."

Reading smirked. "To be young." He jerked his chin at the screen. "Well?"

Tommy skimmed the few lines of text. "It's a continuation from the previous page, which I don't have. But it says, 'I pray to the good Lord that I have done enough to protect mankind from the danger such power poses. If the life I have led for all these years was worthy of our Lord's wishes, then I believe I will have that answer in short order. I pray this is true, for I miss my wife, my children, and my brothers. It has been far too long.'" He looked up. "Man. That's deep."

Reading agreed. "You better get that down to Jim and Laura. Start translating those pages. Hopefully, it has the answers they're looking for."

"What do you think it is?"

"No idea. Something important that sounds foolish. That's all I know. I couldn't make out from the photo what he was holding. It wasn't very big."

"And it looked like wood. Why would that be important?"

Reading snorted. "With those two, what they consider important could mean nothing to us."

Tommy grinned. "Don't let them hear you say that."

Reading eyed him. "Remember, I'm the elder here."

Tommy tilted his head forward and stared up at him. "Which makes your words all the more hurtful."

Reading pursed his lips. Tommy was right. "Better get moving."

"Yes, sir." Tommy scrambled across the bench seat and stepped onto the pavement.

Reading slapped him on the back. "Good work."

Tommy beamed at him, then hurried away as Reading's phone rang. He glanced at the call display and saw it was his boss. He did the mental math—it was late in London. She wasn't a fan of his and no doubt wouldn't be pleased about being bothered at this hour. He took the call. "Hello, ma'am."

"What have you gotten yourself involved in now?"

"Nothing much. It looks like some sort of theft at an archaeological site. The Vatican's eager to discover what happened, and because I've dealt with them before and happened to be here, they've asked for my help."

"It's those damn professors again, isn't it?"

"Isn't it always?"

"Those two aren't good for your career."

"Tell me about it. But I can assure you, they've done nothing wrong here—merely discovered a theft that happened today from what was supposed to be a secure site. I just need the word from you so my badge is good."

"You have it. It's not every day the Inspector General of the Vatican calls me at home."

"Thank you, ma'am."

"I'll update the system to show you on duty. I'll let Michelle know as well."

"Thank you, ma'am."

"Now sod off. I was in the middle of a perfectly delightful dream with Idris Elba."

Reading grinned. "From what I understand, he's a very busy man."

"You have no idea."

The call ended, and he fished out his Interpol ID.

Time to go to work.

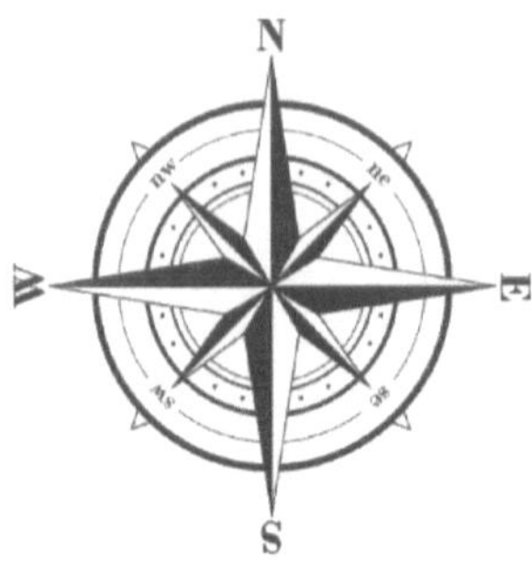

Discovery Site, Water Tunnel No. 3 Project Utility Corridor
New York City, New York

It was a team effort. Laura carefully flipped the pages of the journals, Mai took a photo and sent it to Tommy, who would then decode the page and send it to Acton, who would read it aloud. They were working their way backward through the journals, the mystery revealed in reverse.

"'This mission, centuries long, has finally come to an end. And for that, I am thankful.'" Acton looked up from his tablet. "Centuries? Are you sure that translation is right?"

Tommy glanced up from his laptop. "It's not a translation. I'm decoding it."

Acton's eyebrow shot up. "Wait a minute. You mean these have been in English? You're not translating them from Latin or French?"

"No. It's all in English, at least so far."

Acton pursed his lips, staring at the text. "I have to admit that surprises me."

Laura agreed. "Me too. Could this all be a hoax?"

Acton tapped the screen. "'This mission, centuries long, has finally come to an end.' What does that even mean?"

Laura folded her arms and pinched her chin. "Generational. There's the theory that some Templars escaped and headed for North America. Could that be what this is about? He's the last of the descendants?"

"It must be. And I suppose over time, if they were living here in New York City, the descendants would lose their mastery of Latin and switch to English."

"But there's no real evidence of any of that."

"What about Oak Island?" asked Marconi, standing nearby, his phone pressed to his ear. "I watch that show all the time. They found evidence of Templars on that island."

Acton grimaced. "You do realize reality TV is mostly bullshit."

Marconi stared blankly at him. "You mean even shows like that?"

"Anything's possible. Then again…" He waved a hand at their surroundings. "I think we've just confirmed that anything is indeed possible."

Tommy muttered a curse, tapping away at his laptop before looking up to find everyone staring at him.

"What is it?"

Tommy shook his head in disbelief. "I don't know. I'm starting to wonder what the hell's going on here."

"What do you mean?"

Tommy tapped a few keys then gestured toward Acton's tablet. "Read this one—the first line."

Acton opened the decoded text. "'I have been told today that within a week, I'll be burying my third child. I've come to believe that this is a curse placed upon me by the Lord Himself for abusing the power of the Grail these past five-hundred years. I've known my days are numbered for some time now, and I'm at peace with that, though I'm disappointed I will leave no legacy behind. As we suspected, the Grail is a power no man should possess.'" He looked up, his mouth agape. "This has to be a hoax, right?"

Laura stared at him, then at the body of the man who had apparently written these words. "It has to be, but…it's exactly what you suspected."

"That was a fantasy. I never expected it to actually be true."

Marconi raised his eyebrows. "Wait, are you saying that what was stolen is the Holy Grail? As in Monty Python?"

Tommy snorted. "They didn't invent it. It's from the Bible."

Laura shut down his statement. "No, there's no mention of the Holy Grail in the Bible. It's a myth created centuries later, around the cup that Jesus drank from at the Last Supper."

"Well, the cup is real, isn't it?" asked Tommy. "I mean, if the Last Supper happened, he had to drink from something, so there *was* a cup."

"If we assume that there was a Last Supper, then yes, we can safely assume there was a cup." Laura pulled out her phone, bringing up the photo of the Templar before the theft. "If it was just a common cup— nothing special—it could look just like this."

Acton brought up the photos, zooming in. Little of it was revealed, the cup clasped tightly in the man's large, scarred hands. It appeared to be made from wood, exactly what he would expect. Jesus might have been the King of the Jews, but he was by no means a traditional king surrounded by wealth.

"Wait." Laura pinched the bridge of her nose. "This has to be a hoax. This can't be real."

Acton threw up his hands. "I don't know. If it is a hoax, it was perpetrated over a hundred and fifty years ago. And to what end? No one was meant to find this." He indicated the journals. "Keep decoding. We need to know what the hell is going on."

"But what if it's real?" asked Marconi.

Acton frowned. "Then someone out there has the Holy Grail—and all the power it contains."

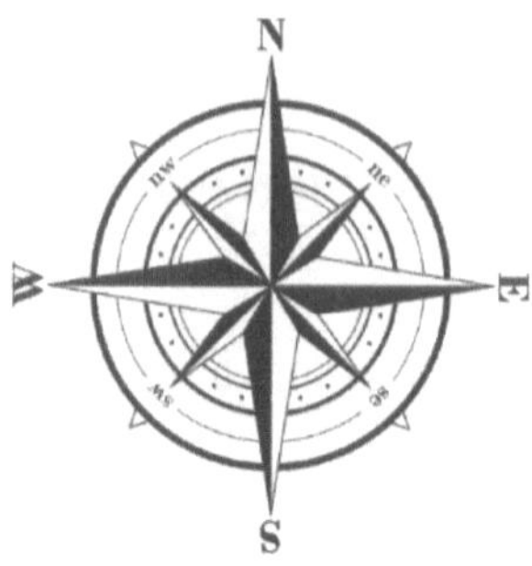

Street Level, Water Tunnel No. 3 Project

New York City, New York

Reading sat in their SUV, his eyes closed, his breathing steady. He exhaled at the count of ten, then opened his eyes and smiled at the numbers displayed on the pulse oximeter. His O2 stats were above 95, and his heart rate was back down below 90—high for some people, but good for him with his history.

He removed the small device and slipped it back into his pocket. Whenever he wasn't feeling well, he checked his vitals to determine whether it was psychological or physical. Unfortunately, far too many times he found his heart rate above 100. Sinus tachycardia, his cardiologist had called it.

He would be lying if he said it didn't bother him. He was too young to die. Far too young, even if he felt old, even if he looked it in the mirror each morning. He had expected to be on this planet for another good twenty or thirty years, but now he prayed for just another ten. Things were as good as they ever had been with his son, and the young man's career was just beginning. He wanted to witness for himself what his son would become, who he might marry.

Oh God, I want grandchildren.

His eyes burned. He wiped away the lone tear that had escaped.

Enough of this self-pity.

He sucked in a deep breath, holding it for a moment, regaining his composure. He hated what his life had become. Constantly worrying if every little chest pain, every little palpitation, was a sign of another heart attack. He feared that the next exertion would be the one that pushed him over the edge. It wasn't how life was supposed to be, yet now it was his life.

And there appeared to be little he could do about it.

He sighed. He could feel sorry for himself later. Right now, there was a job to do. Something was missing from the discovery site, and what Acton had suspected was confirmed by the journals.

"Bullshit," was what he had said.

And it was.

He wasn't a very religious man, but as the old saying went, there were no atheists in foxholes. Now that he had faced death, he found himself thinking more about spiritual things, about life after death, about whether there was a God. He wasn't sure if there was, if any of it was real, though it was certainly more comforting to think that if he only had a few more years of life left, there was something after all this where he would once again see the loved ones he had already lost, and, eventually, everyone he would leave behind.

Please God, let it be real.

He growled audibly. This wasn't him.

A tap on the window had him flinching and his heart racing. His head spun to see Marconi standing there, wagging his tablet. Reading lowered the window.

"Sorry if I startled you. I just wanted to let you know I got that list together for you. Everyone who could have possibly had access to the site today after your people arrived. I emailed it to you."

Reading picked up his tablet off the dash and pulled up the email. Less than ten names were on the list. "You're sure this is it?"

"Yes, like I said, we sealed it off as soon as we found it. We called the local archdiocese, who sent people over. That was it. Nobody was in there until you guys arrived."

"Could somebody have snuck in?"

Marconi shrugged. "Definitely possible. But it couldn't just be anybody. It's not like you can wander in off the street. This is a construction site, fifty feet underground. No unauthorized personnel are allowed."

Reading quickly read the list of names. Not surprisingly, the only one he recognized was Marconi's. "Anybody here a troublemaker?"

"No, they're all good people."

"I need to speak to every one of them."

"I'll arrange it. When would you like to do it?"

"Now."

Marconi frowned. "Okay, I'll do my best. Where should they meet you?"

"Right here."

"I'll start rounding them up and sending them your way." Marconi turned, then held up a hand, whistling. "Yo, Johnny! Come here!"

A man in a hard hat turned and waved. "What's up, boss?" he asked as he jogged over.

"This is Inspector Reading from Interpol. He has some questions for you. Agent, this is Johnny Russo."

Russo's eyebrows rose. "Am I in trouble?"

Reading eyed him. "Should you be?"

"I hope not."

Marconi slapped Russo on the back. "Don't worry, it's just routine." He headed off to find the others, and Reading settled in for what turned out to be a useless effort. Everybody, of course, denied stealing the wooden cup. Nobody had seen anything unusual or spotted anyone who shouldn't have been there. His decades of experience suggested to him they were all telling the truth, except when asked if they had told anybody about what they had seen. Everyone denied it at first. But some eventually admitted they had taken pictures for themselves and posted them on social media or sent them to friends. The fact no one was here yet suggested none had much of a following.

As he dismissed the latest witness from the list, he exhaled loudly. He was investigating the theft of a wooden cup. How far had he fallen? He used to investigate the grizzliest of murders for Scotland Yard, and now here he was, investigating who had stolen a wooden cup. Yes, his friend thought there was a distinct possibility this was the Holy Grail. But to him, the Holy Grail was a Monty Python movie, something from

Excalibur. According to Acton, the most accurate depiction was in Indiana Jones and the Last Crusade.

A wooden cup.

He frowned. Could it be real? They had, after all, found what was believed to be the Ark of the Covenant. If something like that were real, then couldn't the Holy Grail be as well? But Acton had said there was no reference to it in the Bible. Yet it did make sense. If there was a Last Supper, the man had to drink out of something. The journals suggested it had the power to heal, to maintain life.

That had to be nonsense.

But somebody believed it.

The question was, did it really matter? There was no way it was true, so the fact was, somebody had ripped off a wooden cup. Yes, there might be historical significance to it, but he had to treat it like a regular theft.

Marconi approached, wagging his tablet. "I'm sorry. I can't find Reggie."

Reading glanced at the list—it was the seventh name, Reginald Warner.

"I've asked around, and nobody's seen him for at least a few hours."

"What do we know?" Reading asked.

Marconi shifted uncomfortably. "Well, when the initial representatives from the archdiocese arrived, he was with me. We showed them where the chamber was."

"So, he saw what was inside."

"Yes."

"Was he left alone there?"

"I'm not sure if he was alone, but I left him with the reps. I had business to attend to outside."

"Did you see him after the delegation left?"

"No."

"And you didn't think that was odd?"

"This is a big site. A lot of work happening. A lot of people, both below and above. And I was busy with this…whatever this is. Religious artifacts, Templar Knights, Holy Grails, blood of Christ, miraculous powers. It's all bullshit, isn't it?"

Reading grunted. "Who the hell knows? All I know is something was stolen, and it's my job to try to find out who did it and recover it. Right now, our best lead is this missing man. I'm going to need everything you have on him."

"You got it." Marconi stepped away, dialing his phone.

Reading sent the name of the missing employee, Reginald Warner, to his partner, Michelle Humphrey at Interpol, and the local NYPD contact.

Just because you hold a civil service job doesn't mean you're always respectable.

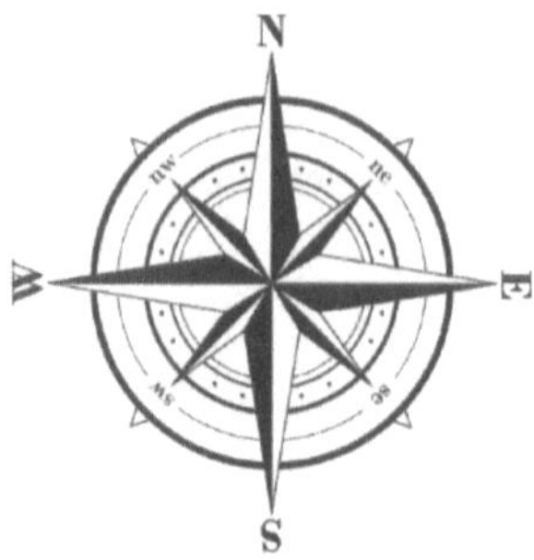

Jerusalem

AD 33

Hannah's heart hammered, her hands trembling as she poured wine into the cup.

Her father stared at her. "What are you doing?"

"I have to try. I have to at least try."

"Try what?"

"If he is who you say he is, I have to try."

Her father let out an exasperated sigh. "Try what?"

She put down the carafe then headed for her mother's bedchambers where the woman continued to groan in pain, her agony released now that their guests were gone—the poor woman stifling her agony as much as she could while they were here.

Berenice's jaw dropped. "Is it because of what he said about the cup and eternal life?"

Hannah ignored her as she pushed open the door, her mother lying on the bed, the coverings tossed aside, her entire body drenched in sweat as she writhed from the torturous pain.

"What are you two talking about?" asked her father, following them into the room.

Berenice responded. "He said something like, 'He who drinks from this cup will enjoy eternal life' or something. I can't remember. I was so busy trying not to drop the plates."

Her father froze. "He said that?"

"Yes, or something like that."

Footsteps shuffled behind Hannah—obviously her father's. She sat on the edge of the bed and worked her hand under the back of the poor woman's head, lifting it up slightly. "Mother, I want you to drink this."

Her mother mumbled something incoherent. Her father stood at the end of the bed, Berenice on the other side.

"You have to try, Mother. Please." She pressed the cup to the dried, cracked lips and tipped it slightly.

Whoever eats my flesh and drinks my blood has eternal life.

The pale purple liquid ran over her mother's lips.

Please God, let this work. Let him not be an imposter.

Yet her mother's lips remained sealed.

"Mother, please. You need to open your mouth and drink this."

Berenice's arm darted out, her finger pointing. "Look!"

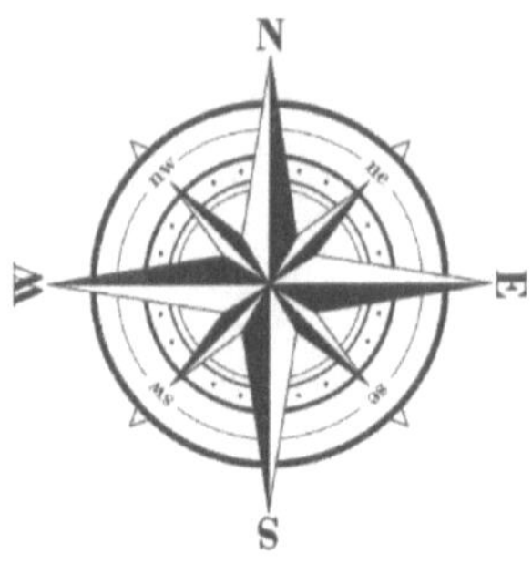

Queens, New York City, New York

Present Day

In the old days, when Reading was with Scotland Yard, he could count on his warrant card to get him through most doors. But now, as an Interpol agent with no actual power, he found himself waiting, waiting for a ridiculously complex process to play out.

He was outside the home of Reginald Warner. Marconi, the man's supervisor, was inside, along with Warner's union rep, as well as two NYPD uniforms. The screen door swung open, and Marconi finally beckoned him.

"It's about bloody time." Reading climbed out of the SUV then shuffled up the walkway, his hip bothering him. He climbed a few steps and took hold of the screen door as Marconi stepped aside.

"You're not going to believe this."

"What?"

"I think it's best you hear it from the horse's mouth."

Marconi led them into the living area where a man and woman sat on a couch, holding each other. Their eyes were red, their tear-stained cheeks suggesting they had been crying for some time. A young child slept beside them, her head in her father's lap.

"I'm not going to be arrested, am I?" asked the man, revealing he was their subject, Reginald Warner.

The officer in charge pursed his lips. "That's not up to me."

Warner finally noticed Reading. "Who are you?"

"Interpol Agent Hugh Reading."

Warner's wife gasped. "Interpol?"

Reading gave a disarming smile, holding up a hand and taking a seat across from them. "Don't worry, I'm not here for you. I'm here at the request of the Vatican. I take it something happened. Why don't you share it with me, and then we'll figure out together what the next step is?"

Warner's head bobbed. "Yeah. Yeah, let's do that."

Reading turned to the officer. "Has he been read his rights?"

"He has."

"Good. Mr. Warner, why don't you tell me what happened?"

"I was at the site, just watching those church people go over it. It was pretty cool, I have to admit. I've always been a bit of a Templar nut." He shrugged. "Who isn't? They were there less than an hour, taking photos, then they left." He flicked his wrist at Marconi. "Frank had gone topside, so I figured I should wait to make sure nobody went inside, so I just took the opportunity to look around, take some pictures of my own. It's not every day you see something like that. I know I shouldn't have, but well, you know."

His wife patted his hand. "It's okay, dear. I don't think they care if you took a few photos."

"Did you send those photos to anyone?" Reading asked.

"No. I never had a chance, and besides, I didn't want to get in trouble, so I never really intended to."

"All right, go on. What happened next?"

"Maybe fifteen minutes later, I got a phone call from my wife's phone."

"But it wasn't me," interjected Warner's wife.

"No, it wasn't, just her number. I guess they spoofed it, I think it's called. It was a man's voice. He said he had my family, and he would kill them if I didn't do what he asked."

"And what did he want you to do?"

"Take the wooden cup. That's it."

Reading's eyes narrowed, and he looked about. "Where's the cup now?"

"He has it, I guess. I was told to leave the cup inside one of those USA TODAY newspaper boxes, right outside the dig entrance."

Reading turned to the officer in charge, who already had his phone out.

"Way ahead of you, Agent."

Reading smiled. "So, then you came home. Then what?"

"I found my wife and daughter perfectly safe. I wasn't sure what to do. I knew what I did was wrong, but I didn't really have a choice. But it was all a hoax, right?"

"No, it wasn't a hoax, though it appears it was a bluff."

"Yeah, that's what I meant—a bluff."

"A crime was committed here."

Warner cursed. "I knew it."

Reading chuckled. "Not by you. You were coerced into doing it. The crime is the coercion. I'm quite confident you won't be charged, though that's up to the local authorities, not me. When you came out of the dig, did you see anybody out of place? Anybody standing around as if they were waiting for you?"

Warner sighed. "To be perfectly honest, I barely remember anything. I was so terrified, so worried about Judy and my daughter."

Reading rose. "Mr. Warner, I'll need you to come with me. I want you to show us exactly where you put the cup and retrace your steps precisely."

"What about my family?"

The other officer, his partner still on the phone in the hallway, stepped forward. "We'll keep a unit here until this is all straightened out."

Warner rose. "Fine." He squeezed his wife's hand. "I'll be back as soon as I can."

The senior officer entered the room, shaking his head. "Assuming we're looking at the right box, there's no cup."

Reading grunted. "I suspect it was collected within moments of being placed. Are there any cameras in the area?"

"Probably. Some units are being assigned to canvas the area. Hopefully, we'll get lucky."

"Hopefully." Reading headed for the door. "But somehow, I doubt it."

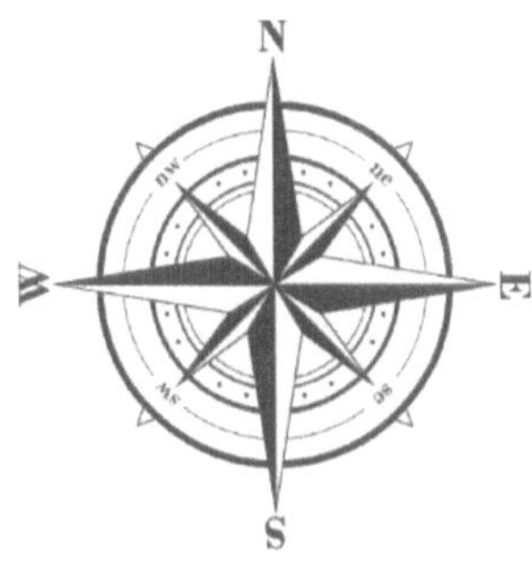

Discovery Site, Water Tunnel No. 3 Project Utility Corridor

New York City, New York

Acton cursed for the umpteenth time as he listened to Reading's update. The phone was on speaker, the signal passed through a cellular relay installed for the construction crew. "So, just to be clear, he's saying that within about fifteen minutes of the delegation leaving, he received a call?"

"Yes," confirmed Reading.

"And then he stole the cup, placed it in a newspaper box where it was picked up likely moments later?"

"Yes, though that part we're not entirely certain about. It's just a theory for now."

"I think we can probably be certain. There's no way it would be left in some place so public for very long. Somebody could have taken it at any moment just out of curiosity."

"I agree, but just for clarity's sake, we can't be certain yet. The NYPD is canvassing for footage now, so hopefully, we'll have an answer on that shortly."

"Good. But let's assume we're right and it was picked up right away. This is a big city. Whoever made that call, or whoever he's working with, would have to have already been here. This wasn't a 'drop the cup in two hours' situation. It was 'drop it right away.'"

Reading agreed. "Good point."

"So, even if someone found out through the grapevine, there's no way they could have arrived here unless by some amazing coincidence they happened to be within fifteen minutes of the site."

Laura stepped forward, raising a finger. "Not to mention, they had to know who to call."

"What do you mean?"

"Well, they called Warner. They didn't call Marconi. So, they knew Warner was the one down here. How could they have possibly known that?"

Tommy's jaw slackened. "It had to be someone from the church delegation!"

"Or Marconi," suggested Mai.

Acton dismissed that idea. "I don't think he would know the significance of the cup. He'd be more interested in the gold. Besides, he's had plenty of time to steal anything he wanted. No, this was someone who knew the significance of the cup."

Laura folded her arms. "But that doesn't make sense. None of the delegation mentioned anything about the cup in their report."

"We didn't notice it at first either. They came in, took photos, and left."

"Maybe one of them did notice."

Acton leaned closer to the phone. "Hugh, ask Warner if anyone struck up a conversation with him. Asked his name, anything like that."

Reading asked their witness. There was a muffled response, then, "Yes. He said one of them asked if he'd be interested in being interviewed. He said yes and gave the man his business card."

"Would he recognize him?"

There was a pause. "Yes."

"Then that's our man. Contact Mario. Get photos of the delegation and show them to Warner. I guarantee you that's who stole the Grail."

"The what?" came Warner's voice through the speaker.

"None of your concern," Reading said, returning to the conversation. "I'll get on it." There was a rustling sound from the phone. "All right, we're off speaker on this end. Give it to me straight. What do you think is going on here?"

Acton exchanged glances with the others. "As much as it makes me feel like a fool to say it, I think this might be the real deal. If not, it's the greatest hoax since the Shroud of Turin."

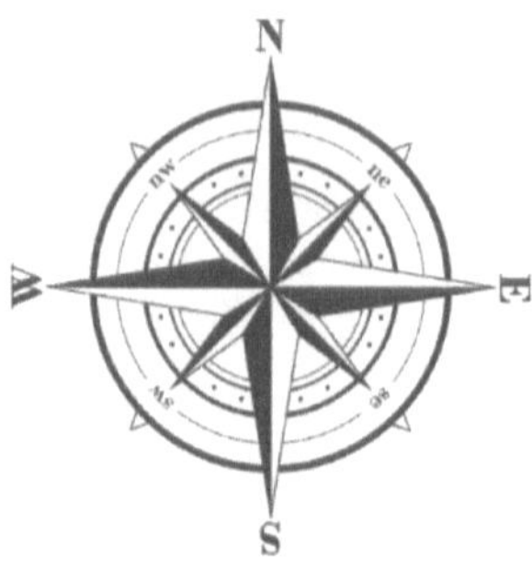

Street Level, Water Tunnel No. 3 Project

New York City, New York

Reading opened the email from Giasson with the requested personnel files. He wanted to believe it was a mistake—that all those now suspected of being involved were actually innocent in this entire affair. Yet his years of experience told him otherwise. Just because you were a man of the cloth didn't mean you were without sin. And something like the Holy Grail could prove too tempting for anyone.

Yet they had to recognize it. That was what confused him. If you recognized something like that, could you contain your surprise, your shock, your excitement? Could you suppress the gasp of recognition, the gasp that would have everyone else in the room turning in your direction?

When he thought of the Holy Grail, he thought of a movie prop. He didn't think of a real cup. And yet, as he read the journal entries scanned by his friends, along with their opinions, he wasn't so sure anymore. The Holy Grail wasn't in the Bible. It came from stories centuries, if not a millennium later. Any man of the cloth, any of those sent in to evaluate the find, would feel the same way—that this wasn't a religious artifact. If they saw it, it would just be a cup. The only thing unusual would be that the man had clasped it in his hands in his final resting place, indicating significance to him. There was no context as to what it was. If someone recognized it as the mythical Holy Grail—and why would they—what did they know that no one else did? And how?

Something more was going on here. And having dealt with the Templars and their secrets, he feared it could be something that stretched back centuries.

"That's him."

Reading held the tablet closer to Warner's face. "You're sure?"

"Absolutely. No doubt about it."

Reading exhaled loudly through his lips. Finally, a solid lead. He sent a quick message to Giasson, confirming the identity and requesting the suspect's current location. The reply came back a moment later, indicating the inspector general was on the job, despite the late hour at the Vatican.

"Did you notice this man outside when you dropped off the cup?"

"No, but like I said before, I wasn't able to really focus on anything."

"Very well." Reading lowered his window and flagged an NYPD officer.

"Yes, sir?"

"I'm done with this witness. Can you arrange transport for him back to his home? Make sure the unit assigned to protect his family remains on site. The suspect is still at large."

"Roger that." The officer opened the rear door and Warner climbed out, turning to Reading.

"Do you think I'm still at risk? My family?"

Reading dismissed the concern. "No. He has what he wants, and I doubt he thought we'd figure out who he is this quickly. We should hopefully have him in custody soon unless he's on the run. If he is, he's nowhere near you. He's heading as far away from here as possible."

Warner smiled weakly. "I hope you're right. Good luck, Agent." He followed the officer and Reading dialed Acton's number. They would have the suspect's location soon enough, and he wanted his friends with him to identify the cup and anything else the man might have stolen.

This should be wrapped up before bedtime.

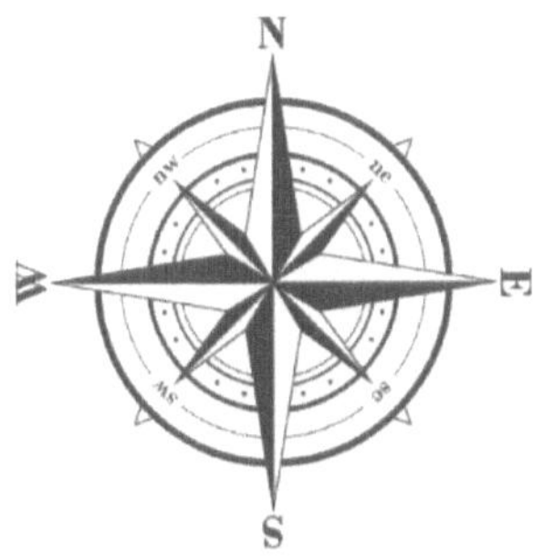

South of Edessa, Mamluk Sultanate

AD 1307

Sir Marcus de Rancourt swung his sword, separating the Saracen's head from his body, urging his steed forward in what might just be his final battle. He had been a member of The Poor Fellow-Soldiers of Christ and of the Temple of Solomon for as long as he could recall, his youth a distant memory. He loved the life it had provided him, but he was too old for the action. He swung again, catching another of their foe, slicing his chest open.

His sergeant and good friend, Simon Chastain, who had served him for decades, grunted behind him as another of the attacking horde fell to the man's blade. "I missed this!"

Sir Marcus chuckled as he tossed his sword in the air, catching it with his left hand, an old injury manifesting itself in his right shoulder for the first time in years. He was out of practice, out of shape, and out of place. This wasn't where they were meant to be. He was supposed to be on the farm back in France, where those he loved and cared about were. But the Order had needed him here, in the Holy Land, one last time. It had been a good life, one he could look back on with few regrets, despite it not playing out the way he had expected.

He wouldn't change a thing.

Arrows whipped past. His squires, David and Jeremy, eliminated four of the enemy coming over the rise. They had stumbled upon a group of Saracens harassing pilgrims, and as a knight in the Templar Order, it was his responsibility to protect them, even if that wasn't the mission. He wore the colors—his white tunic with the red Maltese cross indicating his rank as a knight. It meant he and his sergeant, black replacing the white on his tunic, and his squires in brown, had leaped into action, outnumbered four to one—odds twenty years ago, even ten years ago, he could have lived with.

Yet he was too old for this.

Simon cried out behind him, though to describe it as a cry might insult the proud warrior. Marcus removed the top of a man's head then turned in his saddle to see the best friend he had ever had, gripping at an arrow protruding from his neck, blood flowing freely. More arrows tore past as David and Jeremy rushed to their sergeant's aid, removing four more from the battlefield. Enough bodies lay strewn about that those who remained slowly fell back, apparently uncertain as to what to do, their leader evidently one of those who had just died.

Marcus growled at them, thrusting his sword forward, and they scattered, disappearing over the ridge. He dismounted and rushed over to his friend as David and Jeremy lay him on the ground. Marcus took a knee, his heart aching, his chest heaving, and clasped his friend's hand firmly.

"Now, why did you go and do something stupid like that?"

Simon chuckled then coughed, blood sputtering from his mouth. His friend was dying. This was it. After all these years, after so many battles, his friend would finally be free of the burdens placed upon him. He glanced up at his squires, trained for these things, but both shook their heads. There was no hope. It was indeed over. There was nothing anyone could do.

He stared down, smiling. Simon struggled to say something, and Marcus leaned closer. "What is it, my friend?"

Simon stared up into his eyes, blood trickling from his mouth, down his cheeks, and into his ears. "At least I won't have to shovel shit anymore."

Someone darted toward them—a woman. She dropped to her knees beside Simon, then beckoned to her group. "Quickly! Bring the cup!"

A young woman rose, rushing forward while reaching into a bag slung over her shoulder. She produced an ordinary cup then joined the older woman on her knees. She pointed at Simon's horse. "Get his canteen."

David looked at Marcus with a questioning look, and Marcus jerked his chin. "Do as she says."

There was no point in not humoring them, though their efforts would be futile. There was nothing that could be done for his dear friend. David retrieved the canteen then handed it to the young woman who poured some of the contents into the cup before swishing it around. She closed her eyes and tilted her head back, her lips moving, the older woman doing the same, before they both ended whatever prayer they had recited with an audible "Amen."

The young girl poured half the cup's contents over the neck wound, then the rest into Simon's still open mouth. His eyes shot wide, his hips surging upward off the barren ground, and he gasped, loud and strong, before collapsing back to the dirt. Marcus and the others watched in awe as the arrow was slowly forced from their friend's neck before falling harmlessly to the ground—the wound gone.

Simon stared up at him, puzzled. "What just happened?"

Marcus stared in disbelief. "I don't know." He spun toward the two women. "What magic is this?"

"It's not magic," the old woman said. "This is the cup of Christ. The cup from which he drank at the Last Supper. Any who drink from it will enjoy eternal life."

Marcus dropped onto his haunches as Simon sat up, rubbing his neck, then gingerly turning his head from side to side.

"Eternal life?" David's eyes were wide, his excitement clear.

The young woman stared up at him. "Eternal life can be a curse. Trust me, you want no part of it."

Marcus regarded the two women. "Are you saying…" His voice drifted off. He couldn't form the words. They were too fantastic.

The young girl stood. "Some things are better left unspoken." She walked away then kneeled beside an old man, dead when they arrived.

"Forgive my daughter. You have no idea what she's been through." The girl's mother rose and joined her at what must be her husband's side.

Marcus stood and hauled Simon to his feet, the old warrior still rubbing at his neck.

"Does it hurt?" asked Jeremy, the youngest of the bunch, though no one would call him that anymore.

"Not at all. In fact, I feel incredible, like twenty years have been taken off my life, but in a good way."

"I don't understand. What she said can't be true, can it?"

Marcus eyed his friend's neck, the only evidence there had ever been a wound, the blood still staining his skin and tunic. "I believe my own eyes. And there's no denying that arrow"—he pointed to the offender lying on the ground, blood staining its tip and part of the shaft—"was stuck in your neck. You were dying, my friend. You should be dead."

Simon grunted. "Yet here I stand."

Marcus joined the two women and took a knee. There were no tears here, something he found curious. He gestured toward the stomach wound that had felled the man. "Can't you use the cup on him?"

The young woman dismissed the suggestion. "No, that's not how it works. It can cure the ailing, but not the dead."

"Why not?"

The mother looked up at him. "Because they are with God and are not in need of saving."

He exchanged a look with Simon, who pursed his lips. "Some might prefer to be with God."

The young girl rose. "Would you have preferred that I not save your life?"

The question was snapped, and Simon took an involuntary step back as the mother reached up and squeezed her daughter's arm. "Now, now, Hannah, there's no need for that."

Hannah's shoulders slumped. "You're right. I'm sorry, sir."

Simon scoffed. "I'm no 'sir.'" He jerked his chin at Marcus. "White tunic means nobility. I'm a sergeant."

"I'm sorry, Sergeant. I'm just so tired of this, tired of it all." She inhaled sharply and held out the cup to Marcus. "You take it."

"What?" It was Marcus' turn to step backward.

"Take it. I don't want the responsibility anymore. It's too much."

"What would you have me do with it?"

"Protect it. If it falls into the wrong hands, that person could live forever and use it for evil purposes. I should have never taken it that day. It should have just been washed out and put away along with the other cups his friends used. But I was desperate." The young woman's voice cracked, and her mother wrapped an arm around her shoulders.

"You did nothing wrong."

Tears rolled down both their cheeks.

"Please take it. I don't want it anymore. I just want to die like everyone else, like everyone I've ever known. I want to be with my father, with David, with everyone else to whom I couldn't tell the truth." Hannah closed her eyes, her chin dropping to her chest. "I want to meet Him again and thank Him for everything He did for my family and for our world."

Marcus took the cup, uncertain as to what to say. "If we take this, you'll no longer be protected."

The mother hugged her daughter. "We understand, and it's what we want. It's been so long. We just want it over with. While the idea of eternal life sounds wonderful, it in fact is a curse, one we were willing to pay to be together, but these are things that should never be toyed with. Life and death, that's the power of God, not man. We were never supposed to wield it. Choosing who lives, who dies, whose suffering you relieve—it's too much of a burden for one family to bear."

Simon glanced at the wooden cup. "Did you ever think to simply burn it?"

The daughter glared at him. "We're not fools! Nothing works! The power of God is held within that cup. I've come to believe it was a test. A test I failed."

"We all failed it, dear."

"Well, it's over now." Hannah stared at him. "I don't suppose you would do us the courtesy of ending our lives."

Marcus' eyes shot wide. "I'll do no such thing!"

"Of course. I didn't expect you would." Hannah pointed at the cup. "Be careful. The temptation to use it is too great for any man to resist, though perhaps a Templar who has given himself to God might do so. Just remember, while what it offers may seem good, it is anything but. Beware, lest ye be damned as we were."

She turned and walked away, her mother following, both heading in the direction the Saracens had retreated toward. Simon opened his mouth to warn them when Marcus held out his hand, stopping his friend.

"Let them be. It's what they want. It's the only way for them to be free." Marcus regarded the cup, and Simon voiced what he was sure they were all thinking.

"What does this mean for me?"

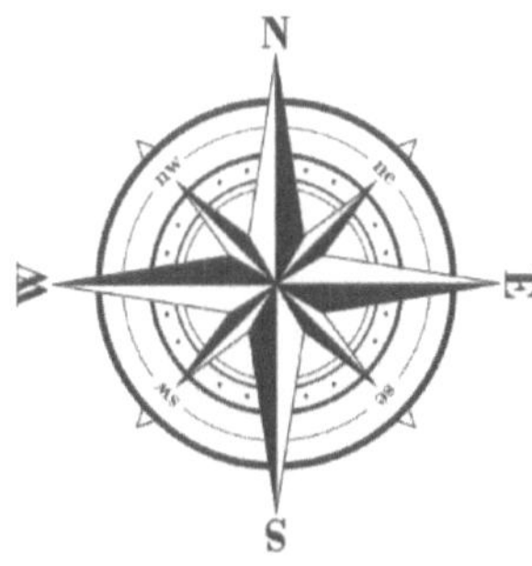

En Route to Moreira Residence

New York City, New York

Present Day

Laura drove with Reading in the passenger seat, Acton in the next row with Tommy and Mai, flipping through the journals on their tablets.

Tommy looked up. "Can you imagine what it must have been like to live through all this history?"

Laura glanced at him in the rear-view mirror. "It sounds bloody horrible."

His eyebrows shot up. "Horrible? Why?"

"From what we've seen so far, it looks like only four of them used the Grail. And you saw some of the passages where he was lamenting the loss of his friends and those he considered family back on that farm. Can you imagine outliving everyone you ever knew, you ever loved?"

Mai shivered. "That does sound horrible."

Acton frowned. "I suppose that aspect would be, but if you could live for another thousand years, see what becomes of the human race. I think that would be fascinating."

Tommy looked up from his laptop. "I think I'd rather sleep for fifty or a hundred years at a time, then wake up and see how things turned out, then go back to sleep. I think living for a thousand years would drive me nuts."

"Me too," agreed Mai.

Laura glanced over at Reading. "What do you think, Hugh?"

Reading looked up from his tablet. "Me? Yeah, sounds rough. Count me out. It's all bollocks anyway."

Laura snorted. "It's just a little bit of fun. Forget the Grail—would you want to live for a thousand years?"

"Nope. I have no interest in living like this for another thousand years."

"But from what we've read, the Grail heals you, makes you feel younger."

Reading chewed his cheek for a moment, his head turning slightly away from everyone. "So…it could fix my heart?"

"Maybe." Laura shrugged. "Are we talking fantasy now, or the Grail?"

"The Grail." Reading's voice was subdued.

Acton leaned forward. "Are you okay, buddy?"

Reading nodded a little too rapidly. "Yeah, I'm fine."

Acton patted him on the shoulder then leaned back, concerned about his friend. He had had a couple of serious health scares recently, both involving his heart, and Acton swore the man had aged five years in the past one. Reading was a shadow of his former self. Almost frail, or at the very least, much more hesitant, more timid than before. Some of it could be age, but he had the sense Reading was scared, and he couldn't blame him.

Laura stole a glance at him in the rearview mirror, his wife clearly thinking the same thing.

Acton lightened the mood slightly. "I'll tell you what, buddy, when we recover the cup, you get the first drink. Fix up that ticker of yours."

Reading sniffed loudly. "I don't think so. I have no interest in living for eternity."

"Apparently, it doesn't work like that. You have to keep drinking from it to live forever. Drinking from it heals you, but from what I've read so far, age-related ailments eventually return. Whatever was broken remains fixed."

Reading turned his head slightly. "You mean…"

"Who the hell knows? Remember, this could all be bullshit like you said."

Reading grunted. "Definitely bullshit."

Laura reached over and patted Reading's forearm. "I say even if it is bullshit, you take a drink anyway. Can't hurt. Plus, it might be kind of neat to be able to say you drank from the Holy Grail."

Tommy's eyes brightened. "Oh, that would be so cool. Can we all do that? I could do a live broadcast. My followers would be so into it."

Acton rejected the idea firmly. "Hell no. If this is the real deal, nobody can know."

"Why not?" asked Mai.

"Can you imagine how dangerous this thing could be? Wars could be fought over it. Even if you gave it to the government to protect, you know it will be used. And if people knew about it, they'd demand it be used to save the sick and the dying. There'd be riots in the streets. And if it fell into the wrong hands, God only knows what could happen." He tapped his tablet with the decoded journals. "No, these Templars were right. This has to be kept out of the hands of mankind. It's just too dangerous."

Tommy regarded him. "But we're all still going to take a drink, right? Fix whatever ails us, reboot the machine?"

Laura, turning and following the squad car ahead of them, said, "I wonder if it might fix those stomach issues I've been having lately."

Acton sighed. "This is why power like this shouldn't be available to people." His entire body ached from countless fights, falls, stabbings, and gunshot wounds. One drink from the Grail could take that all away. It was so tempting. It was too tempting. Could they be that selfish? Recover the cup, each take a drink, then hide it away, perhaps in the Vault, buried deep under the Vatican?

He inhaled deeply. "Now you see the dilemma possessing the Grail poses. Who are we to enjoy its benefits when so many others are suffering far worse than us?"

Tommy's face slackened. "You're right." He slapped the back of Reading's seat. "But he should get to drink. If one of us gets to, he should."

Reading twisted slightly. "I appreciate the sentiment, lad, but I think Jim's right. This is something best not messed with."

Laura gestured ahead. "It looks like we're here. If we're about to recover the Grail, the police will probably want to take it as evidence. If we're going to use it, this could be our last opportunity." She came to a halt behind the squad car and shifted their SUV into park. She faced Reading and took him by the hand. "If there's any chance this is real, and not complete and utter nonsense, I think you should drink from it. None of us is suffering from anything beyond normal aches and pains. You have heart issues. If it's real, if it does indeed contain the power of God, then the fact He put it in our path must mean He wants you to use it."

Reading looked away again, slowly shaking his head. "I just wish we knew. Trying it without knowing seems the act of a desperate man."

Acton's chest ached at the defeat in his friend's voice. This wasn't his friend. This was a broken man, a shell of what he once was. It didn't make sense. The last medical checkup only a couple of weeks ago had apparently gone well. He was improving. He was recovering. Everything was headed in the right direction. His friend was in a funk, and if he couldn't be pulled out of it soon, it could turn into all-out depression. When this was all over, regardless of whether the Grail was recovered and it worked, he had to do something to help his friend psychologically.

A smirk crossed his face as the perfect solution occurred to him.

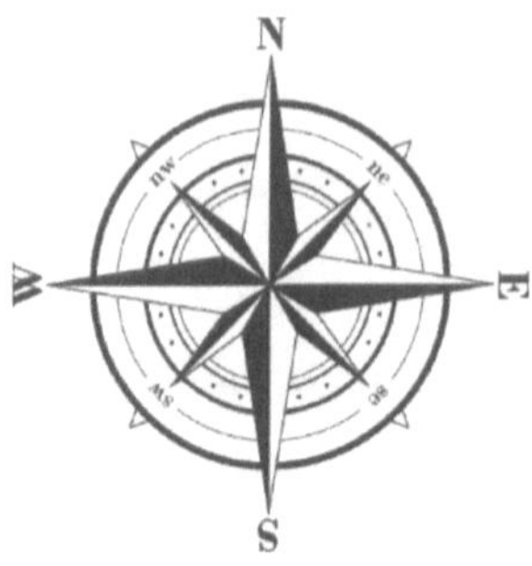

South of Edessa, Mamluk Sultanate

AD 1307

Sir Marcus kneeled in front of the graves, praying silently for the souls of Hannah and her parents, their long, torturous journey, if they were to be believed, finally over. Yet he didn't know what to believe. His sergeant, standing by his side, should be dead. Of that, there could be no doubt. His wound was gone, and he claimed to feel better than he had in years. Yet Marcus had seen people caught up in religious fervor before—someone who hadn't walked in years standing and shuffling down the aisle, though a week later once again in their crippled state. He had witnessed feats of incredible strength in battle, in moments of panic. He had experienced it himself, and it could explain away many so-called miracles.

Yet never in his life, in all his years serving and fighting with the Order, had he seen a wound heal spontaneously.

He had no explanation for that beyond the work of God, and it could be no coincidence that the cup had delivered the miracle. If the women were to be believed, and it was from the Last Supper, almost 1300 years had passed since that event. Could these women truly be that old? He had so many questions for them, yet their answers had died with them, though not at the hands of the Saracens, as they had wanted.

Their screams had been those of terror. He had climbed the ridge to see their clothes ripped off their bodies, the Saracens no longer interested in merely robbing them, but now hellbent on raping them. He couldn't stand by and let that happen and had ordered David and Jeremy to put an end to the women's suffering. Arrows were loosed, the women quickly dead, the Saracens scattering once again.

David fit the last stone in place then rose, clasping his hands in front of him and bowing his head before Hannah's grave, Jeremy before the mother's, each praying for forgiveness for taking the lives of these innocent women. Marcus rose and made the sign of the cross, signaling the end of the proceedings. He bent over and picked up the cup sitting in the sand and eyed it.

"What are we going to do with it?" asked Jeremy.

"I should think we would take it to the Grandmaster," replied David. "This is too important for us." He bowed his head slightly. "No offense, master."

Marcus chuckled. "None taken. And you're right. This is too big for us, but I fear it's too big for any of us."

Simon cocked an eyebrow. "Even the Grandmaster?"

"Even a king. Man wasn't meant to wield such power—to heal wounds, to prevent death. That's the power of God, not man. No one should possess such capabilities. Can you imagine a battlefield where someone merely poured water on the wounds of fallen warriors, who could then rejoin the battle fully healed, perhaps in even better shape than before?"

Simon drew his sword, swinging it around. "Sounds good to me. We'd never lose."

"Yes, exactly. And what happens if the enemy gets their hands on the cup? Then *they* would never lose."

Simon grunted. "Hadn't thought of that. Perhaps you're right. Then what do we do with it? You heard what she said. They tried burning it, they tried destroying it, and they couldn't."

"What if we hid it somewhere?" suggested Jeremy.

"Where would you suggest we hide it?"

The younger man shrugged. "In a cave somewhere?"

David held up a finger. "Perhaps at sea?"

"Wood floats, you fool," grumbled Simon.

David gave him a look. "I'm well aware of that. Obviously, we would weigh it down with something."

"And if it came loose, it would bob to the surface and be found."

"But does that matter if they don't know what it is?"

Marcus dismissed the idea. "All it would take is for somebody to drink from it. They'd quickly discover its capabilities, if not its pedigree, as I'm sure Simon can attest to."

The gruff warrior agreed. "You're right. Even if it weren't for the wound, you would have to be perfectly healthy not to feel its effects." He continued to swing his sword. "I feel incredible." He stabbed the tip of his blade into the sand, his chest heaving.

"You feel younger, yet you're still fatigued?"

"Yes, but after all that, I should be far more tired. I wonder…" He drew his dagger and ran it across the palm of his left hand, drawing blood. The wound healed within moments.

Marcus frowned. "I wonder how long that lasts."

"What do you mean?"

"I mean, will you be healed forever, or does the power need to be replenished from time to time?"

David waved a hand at the graves. "The fact they're dead suggests the latter, doesn't it? They didn't die instantly. It took a little while. You saw how quickly the sergeant's wound was healed. They should have been healed as well. There was enough time before they died."

Marcus' head bobbed. "I think you're right." He jerked his chin toward Simon's hand. "I want you to repeat that test each morning so we can see how long the cup's effects last."

Simon shrugged. "Fine. And when it doesn't?"

"We'll conduct another experiment."

"What's that?"

"We'll pour water from the cup on the wound only, not have you drink it, and see how long the effects last."

Simon turned to the west. "Someone's coming."

Marcus cocked an ear but heard nothing. "Are you sure?"

Simon tapped his ear. "I seem to be hearing better."

"Remarkable."

They mounted their horses, preparing for what might be another horde of Saracens. Marcus tucked the cup out of sight, then spotted the top of a Templar flag. He smiled as a dozen of their brothers crested the rise. They came to a halt, and the lead knight bowed his head slightly at Marcus.

"I am Sir Bertrand de Torroja. To whom do I have the honor of addressing?"

"Sir Marcus de Rancourt."

The man's eyebrows rose slightly. "Sir Marcus, it is an honor. The Grandmaster speaks highly of you, and I thank the Good Lord that we found you."

Marcus exchanged a glance with Simon. "You seek us?"

"Yes, you among others. I come bearing bad news."

"And what is that?"

"The Order has been betrayed, not only by the King of France and those who support him, but the Pope as well."

Marcus tensed. "What are you saying?"

"I'm saying, sir, that the Templar Order has been outlawed, disbanded, and all its members have either been arrested, killed, or are now being hunted. We've been ordered to turn ourselves in for trial."

Simon spat. "Over my dead body!"

Sir Bertrand smiled. "Good. I hope your sergeant's attitude is the attitude of all your men."

"It is." Marcus glanced over at David and Jeremy, who both nodded vigorously.

"Excellent. Then join us. We're heading to the sea where boats have been arranged. The Order will survive."

"Where are we heading?"

"To the north, as far away from Rome and Paris as we can get. The Order must survive, then seek its revenge. We cannot fail, not with the Good Lord on our side."

Bertrand turned his horse around, leading them southwest, with Marcus and the others following. He glanced down at his saddlebag containing the holy relic. His mind raced as he struggled with what to do. If the Templar Order used the power of the cup, they would be unstoppable. No pope or king could bring them down. Yet how could a Templar army, impervious to its enemies, be good for mankind?

He cursed.

Why, Lord, have you given me such responsibility?

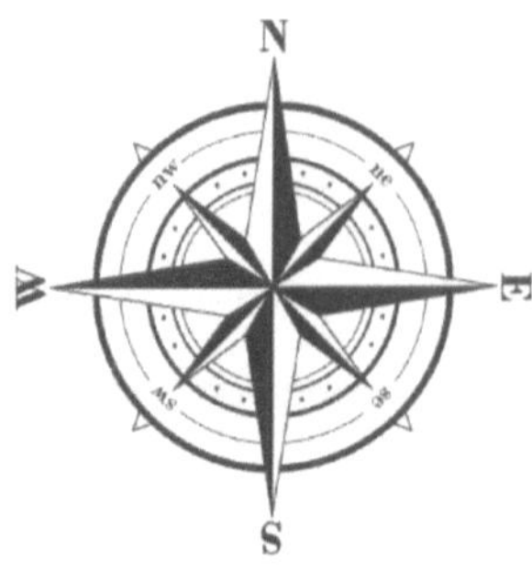

Outside Moreira Residence

New York City, New York

Present Day

Acton climbed out of the SUV when the all-clear was given. It was evident from the reactions of the officers who had gone inside that all wasn't as it should be. "Something's wrong," he said to the others as they strode through the lobby and toward the elevators.

"Our suspect has been assaulted. Looks like two gunshot wounds to the stomach," an officer reported.

Laura gasped, her hand darting to her chest. "Is he going to be all right?"

The officer frowned. "I doubt it. EMTs are on the way, but he's lost a lot of blood."

They boarded the elevator and headed for the sixth floor.

"Is he conscious?" asked Reading, staring up, counting off the floor numbers.

"Yes, but barely. If you're going to get anything out of him, you're going to have to get it now. Once he's out, my guess is he's out permanently."

Acton cursed. "There's no way this is a coincidence. He steals the artifact and then gets shot in his apartment later the same day?"

"Karma?" suggested Tommy. "We aren't just dealing with a regular artifact."

Acton shot him a look, silencing him, the young man's cheeks flushing the moment he realized what he had said in public. They had all agreed this had to remain among themselves. If what they suspected they had found became known, who knew what could happen?

The officer eyed Tommy. "Just what is this guy supposed to have stolen?"

Reading saved the moment. "Just a Templar relic. Only important to the nerds." He jerked his thumb toward Tommy. "This one's a little too much into cosmic balance and spirituality."

The officer snickered. "So is my wife. I love the woman, but my God, enough with the crystals already. The whole damn house is covered in them."

The elevator doors opened, ending the conversation.

Tommy leaned closer to Acton. "Sorry," he whispered.

Acton patted him on the back. "Don't worry about it."

They were soon inside Father Luiz Moreira's apartment, and Acton momentarily closed his eyes at the sight. Moreira, a member of the delegation sent by the archdiocese to assess the Templar find, was on his couch, his face ashen, an officer pressing a throw cushion against the man's stomach, blood staining his pants and the couch.

There was no way he would survive.

Acton turned to the others. "Look for it."

They split off, and Acton took a knee beside the man. "My name is Professor James Acton. I was sent by the Vatican to inspect the find. You took something you shouldn't have, and that's okay. I'm certain God will forgive you when you meet Him, but I need to know where the artifact is."

The man stared at him, his breathing rapid. He had minutes at most. "Do you think God will forgive me?" Moreira's voice was weak.

"Did you hurt anyone?"

Moreira shook his head. "No, but I did scare someone."

"Then I'm sure he forgives you, as God will. Now, the artifact. Where is it?"

"I recovered it like I was ordered to."

"Ordered by whom?"

"Father…"

"Your father?"

"Father…" Moreira's head lolled to the side and Acton reached out, lifting it up. Moreira's eyes fluttered back open.

"Where is it now?" Acton asked, abandoning his line of questioning.

"He took it."

"Your father took it?"

"No, a man. I don't know who he was. When I notified him that I had recovered what we had been looking for for so long, he told me to wait, and that someone would come to pick it up. But when he arrived…he shot me and took it."

"What does he look like?"

Moreira gasped in agony, glancing weakly over his shoulder. "Camera…in the frame. Damn kids kept breaking in…" His voice drifted off, his head slumping to the side, his rapidly heaving chest letting out one last sigh.

Acton reached forward and checked for a pulse, finding none. He shook his head at the officer, who removed his hand from the cushion and stood, the dark brown overstuffed pillow falling to the carpet, soaked in blood.

Moreira had never stood a chance.

Acton rose, rounding the couch and examining the half-dozen picture frames, finding the one in the middle aimed directly at the door, a tiny camera lens hidden in the design. He prayed the technology had worked, because things had now gotten far more serious. Someone was dead—killed by someone who knew what had been found. But what concerned him more was that it sounded like Moreira, and others, had been searching for the Grail for some time.

But why would they ever think it was in New York City?

Detective Shakespeare entered the apartment, bustling with too much unauthorized activity, though at least this time there was a body. And it was fresh, instead of the stale one from this morning. "Who the hell are all these people contaminating my crime scene?"

Everyone turned toward him. A graying man, who had the bearing of someone accustomed to being in charge, stepped forward, extending a hand. "Agent Hugh Reading, Interpol."

Shakespeare took the man's hand, his eyebrows rising. "Interpol?"

"Yes, I and my colleagues"—Reading waved a hand toward four people in the far corner, two men and two women, huddling around a laptop—"are here at the behest of the Vatican."

Shakespeare muttered a curse. "Please tell me this doesn't relate to that Templar thing this morning."

Reading cocked an eyebrow. "As a matter of fact, it has everything to do with that."

Shakespeare stepped over to the body, carefully avoiding the pool of blood on the floor. "Explain it to me."

"While the city was digging a tunnel for the subway, they stumbled upon the room—"

Shakespeare cut him off, rolling his hand in the air. "Skip the preamble. I know about that already. I was at the scene this morning and said it wasn't homicide's concern and to contact an archaeologist."

One of those in the far corner raised his hand. "That would be us. My wife and I are the archaeologists that were eventually brought in."

Shakespeare turned to Reading. "Do I need to know their names?"

Reading smirked slightly. "Definitely."

Shakespeare pulled out his notepad, quickly sketching the scene, indicating where the various players had been when he entered the room. He jerked his chin toward the archaeologist. "Your name?"

"Professor James Acton, Saint Paul's University."

He scribbled it down. "And you?"

"Professor Laura Palmer, Smithsonian."

He noted the British accent. "And you two?" he asked.

The young man operating the laptop looked up. "Oh, we're not archaeologists."

"But you have names, don't you?"

"Tommy. Umm, Thomas Granger. I work at Saint Paul's University."

The young woman waved awkwardly. "I'm Mai Trinh. I work at the university as well."

"All right, so you were all called in because of what was found this morning?"

Heads bobbed.

"So, how the hell did we end up here?"

Reading took over, delivering the facts without commentary. "Your officers found him like this. He was still alive. One of them came and got us. We were able to talk to him briefly."

"Did he say who did it?"

"It was a little confusing, but it was implied he was working for his father. But before he died, he indicated this." Reading waved toward Acton, who held up a picture frame.

Shakespeare's eyes narrowed. "What's special about it?"

"It has a camera in it." Acton stepped over to a table in front of the window and tapped where it had been. "It had a direct view of the door."

"Hi-ho! We've got a fresh one here!"

Shakespeare turned to Vincent "Vinny" Fantino, head of the crime lab, standing in the apartment doorway. "Hey, Vinny. Meet Luiz Moreira.

Looks like he was shot in the stomach and bled out. See what you can tell me." He pointed at the frame still held by the professor. "And bag and tag that. Apparently, it's a camera. It might have recorded the crime."

"We're on it." One of the team members pulled out a large evidence bag and the young man held up a memory card.

"You'll want this."

Shakespeare eyed him. "Did you tamper with evidence?"

Reading stepped in. "We figured time was of the essence, so we wanted to confirm what was on the card."

"And?"

"You can see the shooter clear as day."

"Well, we'll be taking over now. You know very well Interpol has no authority here. All you can be is an observer."

Reading held up both hands. "No problem, Detective. I'm merely here as a representative of the Vatican, keeping in mind that I do have access to databases you don't."

Shakespeare grunted. "Don't worry, Agent. If I can use you, I will. But I just can't have civilians handling the evidence."

"I understand completely."

The frame was sealed, along with the memory card. Shakespeare jerked his thumb over his shoulder. "Analyze that card right away. Run any faces you see on it."

"You got it, boss."

The young woman left and Shakespeare gestured toward the door. "I'll need you to vacate the premises. We don't want to risk contaminating the crime scene. But stick around. I'm going to need statements from all of you."

"No problem, Detective. We have a car downstairs. I'll have them begin on their statements immediately."

"You do that. I'll be down shortly to go over them with you."

Reading gestured to the others, and they all quickly left the small apartment. Shakespeare turned to find Vinny examining the victim. "What can you tell me?"

"Two shots to the stomach. High caliber weapon. Whoever did this wanted him to die, but wasn't concerned with how long it took."

"How long would it have taken him to bleed out?"

"As little as ten or fifteen minutes, an hour at most."

"Why wouldn't he call for help?"

"I haven't found a cellphone on him, and I don't see a landline here."

Shakespeare scanned the room. "I don't see one either."

One of the team entered the room from the bedroom. "I think this dude's a priest."

"What makes you say that?"

"A whole bunch of black robes and white collars in his closet."

Shakespeare reexamined the room. "That might explain why he's living like a pauper."

"So, what did this guy do?" asked Vinny.

"He apparently blackmailed a city worker into stealing an artifact from something they stumbled upon this morning."

"Oh, that Templar thing?"

Shakespeare regarded him. "That would be the one. How did you find out about it?"

"Buddy, everybody's talking about it. It's all over the news."

"Lovely. Let's hope we can get an ID on the shooter from that nanny cam. I'd kind of like to get this wrapped up before it turns into a media circus."

"Too late."

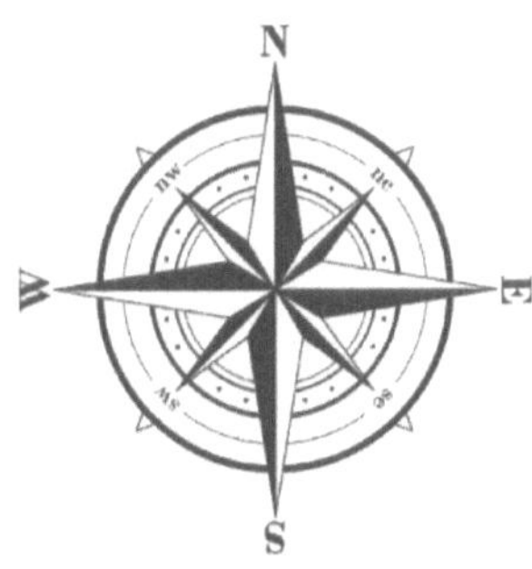

Outside Moreira Residence

New York City, New York

Acton replayed the murder on his tablet, cringing once again as the two shots were fired. The fact a suppressor was used indicated this was a professional hit. This wasn't a crime of opportunity. He turned to Reading. "Any luck?"

Reading frowned. "Not yet. It'll take time. Michelle will run it through all the databases we have access to."

"What kind of priority will it be given?"

"Not very high, I'm afraid. That goes to terrorism cases, international crime syndicates, cartels. Right now, this is just a single murder on an investigation the responsible jurisdiction hasn't requested their help on."

Acton pursed his lips. "So, this guy could be long gone before your people even look at it."

"If he's a pro, he's probably long gone already."

Acton checked his watch. "I doubt it. It's been at most an hour, hour and a half since he shot the guy. This is New York City. It's not exactly easy to get around here."

"What about Kane?" Tommy suggested. "Maybe he can do something with this."

Acton chewed his cheek for a moment before looking at his wife. "What do you think?"

"He's right. Kane's absolutely got the ability to have it checked out faster than us."

"I know, but I hate going to that well when it's not an emergency."

Laura scratched her chin. "True. But we're only asking him to run a face. We're not asking for Delta or anything like that."

Acton exhaled, his lips puffing out. "You're right. Let's do it. If there's any chance this is really the Holy Grail, then this just might be the biggest emergency we've ever faced."

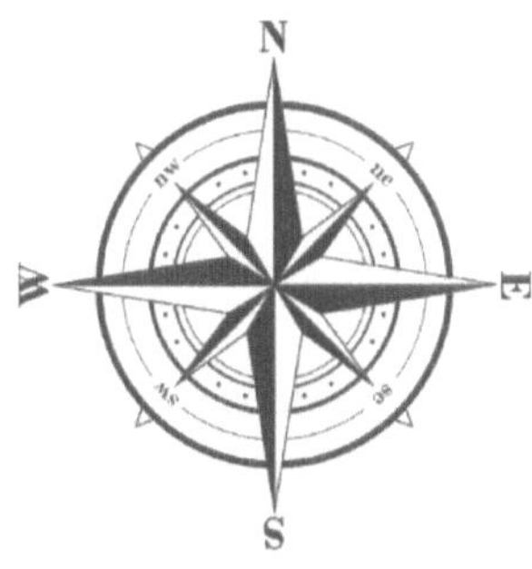

Port of Latakia, Kingdom of Armenia

AD 1307

"Sir Marcus, this way!"

It was chaos. Absolute, utter chaos. Word had spread throughout Christendom and beyond. The Templars' betrayal and loss of status were now known to all, rewards placed on all their heads, especially anyone wearing the white tunic like he did. But the members of his order were proud and refused to hide. White, black, and brown tunics were everywhere. The last of the Order in this part of the world battled through the crowds to get to the boats that would ferry them away from those determined to collect on those bounties.

He followed Simon, who, on any good day, outmatched the common man. But today was an exceptional one. He plowed through those in front of him with vigor Marcus hadn't seen in twenty years. It was the cup—the power of the cup, the power of their Lord. And it was awe-inspiring. If Marcus had ever had any doubts regarding his faith, they had been laid to rest over the past several days. Simon was alive, yet shouldn't be. And not only that, he appeared younger, and was clearly far stronger than before he had taken an arrow to the throat.

Simon was a changed man.

"Get the hell out of my way!" shouted the big man, his voice deep, gravelly, still as intimidating as ever, especially now that it had such energy behind it. The crowd parted slightly, and they charged through on their horses. Simon turned in his saddle, gesturing ahead. "Blockade. Looks like they're forcing everyone to dismount."

Marcus cursed. "Including those of the Order?"

"Yes."

Marcus cursed again. "Get as close as you can, then we'll go on foot."

Sir Bertrand and his men had left them at the edge of town. Marcus was but one name on a list the knight had been sent to find. Arrangements had been made for safe passage on a boat that could only wait for so long. If it became too dangerous, the captain had orders to sail to a rendezvous point only he knew.

There was no time to waste.

They continued forward through the mass of human flesh desperate to escape. Marcus spotted a cloister of nuns and finally realized who these people were. They were people who had worked for the Order. Not all were knights, sergeants, or squires. There were stable boys, cooks, cleaners, seamstresses, translators—everything. Tens of thousands worked for the Order in capacities that shouldn't matter to the powers that be. But if the stories Bertrand had told of mass arrests, of executions, of show trials, accusations of witchcraft, heresy, and more, this was a purge designed to eliminate the Order entirely.

All because King Philip couldn't pay his debts.

Simon dismounted, unable to proceed any farther. Marcus and the others did as well, everyone retrieving whatever they could carry from their saddlebags. Marcus pulled out the cup, eying it for a moment before stuffing it inside his tunic and under his chainmail. It was uncomfortable, but he couldn't risk it being knocked out of his hand or dropped should it become necessary to wield his sword. The four of them pressed onward, Simon and the squires forming a wedge in front of him, and they were soon at the blockade.

A Templar on the other side pointed at them, jerking his thumb toward the docks visible ahead. "Let them through!"

They passed and approached the man, sheets of parchment tacked to a small board gripped in his hand.

"Your name?"

"Sir Marcus de Rancourt."

His name was found on the third page, a checkmark quickly drawn beside it.

"This is my sergeant."

"We don't care. They'll take all the names at the boat. Here, we're just trying to see how many make it before we pull out."

"How many have made it so far?"

The man grimaced. "Not enough."

Marcus' heart sank. "Any word of what's happened in Europe?"

"Nothing good."

"What of the headquarters in Paris?"

"Fallen. I'm afraid there's not much left of the Order, especially in France." The man spat. "Betrayed by our coward of a pope. I don't care what oath I might have sworn. If I lay eyes upon him, mine will be the last face he ever sees."

Marcus gripped the man's shoulder, giving it a squeeze. "Not if I get to him first."

The man jerked his chin toward the boats. "Hurry, we've received word of troops on the outskirts. As soon as they approach, the boats are ordered to leave. Get yourselves on one as quickly as possible. You don't want to risk being left behind. I know I have no intention of surrendering."

"Nor do we," growled Simon.

Marcus shook the man's hand. "Good luck to you." He turned to the others. "Good luck to you all." He signaled his team, and Simon resumed the advance toward the boats, though beyond the barricade, things were far calmer. He felt safer here, surrounded by members of the Order, men he could trust—men who would die for each other should the need arise.

Squires ahead held up signs with the names of boats. "That's us." Jeremy made a beeline for the fellow squire, who pointed to their left.

"Two down. You can't miss her."

"Thank you."

They continued forward, quickly finding the boat and heading up its ramp, a crewmember standing at the top asking for Marcus' name.

"Sir Marcus de Rancourt."

This time, his name was near the top of the list.

"Pleased you made it, Sir Marcus. And the name of your sergeant?"

"Simon Chastain. And my squires—"

The man cut him off. "No squires, only knights and sergeants."

"Bullshit," rumbled Simon.

Marcus held up a hand, silencing what, no doubt, would be a colorful tirade. "These are my squires. They've been with me for decades. Where I go, they go."

"No exceptions."

"Very well." Marcus turned. "Let's go."

David stopped him. "Sir, you must go. It's not safe here."

"It's not safe for you either. We're a unit. We're family."

"Yes. And members of a unit, members of a family, sacrifice themselves should it become necessary."

"Not today. Today it's not necessary."

"Sir Marcus, I'll need you and your sergeant to stand aside, and for your squires to depart immediately."

"Troops have breached the city!" shouted someone from the pier.

"Prepare to cast off!" ordered the captain from somewhere out of sight.

The man with the manifest indicated the ramp. "You have to leave now."

Marcus scowled. "Then we'll all be leaving."

"What's going on here?" boomed a voice.

Marcus turned to see Sir Gilbert Gaudin, a man he knew well from years ago. The glint of recognition was soon joined by a broad smile as the man extended his arms, grabbing Marcus by the shoulders.

"Sir Marcus, how relieved I am to see you're alive!"

"And I you, Sir Gilbert. It's been too long."

"Far too long." The man let go of him. "What's going on here? What's the problem?"

"I'm being told my squires aren't welcome. Where they can't go, I won't go."

Sir Gilbert turned to the gatekeeper. "I see a knight. I see a sergeant. I see two crewmen, don't you?"

The man gulped. "Yes, sir."

"Then do we have a problem here?"

"No, sir."

"Very well." Gilbert turned to David and Jeremy, lowering his voice. "Rid yourselves of the tunics, and unfortunately, you might end up swabbing the decks, but at least you'll be alive."

David and Jeremy both bowed deeply. "Thank you, sir," said the elder David. They rid themselves of the brown tunics denoting their rank as squires, then were directed below decks.

Marcus turned to Gilbert, shaking his hand. "Thank you. They've been with me over twenty years. To abandon them would be as if I abandoned my own brothers."

"I understand." Gilbert lowered his voice. "My own squires are below." He grinned. "They'll be relieved to know someone else will be shoveling shit for this voyage."

Simon grimaced. "I'd rather swim back home."

"I'm afraid we have no home to swim back to." Gilbert led them away from the ramp as it was pulled back on board, the lines cast, long poles manned by the crew pushing them away from the dock as the sails unfurled.

"Where are we going?"

"To a secret rendezvous point. It'll be a long, difficult journey. We have several stops along the way where we'll resupply, but ultimately, we're heading north."

"North as in through the Straits of Gibraltar and up the Atlantic coast?"

"Exactly."

"Just how far north are we going?"

"To the land once ruled by the Vikings."

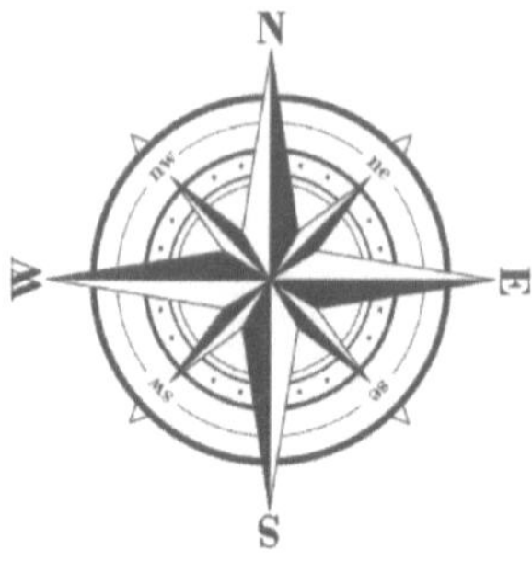

Doha, Qatar

Present Day

CIA Operations Officer Dylan Kane sat behind the wheel of his rental, his seat leaned back slightly, his eyes closed. This was the type of stakeout he didn't mind. After he had deployed the micro-drones and ensured they were in place, someone else was doing the staring for him—his best friend. CIA Analyst Supervisor Chris Leroux and his team back in Langley were on the other end of his comms, watching all exits to the Iranian embassy just down the road. Hezbollah, Hamas, and Houthi representatives had been spotted entering earlier today, no doubt to plan more carnage against the Jewish state.

The entire situation pissed him off. How the hell was Israel getting blamed for what Hamas did on October 7th? The useful idiots protesting, demanding a ceasefire, didn't even understand what the word "ceasefire" meant. They were too busy drinking the terrorist Kool-Aid, displaying complete ignorance not only of the geography of the area but the history. This was not the Palestinian homeland, it was the Jewish homeland. Ancient Judea pre-dated the Palestinians by thousands of years, and if the Romans hadn't forced them out, it would have always been Jewish.

This conflict had to be brought to an end, especially with Iran possibly having nukes in short order. And there was an easy way to do it. It had nothing to do with Israel stopping what it was doing and everything to do with organizations like Hamas and Hezbollah laying down their arms. Their only reason for existence was to kill every Jew on the planet, to destroy the State of Israel, to erase it from the map. "From the river to the sea," chanted by so many morons, meant just that. The elimination of the Jews between the Jordan River and the Mediterranean Sea. Exactly where Israel was on the map. How was that acceptable in anyone's mind? If they would let go of their hatred and simply live in peace, this would all be over. But now that wasn't an option, so all that was left was to kill all the terrorists, which he wholeheartedly supported.

His CIA-customized TAG Heuer watch sent a coded electrical pulse into his wrist, detectable only by him, indicating he had a message on his private network. He pulled out his phone and logged in, rolling his eyes at a message from his former professor, James Acton. The man and his wife were constantly getting into trouble, though it was mostly because they stood up for what was right and put their own lives at risk when others wouldn't. He opened it, his eyebrows slowly climbing as he read about the Templars and a stolen artifact. He continued reading, his mission forgotten, then cursed at the revelation someone had already been murdered.

The body of a Templar found underground in New York City, buried possibly 150 years ago. That was curious. No mention was made of the artifact. Also curious. What might a Templar have worth killing over?

He inhaled sharply. "Holy shit!"

He dismissed the idea. It couldn't be. He quickly fired back a message.

Are we talking Indy 3?

A thumbs-up was the reply.

His stomach churned with the implications. But it couldn't be real. Even if someone thought it was the Holy Grail, it couldn't be real. Could it? He had heard about some strange goings-on over the years with things the professors had found—crystal skulls, the Ark of the Covenant—but this would take the cake.

He pulled up the video attached and watched it, cursing aloud.

"Lance Manion, Control Actual. Are you okay, over?"

Kane snickered like a schoolboy at the Sam Malone-inspired callsign. He forwarded the video and the email chain to his friend. "Yeah, I'm all right. I just sent you something from our professor friends."

A groan sounded on the other end. "What now?"

"You're not going to believe it. Keep it to yourself. Let's see if we can identify the shooter in the video."

"Shooter? Are they all right?"

"Yes, they're fine for the moment. But I have a funny feeling that if they keep heading in the direction I assume they're going, things could get ugly. Very ugly."

A heavy sigh resulted in a burst of static from Leroux. "What part of the world are they in now?"

"One of the most violent places in the world, if you believe some of the politicians."

"You don't mean?"

"Yep. New York City."

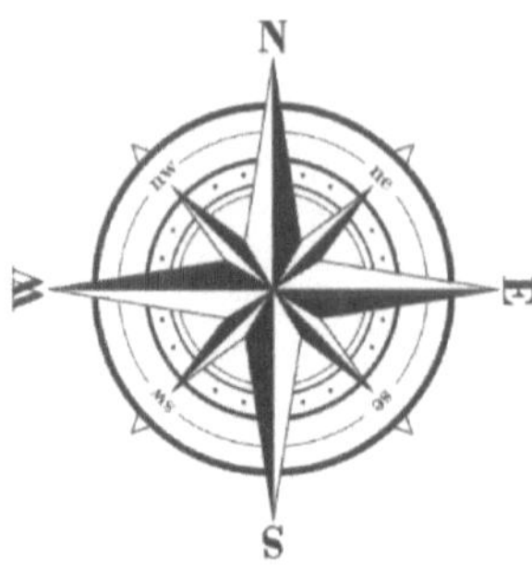

Operations Center 2, CIA Headquarters

Langley, Virginia

Analyst Supervisor Chris Leroux reread the email chain his friend Kane had just sent him. He still couldn't believe it. After the first read-through, he had forwarded the video to his second-in-command, Senior Analyst Sonya Tong. The murder was irrelevant—none of his concern. In fact, none of this was his concern. He was CIA. Their jurisdiction specifically excluded American territory. This was a New York City murder. NYPD, FBI, DHS. But not CIA. They shouldn't be looking at this, yet when it came to the professors, a little leeway was always shown. The country owed them, and they had sometimes come through when the country couldn't.

But they weren't in danger here. This was a theft and a murder, or so it seemed on the surface. Could the professors be right? Could what was stolen be the Holy Grail? His immediate inclination was to dismiss it as nonsense, but he had followed enough of the professors' exploits to know that strange things—some very strange things—were possible. He wasn't particularly religious, though he supposed he believed in God. If Jesus were real, and if the events of His life as described in the Bible had occurred, then the Holy Grail—if it merely referred to the cup Jesus drank from that day—certainly existed at some point. Was it inconceivable it had been protected over millennia? He supposed not. But did it contain the power of Christ?

That, he found impossible to believe.

He fired off a secure message to Tommy Granger, someone who had done side work with him in the past.

Is this for real?

Tommy replied within moments. *The professors certainly think so.*

Is there proof?

Journals that go back to the 14th century, written by one man.

How is that proof?

The journals span over 500 years.

Leroux stared at the screen in disbelief. *How do they know they're not fake?*

We don't know conclusively yet, though they appear genuine. The professors seem very concerned about the Grail falling into the wrong hands.

Why?

If it's real, it could mean immortality for anyone who possesses it, including our enemies. Imagine if Putin could live forever.

Leroux's skin crawled at the notion. He still thought it was insane, yet the vast majority of the country believed in God, believed in Jesus, and many believed in the Bible as gospel. Was it his job to dismiss the beliefs of those he served simply because it was based on faith and not science?

He sighed. This was too big a decision for his pay grade.

He typed one last reply. *Keep me posted.*

He rose, heading for the double doors leading out of the state-of-the-art operations center. "Anything yet?" he asked Tong.

"Nothing."

"Fine. I'm going to see the Chief. Let me know as soon as you get a match."

"I'm on it."

He exited through the doors, designed to prevent any stray signals from getting in or out, then made his way to the elevators, crafting the words he would use on his boss, Deputy Director of CIA for Operations Leif Morrison. How the hell do you tell your boss that someone might have just found the MacGuffin from *Indiana Jones and the Last Crusade* without being laughed out of the room?

The elevator doors chimed, and he jogged the final few yards as they opened. He boarded, lost in thought, ignoring everyone—even those saying hello. He pressed the button for Morrison's floor then receded into the corner, his arms folded, his chin pinched.

What the hell am I gonna tell him?

The truth. As he knew it. But what was he asking for? He wasn't sure. This certainly wasn't CIA jurisdiction, and they wouldn't even know about it if it weren't for the fact Kane and the professors were friends. And this wasn't Nazi Germany, where the Führer had sent out archaeology teams around the world to find mystical artifacts that might give them the power to win the war. This was the United States, where too much of the population believed in Facebook.

He had to tell someone—someone who could make the decision—because, like Tommy said, what if it was real?

He reached Morrison's floor and cleared security. The Chief's receptionist smiled at him as she picked up the phone. "Chris Leroux to see you, sir…yes, sir." She hung up and gestured toward the door. "He'll see you."

"Thank you." Leroux knocked twice then opened the door. Morrison smiled, gesturing toward a chair in front of his desk.

"What can I do for you, Chris?"

Leroux stood by the door, his hand still gripping the knob, uncertainty overwhelming him. He felt like a fool.

Morrison's eyes narrowed. "What's wrong?"

Leroux's shoulders slumped and he sighed heavily, releasing his grip on the knob and finally closing the door then sitting. "I'm not sure how to say this. It's strange. It's crazy." He cursed. "It's ridiculous, but I have to tell someone, just in case it's not."

Morrison leaned forward, his elbows on his desk. "I don't think I've ever seen you like this."

"I don't think I've ever heard anything like this before."

"What is it? Just start from the beginning."

Leroux nodded. "You're right. Just the facts. Here it is—I got an email from Kane. There's been a murder in New York City, and the professors—"

"*The* professors?"

"Yes. They're involved."

Morrison leaned back, steepling his fingers and resting his chin on the tips. "Wait. You're not saying the professors murdered someone."

"No, no, no, not that at all." Leroux exhaled. "I'm not explaining myself properly. Hell, sir, they think they found the Holy Grail!"

Morrison's eyebrows leaped. "Wait a minute. Didn't you say the murder was in New York City?"

"Yes."

"Where did they find this Grail?"

"In a sealed-off room underneath New York City, with a Templar buried in a sarcophagus and five hundred years of journals apparently written by the same man."

"Bullshit."

"That's what I thought too, sir. But I reached out to Tommy Granger, and he said the professors believe it could actually be the real deal."

Morrison leaned forward again. "Wait a minute here. Let me get this straight—they think they found the Holy Grail underneath New York City, in the possession of a Templar who lived for over five hundred years?"

Leroux threw up his hands. "I told you it sounded insane."

"So, this murder, does it involve us at all?"

"Not that I'm aware of."

"So why did they reach out to Kane?"

"They have the murder on tape. Clear shot of the killer's face. So they asked him if he could help identify the killer."

"Isn't that NYPD's job?"

"Yes, but knowing the professors, they're probably trying to get a jump start on the bureaucracy. If the Grail has indeed been stolen, and it is real like they suspect, we can't let it get out of our hands, can we?"

Morrison squeezed his temples, his eyes closed. "We're supposed to deal with national security threats—spies, terrorists, hackers. Not religious artifacts with the power of God."

"Now you see why I came to you."

Morrison grunted. "Thanks for that."

Leroux chuckled. "You're welcome."

"What action have you taken?"

"I have Sonya running the face."

"Anything so far?"

Leroux double-checked his phone. "No. Still searching, but that's it. It's not our jurisdiction. Are we going to let anybody know?"

Morrison shook his head. "Who would we tell? Monitor the situation. Let me know if it changes."

Leroux rose. "Yes, sir." He headed for the door, but Morrison stopped him.

"And Chris?"

"Yes, sir?"

"Keep this under your hat. If word gets out that the Holy Grail might be out there, God knows what kind of shitstorm that will bring."

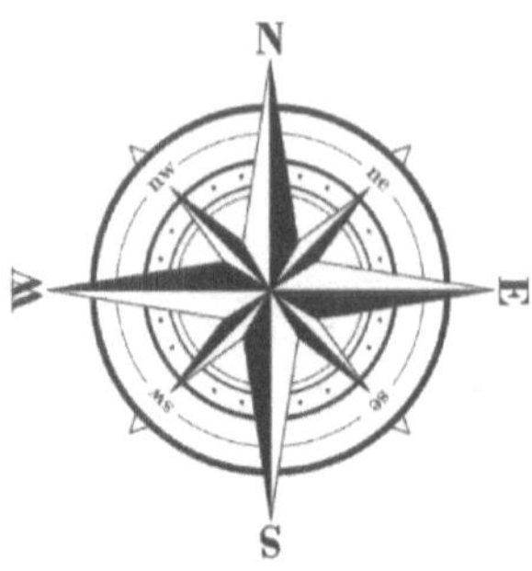

Doha, Qatar

Kane pursed his lips as he read the message from Leroux. The CIA would attempt to identify the killer, but that was it. Morrison hadn't authorized anything beyond that. The response didn't surprise him. It wasn't the CIA's jurisdiction, and running the face was a courtesy rarely extended. It was about all he could hope for at this point.

But with the professors involved, he was concerned for their safety. Somebody was already dead, and he didn't want them to wind up in this week's obituaries. Regardless of whether the Grail was real, someone obviously thought it was—and was willing to kill for it. And if the professors thought it was real as well, knowing them, they would be willing to die for it.

He sent a message to Tommy. *I suggest you return to Maryland so you and Fang can get to work.*

Tommy replied. *Just a sec.*

Knowing the young man, he was clearing it with Mai and the professors. Acton and Laura would likely be eager to offload Tommy and Mai for their own safety, and his theory was confirmed by Tommy's next message.

Mai and I are on our way. Where should we meet Fang?

She'll get in touch with you. Bring everything you know so far with you.

Will do.

He dialed Lee Fang, the love of his life, and former Chinese Special Forces operator. She answered on the third ring, sounding groggy.

"Did you go to bed early?"

He could hear her stretching like a Cheshire cat. "No. Well, yes, I guess. I fell asleep on the couch. Watching TV is boring without you to cuddle with."

A warmth spread through his body. "Yeah, I hear you. Don't you dare jump ahead on Physical 100. I want to see what those crazy Koreans do next."

She giggled. "Don't worry. You've got my word."

"Good. And I might have a solution to your boredom."

"What's that?"

"The professors might be about to get themselves in trouble again."

She immediately sounded alert. "How can I help?"

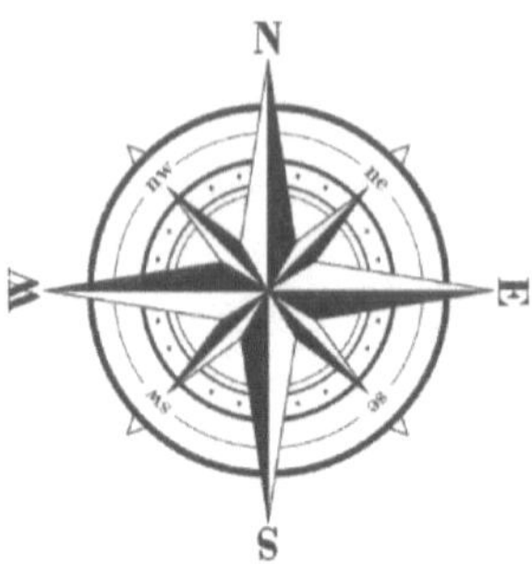

Operations Center 2, CIA Headquarters
Langley, Virginia

Sonya Tong snapped her fingers, directing Leroux's attention to the massive display wrapping across the front of the state-of-the-art operations center. "I got a hit!" An Interpol file appeared, the computer displaying the mapped facial recognition points from the video of the murder, indicating a 100% match.

"Who have we got?" asked Leroux as he rose from his chair, clasping his hands behind his back as he stared at the image.

"We don't have much. His name is Maximillian Kruger, though that's assumed to be an alias. No prints, no DNA on file. He's believed to have been involved in multiple art thefts over the past ten years, several of which were quite violent. Multiple deaths have been linked to him. What you're looking at is the only known photo, from a theft in Buenos Aires three years ago."

"Definitely sounds like our guy." Leroux noticed the tag across the top of the Interpol record. "They've issued a Red Notice on him. That should make things a little easier, depending on wherever the hell he's going. Get this info to DHS, FBI, NYPD."

"Got it. And Kane?"

"Yes." Leroux leaned back. "Now let's see if they can find our guy."

"Good luck with that," muttered Randy Child, the team's tech wunderkind, as he spun in his chair, staring at the ceiling. "This guy seems to be an expert at disappearing." He smirked. "But maybe that's because he hasn't come up against us."

Leroux smiled at the young man. "And he still hasn't. We're not cleared for domestic surveillance. We've identified our target and passed on the info. Our job is done."

Child frowned as he dropped his foot, killing his spin. "Well, that sucks. Since when do we leave a job half-done?"

"Since it's not our job. Get that off the screen. We've got an op to finish."

Tong tapped her keyboard, the Interpol record disappearing, various isolated satellite feeds, one showing Kane still parked where he had been for hours, filling the display once again.

Leroux sat back down, confident he had made the right call, though Child's words gnawed at him. Since when did they leave a job half-finished? They needed to know more about this Kruger. The chances of finding him were slim, based on his past success in avoiding the authorities, but the more they knew, the more their odds improved.

He smirked, an idea forming. He turned in his chair to face Child. "I've got a side job for you."

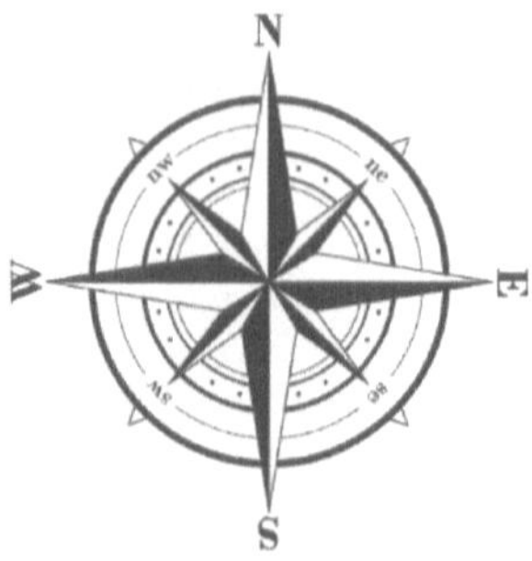

The North Atlantic

AD 1307

Marcus leaned over his ailing squire, Jeremy, at his side for as long as he could remember. He gripped the younger man's hand, picturing him as the boy he had met so long ago. David gripped his friend's other hand, tears shamelessly flowing down his face, while Simon stood at the foot of the bed, revealing no emotion to anyone who didn't know him. But Marcus knew him too well and recognized the pain. While the four of them had served in the Order for years, they had become a family. After being forced to leave for family obligations, the others had stayed by his side, selflessly sacrificing, and had become as close as any four men could. But they were finally about to lose a member of the team, and it broke his heart.

Yet it needn't be so.

He could save his friend.

His free hand clasped the cup, and David noticed. "Can we?"

Jeremy saved Marcus from answering, shaking his head. "No. I'm ready to meet the Lord. I've led a good life, an incredible life, and while I wish I had died on the field of battle, I die content regardless, with my brothers around me, and with the knowledge that you will all soon be safe."

He inhaled sharply, pain racking his body, and Marcus gripped his friend's hand tighter, clasping it with the other. The dawn of recognition of what was about to happen spread across Jeremy's face, and the noble squire stared up at Simon, whose eyes glistened.

"At least I won't be shoveling shit anymore."

A final sigh escaped their friend's body as it slumped into the bedding. David gasped out a cry, draping himself over his best friend, his shoulders heaving silently. Marcus let go of Jeremy's hand, placing it gently onto the bedroll, then patted David's back before saying a silent prayer. He glanced over at the priest standing in the corner of the small sickbay, the man reading from his Bible, his voice a mere murmur, the Last Rites already given after the horrific accident had occurred. A large barrel, improperly secured in the hold, had fallen during a storm, breaking Jeremy's back as he had attempted to tighten the rigging.

The cup pressed uncomfortably against his ribs. Just one drink could have healed his squire, yet they had agreed no one else would use it. Thankfully, it appeared the effects, while long-lasting, weren't permanent. Simon was already complaining about some pain returning to his fingers. It suggested drinking from the cup continuously was necessary to enjoy the eternal life implied by the women they had met that fateful day. Yet the dilemma remained. What to do with the cup? No one should possess this power.

During a stop in Scotland for fresh supplies, he had attempted to burn the cup, yet had failed. He had even tried to destroy it with a blow from his sword, but it had proven as strong as any stone. He had no doubt that over the centuries Hannah's family had possessed it, they had attempted all manners of destruction. So, after his two failures, he gave up, accepting the fact the cup was permanent.

It needed to be hidden away somewhere, or protected somehow.

It was a problem that had haunted him since he had had time to think after setting sail. What possible hiding place could there be that could guarantee it would never be found? He could think of none. And if it couldn't be hidden away, then it had to be protected. But by whom? Three of them remained. Any one of them could die at any moment. They all could die on this voyage, despite assurances from their Scandinavian hosts they would soon arrive at their destination.

He sighed, rising and stepping back away from the body of their friend, a difficult decision having been arrived at. Only the three of them could be trusted to protect the secrets of the cup.

And to do so, a vow had to be broken.

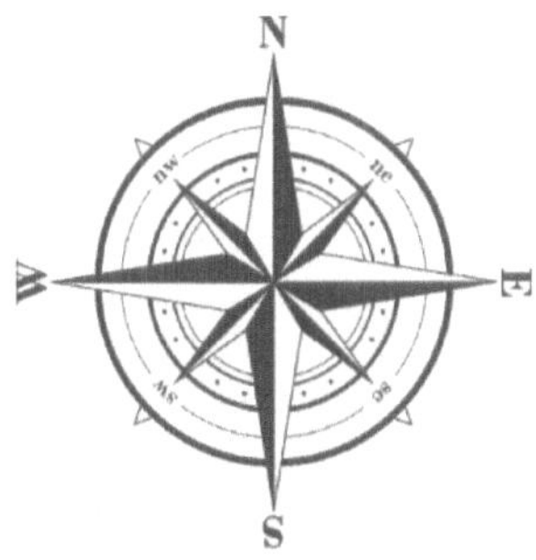

Minsk, Belarus

Present Day

Alexie Tankov, retired Spetsnaz, moaned in pleasure as the tiny import rubbed her naked body over his heavily oiled frame. There was nothing like a good nuru massage—they always ended happily.

There was a rap at the door and he growled. Why was he always interrupted while having fun? "This better be good."

The door opened a crack, revealing a sliver of his best friend's face. "Our friends at Langley have reached out again."

This piqued his interest, and he released an ass cheek, beckoning Arseny Utkin in. Utkin pushed open the door, unable to resist ogling the writhing form of the young Thai girl Tankov kept on staff just for his own use.

"What makes you say that?"

Utkin tore his eyes away from the voluptuous yet athletic form, delivering exquisite pleasure. "Sorry. Same coded message as before, posted on a few Dark Web forums."

"Interesting. Anything big going on that we might be interested in?"

"Apparently, they found some Templar temple under New York City earlier today. I'm pretty sure it's a hoax since it doesn't fit the history."

"Check again. And look up the number. It'll be the same as last time."

Utkin eyed the girl once again before retreating. "I'll get on it."

Tankov waved him away, and Utkin left the room, closing the door behind him. Tankov lowered his head back onto the massage table and closed his eyes once again. Yet relaxation eluded him. He was distracted. The CIA wasn't calling with a warning that he and his men were about to get arrested for stealing artifacts from around the world and selling them to private collectors. For the CIA to reach out meant they wanted something.

There was nothing to gain here beyond a possible get-out-of-jail-free card. They were wanted criminals, but they weren't bad men. What they did was purely for money. No politics, no religion, no agendas. They were hired to do jobs, and they did them. Were they any different than the soldiers they once were? Was killing and violence only condoned if you had the flag of a nation behind you? And even if you did, how people felt depended upon what nation's flag that was. If it was the Russian flag he used to serve, then it was vilified by most of the Western world. But much to the annoyance of those same countries, the Russian flag was hailed across what much of the West liked to call the Third World.

He growled. He had to know what the hell the CIA wanted.

The girl looked up. "Keep going?"

He reached out and guiding her head. "Don't stop, darling."

Utkin sat uncomfortably, Junior having poked his head up with his one good eye to take in the sight. Tankov's woman was gorgeous—every man's dream, though not his. In the looks department, sure, but he wanted a woman he could have a true relationship with, not just a sexual one.

He adjusted the third leg of the tripod, then pulled up the previous records with the contact information for Langley. He punched the number into a secure satphone that Langley couldn't trace—the satellite network was Russian government. Scanning through the thousands of automatic alerts he had set up to find things that might interest their clients, he found nothing that might have piqued the CIA's interest where his team might be concerned.

Except for the Templar hoax, which he couldn't see the Americans contacting them over, he had found nothing. He continued skimming through scores of results, finding nothing, when the door to the conference room opened.

Tankov entered, wearing a robe and a satisfied smile. He dropped into a chair beside him. "You really should get yourself one of those. There's nothing like being with a woman that does everything you want, then you don't have to talk to after."

Utkin shrugged. "To each his own, I guess. Personally, I like the conversation."

Tankov eyed him. "Sometimes I wonder about you."

Utkin gave his friend a look. "Spoken by the man who's obsessed with a certain female archaeologist."

Tankov laughed. "All right, you've got me on that one." He jerked his chin at the laptop. "Find anything?"

"Other than that Templar hoax in New York, nothing. If there's something going on, it's not on the Internet yet, or if it is, it's so obscure it hasn't shown up."

"Fine. Let's find out what the Americans want."

Utkin handed him the phone, pressing the button to dial the number. Tankov put it on speaker, placing it back on the table. The phone rang twice before it was answered by a familiar voice.

"Hello, *Barry*. So good to hear your voice again."

"Mr. Tankov, thanks for getting back to me so quickly."

"Anything for our Langley friends. What can I do for the CIA?" The phone vibrated.

"I've just sent you a text. It has a link. Don't worry, it's safe. We're not interested in you. We're interested in the person whose file that link points to."

Tankov forwarded the text to Utkin. He opened an isolated virtual PC and clicked on the link, twisting the laptop so Tankov could see the Interpol file. His eyebrows rose. "I see. You assume all of us art thieves know each other."

The man on the other end chuckled. "Birds of a feather."

"Uh-huh."

"What can you tell me about him?"

"Not much. If you think I'm bad, he's worse. Far worse. He kills for pleasure. I only kill out of necessity. I assume he's killed, otherwise, you wouldn't be calling."

"He has."

Tankov jabbed his finger at the laptop, and Utkin set to work searching for any recent murder reports. "Has he stolen something?"

"I can't get into any details. Do you have any way of finding out who his client might be, or where he might be headed?"

"I could make some inquiries, but I doubt it will produce anything. The people I deal with typically aren't in a sharing mood."

"So, you have no idea where his base of operations might be?"

"No, except to say that if he's anything like me, it won't be in America or Western Europe."

"Fine. If you hear anything, let me know. Same number."

"And if I do find him? What's in it for me?"

There was a pause. "I'll owe you one."

"*You* owe me one, or the *CIA* owes me one?"

"*I* will."

Tankov chuckled. "Not as valuable, but I'll take it. I'll talk to you soon, *Barry*." He hung up, and Utkin spun the laptop toward him triumphantly with an online article reporting a murder in New York City. That was nothing out of the ordinary except for who was in the photo shown leaving the crime scene.

Tankov smiled. "Hello, professors. I should have known you were involved."

The Grand Hyatt

New York City, New York

Acton dropped into a chair near the window of their suite at the Grand Hyatt as Reading groaned and grunted his way into another. If Acton was exhausted, he could only imagine how tired his friend was. Laura grabbed three bottles of water from the mini-fridge then handed them out. Reading gratefully gulped down about half before sighing heavily. He was clearly tired, but there was a smile on his face.

Laura gave the man's shoulder a squeeze. "How are you doing?"

"Tired. But it felt good to be at a crime scene again."

Laura snickered and took a seat around the table. "You have a strange idea of what's fun."

Reading gave her a look. "Spoken by the woman who is constantly dodging bullets."

She grinned. "I've been known to send a few dodging too."

"Haha. Does this place have room service?"

"Absolutely." Acton grabbed the menu and pushed it across the table toward his friend. "So, we're going to refuel here. What's our next step after that?"

Reading opened the menu. "Sleep."

"I think that's included in the recharge. I mean, tomorrow. What are we doing?"

"Probably very little."

Acton regarded his friend, disappointed. "What do you mean?"

"We have no jurisdiction here. Or more specifically, I have no jurisdiction here, you two have no jurisdiction anywhere. The most I can do is ask questions, and they don't have to provide answers. This is a murder that took place in New York City. It's NYPD's business. Perhaps the Vatican's because a priest was murdered, but even there, all they could do is ask questions."

"Well, at least we can go back to the site tomorrow," said Laura.

Reading closed the menu and handed it to Laura. "Grilled chicken Caesar salad. And no, you probably won't be going to the site tomorrow. It's now part of the investigation."

Acton cursed. His friend was right. It was the site of the original crime—the theft and extortion. There was no way the NYPD was letting them in.

Laura pushed the menu across the table toward him. "I'll have the same."

Acton flipped it open. "Caesar salad isn't exactly a healthy choice, but I guess it's better than a bacon cheeseburger with French fries." He grinned. "Which is my choice."

"Bastard," muttered Reading. "I have to eat healthy, but you get to do whatever the hell you want?"

"Yep, and in front of you too."

Reading flipped him the bird. Acton laughed then rose, stepping over to the phone nearby. He placed the room service order, then sat back down. "So, are we saying we're just going home tomorrow?"

Laura shrugged. "It doesn't sound like there's much reason for us to stay here, but I'd rather not go home."

Reading groaned. "I'm afraid to ask. Why not?"

"The Grail is still out there. We need to find it."

"Leave that to the police. It's their job, and when they get it, nobody knows what it is, so it's not a danger to anyone."

"I wouldn't be so sure about that."

"Who in their right mind is going to take a drink from an unfamiliar wooden cup?"

"Somebody's going to put two and two together," said Acton. "Dylan figured it out within moments of me messaging him. Somebody's definitely going to piece together the puzzle—a Templar crypt, a wooden cup stolen from the site, somebody murdered over it. What would the average person do if they got their hands on that? Pour some water in it, drink, and suddenly feel twenty years younger."

Reading leaned back and folded his arms. "Interesting question. Would you keep it to yourself or would you tell the world?"

Laura's fingertips drummed on the tabletop. "I think you would, at first, keep it to yourself. Then let your family use it, maybe your closest friends, but eventually, word would get out, and then you'd be on the run for the rest of your life."

Acton agreed. "You'd find yourself in the exact same situation the Templars did. You couldn't trust anyone, and you couldn't stay anywhere where there were other people. Neighbors tend to grow suspicious when the guy who's lived on the street forever keeps looking like he's forty when he checks his mail."

"My fear is if it falls into the wrong hands. Like Tommy said, what if someone like Putin got his hands on it?"

"Yes." Reading shifted in his seat. "I think for now the best we can hope for is that the authorities recover the cup, and then it goes into evidence where it will be locked up. The Vatican might make a legal case that the cup belongs to them, though I think it would be a stretch."

"It could end up in the Smithsonian," suggested Laura. "If it does, I might be able to get my hands on it."

Reading cocked an eyebrow. "You're planning on stealing it?"

"If it is the real deal, do we have a choice?"

"We do. Not be criminals."

She eyed him. "You know what I mean."

Reading sighed. "Unfortunately, I do. But if you stole it, who would you give it to?"

"Deliver it directly into the hands of the Pope, then watch him put it in the Vault, where hopefully it will be forgotten over time."

Reading pursed his lips. "Or the Pope might just use it himself."

"I suppose that's possible. It'd be pretty obvious if he did though."

Acton scratched his chin. If the Pope could be trusted, and it was placed in the Vault, a secret archive under the Vatican few were aware of, it might be safe. "You know, there's one thing I was wondering about."

"What's that?"

"Why did the Templar stop using it? He never said. He referred to his time being short, but the cup should have kept him alive forever."

"Maybe he just got tired." Reading sighed. "I know I would. Five hundred years, much of it alone."

"He wasn't really alone at the end. He was married. He had children," said Laura

Reading dismissed her point. "That was at the very end. Maybe the last ten or twenty years. And all of his children died from what he thought was a curse. I think the last of his friends passed, and he held on as long as he could. With that type of loneliness, especially when surrounded by people he had to avoid, it was unbearable. I think he just gave up, stopped drinking from the cup, and welcomed death when it came." He lowered his voice. "I know I will."

Acton noted his friend's deliberate choice of words. Reading was feeling very mortal right now. They would definitely have to get him out of his funk when this was over. Acton's phone vibrated on the table. He picked it up, then flashed the call display at the others.

"It's Tommy." He took the call and put it on speaker. "Hey, Tommy, you're on speaker with Hugh and Laura. Have you guys settled in yet?"

"Yes, sir. We arrived at Kane's secret lair about fifteen minutes ago."

Acton chuckled. He had heard of Kane's off-the-books private operations center and would love to see it one day. For now, he was content simply to take advantage of his former student's paranoid belief that one day his country would screw him—or itself. "Have you found out anything yet?"

"As a matter of fact, I have." He could almost hear Tommy grin through the phone. "When you put the best on the job…"

"Haha. Don't get too cocky. What have you found?"

"Well, while we were driving here, I got to thinking. Remember the victim said it was his father that had him steal the cup."

Acton leaned forward. "Yes, but that's not exactly what he said, is it?"

Tommy groaned. "Please don't tell me you guys have already figured this out."

Reading's eyes narrowed. "Figured what out?"

If he were honest with himself, Acton hadn't figured it out until this very moment. "Go ahead, Tommy."

"He said 'father.' I think he said it twice. He didn't say 'my father,' he said 'Father.' This guy's a priest, so wouldn't it make sense that maybe he's working for another priest? So, Father something?"

Reading threw up his hands. "Of course. Bloody hell. Why didn't I think of that?"

Laura reached out and squeezed their friend's hand. "You can't think of everything. We didn't."

Acton let Tommy have the win. "Okay, what does that give us?"

"Well, I did a deep dive on our murder victim, just from records I could access in the car. He's originally from Brazil. Rio."

Acton's head bobbed slowly. "So, you're thinking that whoever he's working for is from Rio as well?"

"Yes. So, I started doing some digging. I figured if the murderer was working for someone in Brazil, he would most likely be heading south to hand over the cup. So, I started looking for any flights out of New York City or the surrounding area, heading south out of the States."

"There has to be dozens of flights," said Laura. "And all we have is a name that's apparently an alias. There's no way he'd use it to check in."

"You're right. Fang suggested narrowing the search to private charters. The report we got from Langley suggests this Kruger guy is well funded. He's not going to get on a commercial flight with all those surveillance cameras."

Reading leaned forward. "That makes perfect sense. Security is extremely lax at charter terminals."

"Yeah. So, the three of us discussed it here and figured since this was an accidental discovery, if this Kruger guy is a pro hired specifically for the job, it's highly unlikely that he'd already be here waiting. He had to be called in."

Acton agreed. "Makes sense."

"So, I looked for any private charters that took off after the discovery was initially made, landed in or around New York City, then left again heading south within two hours of the murder."

"Well, out with it, lad. What did you find?" Reading was his former self again, and Acton loved it.

"I found *one* flight that matched the criteria. And now that I'm in Kane's ops center, I was able to access CCTV camera footage that shows Kruger boarding a private jet."

"Where is it now?"

"He's still in the air. Flight plan says he's landing in Mexico City."

"Have you told anybody yet?"

"No. I wanted to let you guys know first."

"Good work," said Reading. "Get that info to Detective Shakespeare, NYPD, to me so I can pass it on to Interpol, and to Kane. He can decide if he's passing it on to Langley. I'm sure he will."

Tapping on a keyboard could be heard through the speaker. Their phones all pinged a moment later. "Done. What do you want us to do now?"

"Are you guys equipped for a long stay?"

"We could outlive the zombie apocalypse," said Mai in the background.

"Good. Stay put and start working on gaining access to as many cameras as you can where he's supposed to land. And just out of curiosity, see if, after the initial discovery, anybody from the clergy booked a ticket from Rio to Mexico City. We just might get lucky."

"I'm on it."

Acton picked up the phone. "Talk to you soon, and good work. You're the man."

"I'm the man!"

Acton ended the call, and Laura dialed her phone.

"Who are you calling?" asked Reading as he reviewed the information sent by Tommy.

"Mary. I want her to charter us a flight to Mexico City."

Reading groaned. "I knew I should have ordered the burger and fries."

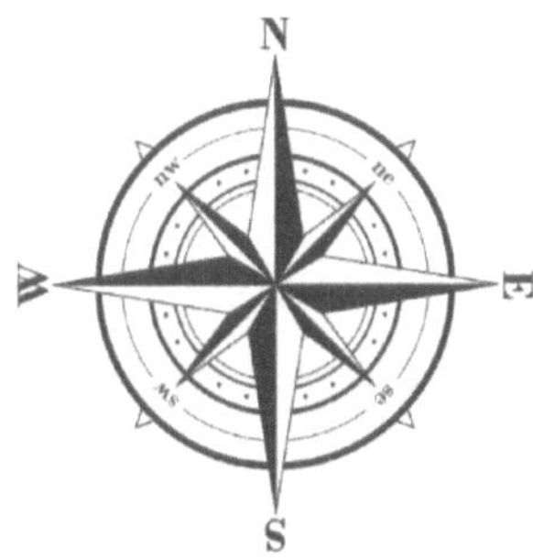

Iceland

AD 1308

David had never recovered from Jeremy's death. The usually boisterous soul had become a mere shell of his former self. He performed his duties, was pleasant enough, but the spark of joy was gone, dead with his friend. This new land they found themselves in—the locals calling it Iceland— was harsh, the winter severe, the landscape unlike anything Marcus had ever seen. Simon was back to his old self—rough, gruff, always cursing some pain in his body, though never requesting permission to drink from the cup they knew would end all suffering.

Marcus still wasn't certain what they would do with the cup, though their new homeland had given him an idea. The land was littered with volcanoes. He had heard of them, of course, but had never seen one. Weeks ago, they had hiked as close as they dared to an active volcano. David had hiked up to the lip, peering over the edge, much to Marcus' annoyance.

"Do you have a death wish? You could have been killed," Marcus admonished.

David had shrugged it off. "Would that be such a bad thing? What kind of life is this? Jeremy's dead. Our brothers are all dead or in prison. We'll never see our family back home again. Do they even know what happened to us?"

Marcus' heart ached at the mention of what had been left behind, of who had been left behind. It wasn't the farm, it was the family they had built there, the helpless, the hopeless taken in over the years, that were always on his mind. His niece, his nephew, Thomas, Isabelle…

He exhaled loudly. He missed them all.

"You're not alone in your feelings," Marcus said, wiping away a threatening tear. "I miss them too. And I sent a letter explaining as much as I could. Hopefully, in time, they'll receive it, though with the Templar messenger network no more, I have no idea whether, or even if, they'll read my words. But we have a duty to perform, one that goes beyond family and friends, beyond even the Order."

David's shoulders slumped. "I know this." He jerked a thumb over his shoulder, back at the lip of the volcano. "I was thinking, what if we threw the cup in that?"

Simon's eyebrows shot up. "Now that's an interesting idea."

Marcus folded his arms, staring up at the glow, the waves of heat reminding him of the desert sands upon which he had spent so many years fighting. "If we were to throw the cup inside a volcano, while it might not be destroyed, it certainly wouldn't be retrievable. Yet we have to be sure. We don't know how these things work—whether they're like pots that simply boil forever, or something entirely different."

Simon scratched his chin. "Maybe we should talk to one of the locals, see if there's an expert on these things."

They had returned to the settlement on their horses, but unfortunately, further research suggested it wasn't an option. Every once in a while, the volcano would erupt, sending its contents down the mountain, which meant the cup could be ejected and subsequently found.

There appeared to be no solution, at least none that he found acceptable at the moment.

There was a rap at the door, startling them all. Marcus eyed his sword, propped up against the wall, but didn't reach for it. They had no enemies here. No one was aware they were Templar. "Come in."

The door opened and Magnus, their landlord, entered, closing the door behind him, running his fingers through his long blond hair and beard, ridding himself of what was hopefully the last snow of the season.

"Greetings, my friend." Marcus gestured toward a chair around the table they now sat at. "Join us."

Magnus did, and David poured him a cup of hot tea steeping near the fire. The man wrapped his hands around the cup and drank from it, sighing as the warmth spread through his body. "You Frenchmen do know how to make a good cup of tea."

Simon grunted. "David knows."

David delivered a rare smile. "An Englishman taught me."

Magnus snorted. "I hear you've been asking about volcanoes."

Marcus leaned back, folding his arms. "Yes. Just curious. We've never seen one before."

Magnus cast his eye around the small cabin they rented. "You've been here for months, yet I still get the impression you don't intend to make this your home."

Marcus frowned. The man was right. They certainly hadn't made themselves at home here, for it could never be home. He shrugged, but said nothing.

Magnus tugged at his beard rhythmically. "I get the sense you're men of action. I'm not going to guess who you are, though I have my suspicions, and if true, you have nothing to worry about from me, and your secret will remain just that. However, if you are men of action and this is merely a stop along your way, I have news that might interest you."

Marcus regarded the man. "And what news is this?"

"Have you heard of the colony established centuries ago in Greenland?"

"No, I can't say I have."

"Far to the west there is a land that my forefathers settled. It's harsh, harsher than here, and with things getting colder, some have grown concerned that we haven't heard from them in many months. We're concerned the colony may have failed. It has been dwindling in size for some time, and there has been trouble with the native inhabitants. A ship is leaving port next week to seek answers by order of the king. Three strong men like yourselves, despite your ages"—Magnus cast a wary glance at Simon, who grunted in protest but said nothing—"would likely be welcome."

"What is the captain's name?" Marcus asked.

"Gunnarr. The ship's name is the Drakkar. If you're interested, I'll let him know to expect you."

Marcus pursed his lips, thinking, then made eye contact with Simon, who gave a curt nod, and David, who shrugged but didn't appear to object. "Tell him to expect us."

Magnus smiled then downed his tea with a satisfied sigh. He rose, then bowed. "Enjoy the rest of your day, gentlemen. And bundle up tight. Nature appears to have one last reminder of who's boss in store for us."

"Thank you for the warning."

Magnus left, closing the door behind him. David asked the obvious. "Why should we join this expedition?"

"Because we know there's nothing to the west. The farther we can get away from God's children, the better. Perhaps this Greenland is where we can find peace."

Simon growled. "Unless there's a god stronger than ours there, we still won't be able to destroy the cup. Which means one day it could still be found."

Marcus chewed his cheek. Simon was right, of course, leaving him with the only conclusion he had come up with so far.

Simon caught his hesitation. "You know it's the only option."

David's eyes narrowed. "What?"

Marcus sighed. "Unless we can think of an alternative, I can see only one option that would guarantee the cup is protected."

"And that is?" David inhaled sharply. "You don't mean…"

Simon rose, pacing in front of the fireplace. "I see no other choice. We know it works. And if those women were telling the truth, they survived over thirteen-hundred years simply by drinking from it. We could do the same and protect the cup."

"But I thought we swore we wouldn't. We let Jeremy die because of that decision. And now we would change our minds and live while he doesn't?" David's voice cracked from the sorrow.

Marcus held up a hand, calming his friend. "We didn't let Jeremy die. He chose to die, and you know that. And I believe if Jeremy disagreed with this decision, he would find a way to let us know."

David jerked his chin toward the storm outside. "Maybe he is."

Marcus smirked. "I would think it'd be something more subtle. But you know we're right."

David's shoulders slumped. "I know. It's just…"

"It's just what?"

"It's just I can't imagine living for another thousand years without my best friend."

Simon halted his pacing. "You'll make new friends."

David stared up at him. "But that's just it. We won't. How can we? Any friends we make will grow old while we don't. Won't that look suspicious? We'll constantly have to be on the move, never able to settle down in any one place. And if we go to this Greenland where there could be no one, it'll just be the three of us, alone, for perhaps eternity." He glanced at Simon. "I don't know about you, but I'm quite certain I'll try to kill the sergeant long before that."

"Not if I get my hands around your neck first," grumbled Simon.

"Why don't we just go back to Europe? Blend in. We have enough money, and, perhaps in time, we could return to the farm."

Marcus dismissed the idea. "No, we can never return. It would put them in danger. And besides, we would have the same problem as we would anywhere. Everyone around us would grow old, yet we wouldn't. Then what are we going to do? I say we continue west, but no longer deny ourselves the power of our Lord Jesus Christ." He pulled the cup out from under his tunic, a metal necklace now wrapped around the base allowing him to conceal it much more comfortably. He poured some of the tea in then held it up. "To your health, gentlemen."

David sighed. "And to the next thousand years of loneliness."

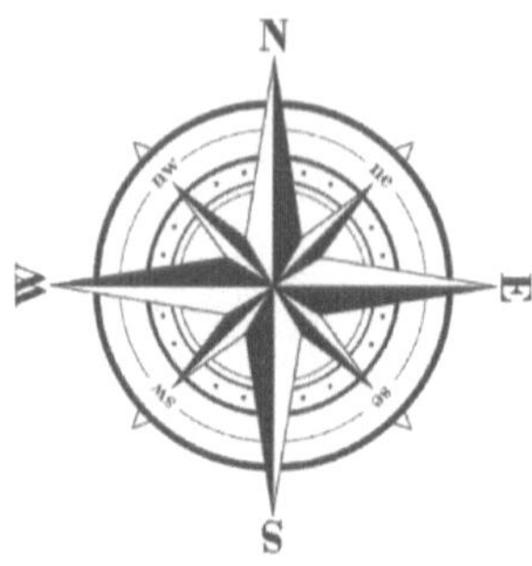

Mexico City International Airport

Mexico City, Mexico

Present Day

Max Kruger cursed as he stared out the window of the Embraer Praetor 500 business jet. At least half a dozen uniformed police were on the tarmac, assault rifles at the ready, as the jet taxied toward the private terminal.

How the hell did they find me? How do they even know to look for me?

This was a simple, though unusual, contract. Several years ago, his mentor had passed it down to him. "I'm too old to be at anyone's beck and call."

Kruger had read the file and had nothing but questions. "Why would the Church have someone like you on retainer?"

His mentor had corrected him. "Not the Church. A specific church."

He had reread the contract, and the man had been right. It wasn't the Vatican. It was the Church of the Holy Grail, based in Brazil. "But the Holy Grail isn't religious doctrine."

"You picked up on that, did you? Good, good. It took me some time to figure that out myself."

"It says here I have to be no more than twelve hours from New York City at any given time. Why New York City?"

His mentor had shrugged. "No idea, but they apparently thought something would be found there eventually, and they wanted me to go in and recover it, no matter what the cost."

"How did they find you?"

"They didn't. The contract was passed on to me by *my* mentor, and apparently his before him. I'm not sure how far back this goes, but at least fifty years, if not much longer."

"Do we even know if this church still exists?"

"It does. I've had it checked out. And besides that, every year the deposit goes into the account. With each handover, the contract was revised, and an updated version sent to the new holder from the church, as mine was, confirming that not only did this particular church want the contract to continue, but that they were still able to fund it."

How they managed a half-million-dollar-a-year retainer, indexed to inflation, was beyond him. Especially considering this particular church's location. Yet every year since he had held the contract, the deposit was made like clockwork.

Yesterday morning, when he had received the call, he just happened to be in England on another job. He had always ignored the stipulation that he remain within twelve hours of New York City. It was ridiculous—it ruled out the bulk of the world he worked in. But when he had received the call, he had managed to fulfill the contract through pure coincidence. He placed his other job on hold, booked a charter flight, and had been in New York City less than eight hours after the initial contact was made.

But that hadn't stopped him from acting while in the air. His contact, whoever that was, had fed him a wealth of information, including what he was to steal. A wooden cup, gripped in the hands of a Templar buried under the streets of New York City.

The wooden cup now hanging around his neck, attached to a chain encircling its flared base.

He hadn't concerned himself with the apparent unimportance of the relic. Instead, he had instructed his contact, who was at the scene, to get the names and phone numbers of anyone guarding the location. That information had come through within minutes, and once he received the all-clear from his contact, he had pounced. Using his resources, he had accessed the man's personnel file. Within minutes, he had the wife's name and number, the child's name and age—everything required to coerce Reginald Warner into stealing the artifact and hiding it inside a USA TODAY vending box where his contact could retrieve it.

It was already secured before he even touched down in New York City. He had retrieved the cup, eliminated the only connection to him, taken the man's phone, then was aboard this very plane within an hour.

How in the hell did they connect me to this?

He frowned as the engines powered down.

Maybe it has nothing to do with this job.

That made sense. There was a Red Notice out on him, after all. Interpol was eager to get their hands on him. Someone might have spotted him at the private airport and reported him. Anything was possible.

But he was prepared for these eventualities.

He sent a text message, and a thumbs-up reply came a moment later.

The flight attendant appeared after the pilot announced they were secure. "I'm not sure what to do," she said, trembling.

He smiled reassuringly at her. "You do your job. Open the door. Greet our guests. They're not here for you. They're here for me."

She nodded, then performed her duties as if nothing were amiss. She stared at him, and he motioned toward the door.

"Go. Make sure you have your hands up. Go slowly. Tell them anything they want to know. You've done nothing wrong." He jerked his chin at the door as the pilot and copilot appeared. "You heard what I said. Go."

Everyone scrambled down the extended steps, and he watched as they rushed toward the police, their hands raised high. They were patted down, then led away into the private terminal by two officers.

Leaving four, plus a man in a suit, holding a megaphone now pressed to his lips.

"Maximilian Kruger, or whatever name you're going by today. Please exit the plane with your hands up."

Kruger sighed. Everything had been going so smoothly.

Inspector Miguel Rios lowered the megaphone and waited. Their suspect was an Interpol Red Notice subject, wanted for at least half a dozen murders, including one committed last night in New York City. He was a dangerous man, an art thief of apparent renown—something they didn't deal with much in Mexico City. Half a dozen Federales were standard in a situation like this, though they had more on standby at the main airport that he could draw upon, should it become necessary. Though with the crew safely inside without incident, he suspected this man was all bark and no bite.

His victims, according to the record, were typically unarmed. So, when facing half a dozen assault rifles with highly trained personnel behind them, surrender appeared to be the order of the day.

He smirked as Kruger appeared in the doorway. "Exactly as I thought." He raised the megaphone. "Descend the steps with your hands up."

Kruger complied, partially—one hand gripping the rail as he descended, the other high in the air. As soon as both feet were on the ground, the offending hand rose.

"Five paces forward."

Kruger complied. The man's bespoke suit caught Rios' eye—something was out of place. He wore a custom-tailored suit, likely costing several months' worth of his meager federal salary, but had a large piece of dull jewelry around his neck. Audacious bling, he might expect—he had seen it before, especially with those who thought life was a rap video. But this was different. Plain, not flashy.

Wood.

Kruger came to a stop.

"Raise your jacket so we can see your waistline."

Kruger lowered his hands, raising his jacket. He slowly spun, no weapon evident.

A sound cracked out from behind Rios. He spun, searching for the source of the odd sound, quickly followed by another. There was a grunt, one of his team collapsing beside the police unit they had been using as cover from Kruger, blood spraying the door. Before his partner could react, he too went down. Rios scrambled around the bumper and dropped to his knees, using the tire as cover as he grabbed his radio.

"This is Rios! We need backup now! Officers down, I repeat, officers down!"

Two more shots rang out, but his other two officers had had the presence of mind to take cover as he had.

"Where are the shots coming from?" he shouted.

Both men shook their heads. "I can't see them!" replied the closest.

"That's kind of the idea," laughed Kruger in flawless Spanish.

Rios stole a glance at the man, who stood exactly where instructed to, his hands up, a smile on his face.

"I can stop this if you want me to."

Rios wanted to tell the man to go to hell, but he already had two dead and was responsible for the lives of two more. This was Interpol nonsense—they were doing some other police force's bidding. No Mexicans had died because of this man.

Until today.

"Call them off!"

Kruger raised a single finger. "Done."

"Now what?"

"Now you let me leave."

"You're just delaying the inevitable. You've killed two federal officers. They won't rest until they have you in custody."

Kruger chuckled. "*They* may never rest, but I assure you *I'll* be sleeping like a baby tonight, far from your country. You'll never find me. No one ever finds me."

"We found you today."

"Yes. I'm curious about that. How did you manage that?"

A car engine revved in the distance, approaching rapidly. It had to be Kruger's men, or reinforcements. Which, Rios couldn't tell. Not yet. He didn't bother looking.

"You screwed up. Everyone eventually does."

Kruger dismissed the statement. "No, I don't think I screwed up. They might have caught me on camera. That's fine. I don't mind that so much these days. There are so many cameras everywhere, there's no avoiding them, and I can change my face easily enough. I want to know how they found me so quickly."

"No idea. I was just sent to pick you up and arrange a handover to Interpol." Multiple engines approached now. He turned slightly to see three black SUVs rapidly closing in. "Friends of yours, I presume?"

"Yes."

"You expected this?"

"No, though I planned for it."

"An expensive precaution."

"I'm paid well by my clients."

"And just who was your client this time?"

"Not that I would ever tell you, but you would never believe me if I did."

Two of the newly arriving SUVs came to rapid halts behind Rios, the third rounding the police units and coming to a stop in front of Kruger.

"What do we do?" asked one of the officers.

Rios lowered his weapon to the ground. "We let them go. Put down your guns."

Both men reluctantly complied. Kruger walked around the SUV, opening the passenger side door.

"It's been a pleasure. I'm sorry about your men. Assuming you continue to cooperate, their families will be compensated."

Rios said nothing, seething in anger. As if any amount of money could take away the pain this man had inflicted.

Gunfire rattled to his right, and his eyes bulged at the sight of half a dozen police units from the airport racing toward them, three of them light-armored vehicles with what appeared to be .50 cals mounted in the rear. Kruger's ride was shredded within moments, the man himself dropping to the ground, writhing in agony, blood spoiling his tailored shirt. The reinforcements turned their attention to the other two of Kruger's vehicles, their occupants returning fire. An RPG appeared from the back seat of one, the projectile soon streaking across the tarmac and taking out the lead LAV. It erupted in flames and black smoke as it flipped onto its side. A second vehicle slammed into it and spun out, its tire catching on a curb, causing it to end up on its roof.

Two of the enemy dropped when something smacked into Rios' back. He fell to the side, struggling for breath as his own shirt rapidly turned red. The gunfire continued, and he reached for his radio, desperate to deliver one last message to his family, but he couldn't reach it—it had fallen to the ground only feet away.

The gunfire rattled for several more minutes as his world slowly faded, and then it finally stopped. Who had won, he wasn't sure. But for him, it didn't matter. This was it. Never again would he kiss his children goodnight. Never again would he hold his wife in his arms. Never again…

Someone walked past him, and he forced his eyes open. If he had the strength, his jaw would have dropped at the sight of a priest approaching Kruger's body. The man kneeled and performed the last rites before rising.

Rios stretched an arm out toward him. "Father…"

The priest turned. "I'm sorry, my son, but there's no time."

And with those words, the priest walked away. Rios gasped his last breath, shocked to see whatever had been hanging around Kruger's neck now hanging around the father's, the man who had refused to perform one of his most sacred duties.

What did I do that was so wrong to deserve to die like this?

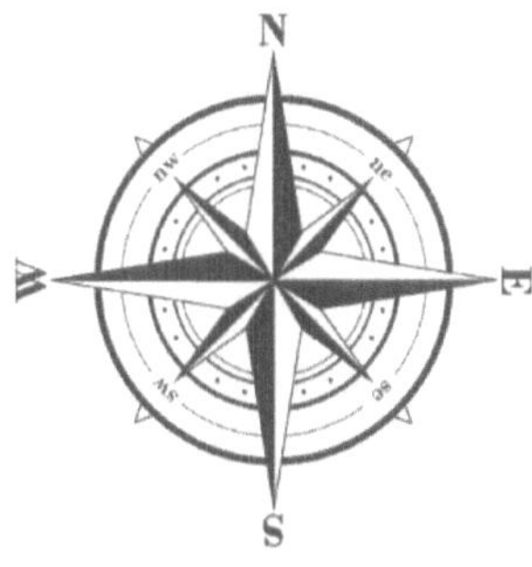

The Ritz-Carlton Doha

Doha, Qatar

Kane lay on the bed in his hotel room, the mission complete. And successful. The micro-drones he had inserted into the Iranian embassy had borne fruit, recording several meetings between Hamas, Hezbollah, Houthi, and Iranian officials, outlining their plans for the coming six months and beyond. This included a continued disinformation campaign, continued attacks on Israel and international shipping lanes, as well as interference in Western elections.

The recordings, along with the photos taken by him showing exactly who the players were, were all back at Langley now. What would happen with it was of no concern to him. Analysis wasn't his job, and politics certainly weren't. He suspected a lot of the intelligence gathered would be selectively leaked. If Mossad knew who some of the players were, they would eliminate them. If Western intelligence agencies were aware of the social media strategies, they could disrupt them—though it was difficult when the massive corporations behind these platforms refused to cooperate or believed that lies, slander, and libel were part of free speech when they weren't. The First Amendment said congress can pass no law abridging the freedom of speech. It meant the government didn't have the right to prevent you from expressing yourself. It didn't mean freedom from consequences, and it only applied to governments. It had nothing to do with private platforms. Facebook, X, and other platforms could censor the nonsense if they were willing.

His watch gently zapped him, the coded pattern indicating a message from his private network. He sat up and logged in through his phone. He brought up the message from Tommy and cursed. There had been a shootout at the airport in Mexico. A lot of people were dead, including their suspect. But that wasn't what had him concerned. It was the fact the professors and Reading were already on a flight heading to Mexico.

This situation was getting increasingly out of control. Bodies were piling up. It didn't matter now whether the Grail was real. It was clear somebody thought it was, and that it was worth killing for. The professors, in their zeal for doing what was right, were heading toward trouble that he feared could get them killed.

He sent a message to Cameron Leather, a former British Special Air Service colonel, who was now the head of the professors' security team, mostly used to secure their dig sites in Peru and Egypt. *Please tell me you're heading to Mexico.*

His phone pinged with a reply moments later. *Four-man team already inbound. Any intel appreciated.*

Contact Fang. She'll provide whatever we've found so far and keep you in the loop.

Thanks. Any more help from your end?

Officially, no. Not yet.

Understood.

Leather and his men were excellent, but what they could do was limited, especially since it was illegal for them to carry weapons. They needed professional help. It was time for a Hail Mary.

He sent a message to an old friend, an old friend who would definitely help if he could.

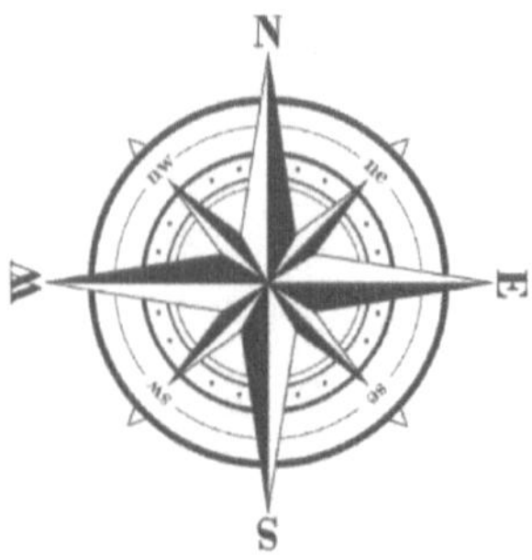

CIA Headquarters

Langley, Virginia

Leroux sat in his office, the op over, Kane scheduled to leave on a commercial flight within the next hour. A backup team was monitoring, just in case something went wrong, but there was no evidence the Iranians or any of their co-conspirators, including the Qataris, were aware they had been observed.

The micro-drones were an incredible technology that eventually would be protected against, though that was an expensive undertaking, leaving most countries simply unable to afford to do it. He was about to head home to spend some time with Sherrie before she deployed on an op, yet he couldn't leave without reading the reports on what had happened in Mexico. Almost twenty dead, fairly evenly split between the good guys and the bad, including their suspect, Kruger.

There was a tap at his door, and he looked up to see Tong standing there. He smiled at her. "I thought you had gone home with the others."

"I could say the same of you."

He chuckled, gesturing at the screen. "You know me. No rest for the wicked."

"I'd hardly describe you like that." She shifted uncomfortably, the comment casual among friends, though possibly misinterpreted with the knowledge they both had feelings for each other that could never be acted upon while Sherrie remained in his life. "I found something I think you're going to want to see."

"Oh?"

"Have you had a chance to review the footage of what happened in Mexico?"

"I was just about to."

"Check your inbox. I queued it up to the key part."

Leroux flipped over to a secure email and brought up the message, opening the attachment. It showed security camera footage from the nearby terminal that had an angle on the events from earlier. Bodies were strewn about, several vehicles aflame. A lone figure walked among the dead. He kneeled beside one of the victims, and Leroux's mouth fell open. "Is he performing the last rites?"

"Looks like it to me."

"Holy shit! That's a priest. What the hell is a priest doing there?"

"I don't know. He came in from out of frame. We need to put in a request to see if there's any other footage available to show where he came from." She pointed. "Watch here."

Leroux leaned closer, peering at the screen. The priest reached down and removed something from around the victim's neck, then placed it around his own. "What is that?"

"I'm not sure. The resolution is shit. If you zoom in, it's all pixels. There's no way to enhance it, it's too small. But you can see there was something dark against the victim's shirt, and now there's definitely something around the priest's neck."

They watched the man walk away and out of frame. They were seeking a small wooden cup, and the photos he had looked at showed it with a metal chain wrapped around its flared base. The man on the ground had to be Kruger. Could he have hung the Grail around his neck? A priest had arranged for the theft of the Grail in New York City, and now another priest had shown up in the immediate aftermath of a gunfight and taken the Grail for himself. This looked more and more like the church was involved, yet he couldn't believe the Vatican was behind this.

"What do you think?"

Leroux frowned. He had been told to keep this to himself, though if he couldn't trust Tong, who the hell could he trust? "Close the door. It's time you're brought into the loop."

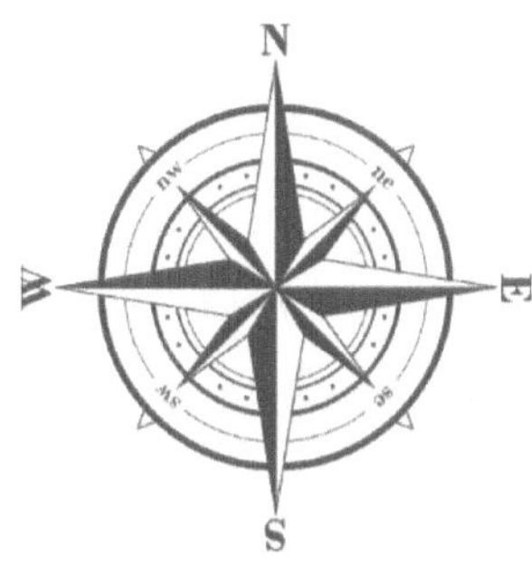

Caye Caulker Beach Hotel

Caye Caulker, Belize

"Thanks, guys. I really needed this."

Command Sergeant Major Burt "Big Dog" Dawson smiled at Sergeant Will "Spock" Lightman. "I think we all needed this. It's been pretty much non-stop all year."

Sergeant Carl "Niner" Sung agreed, draining his far-too-girly drink and holding it up over his head. A cabana boy rushed over and grabbed the empty glass.

"The same, sir?"

"Keep 'em coming."

"Yes, sir."

"I get the sense things aren't going to be slowing down anytime soon," said the Korean-American expert sniper.

They were 1st Special Forces Operational Detachment-Delta, commonly known as Delta Force, America's most elite Special Forces.

Though today, they weren't trained killers. Today, they were beach bums. They had wrapped up an op in Venezuela, and the colonel had given them permission to take four days of R&R. They had hit Belize, a country popular with vets looking to escape the nonsense of what was going on back home, and what many feared was to come.

Dawson loved his country, but he hated what it had become. One half hating the other, split down the middle by algorithms controlled by corporations determined to create division to fill their coffers. It was disgusting. Everyone was aware what was happening, yet nobody wanted to do anything about it. It was as if the country was determined to devolve into left and right, into hatred, and eventually, violence that could spin out of control. How the hell did a civil war work in a modern democratic society? He wasn't sure. All he knew was that he hadn't signed up to kill Americans just because their primary news source and leaders lied to them.

He pushed away the thought. They were here to have a good time, to unwind, to blow off some steam. Most of the team had gone back home to be with their other halves, but Spock, a recent widower, needed this. So, he, Niner, and Atlas had kidnapped their brother, forcing him to enjoy himself for a change.

Sergeant Leon "Atlas" James emerged from the water, his impossibly muscled physique drawing the attention of women and men alike.

Niner sighed. "He is a sight to behold, isn't he?" He publicized his admiration with a wolf whistle, much to Atlas' annoyance. The big man grabbed a towel off the back of his lounge chair and dried himself off.

"I thought we agreed you'd cut that nonsense out," rumbled the big man.

Niner grinned. "You mentioned something, but I never agreed."

Spock set his beer down. "Definitely doesn't sound like something Niner would say."

Dawson agreed. "Definitely not."

Atlas groaned, then sat in his chair, the contraption groaning under the strain of his massive muscles. "You guys aren't helping."

Spock cocked an eyebrow. "Whatever made you think we would?"

Dawson snorted. "I think when we get back to base, you should get your head examined. I think you're getting forgetful."

"Piss off. All of you," said Atlas.

Laughter erupted, and Niner squealed in delight as the cabana boy brought him a fresh drink. The young man flashed him a smile, then left with a little sway in his hips.

Atlas picked up his beer. "I think he likes you."

Niner's eyes shot wide. "Huh?"

"If you play your cards right, he'll keep your bed warm tonight."

"Hey, I'll have you know I'm in a committed relationship."

"Yeah, but is it really cheating if it's with the other side?"

Spock leaned back. "Interesting question."

Dawson's phone vibrated. He fished it out of his pocket and brought up the message. His eyebrows rose.

"Problem?" asked Atlas.

"It's Kane." Dawson brought up the message from his former teammate and rolled his eyes. "Looks like the professors might be about to get themselves into trouble."

Niner groaned. "Not again."

Spock sighed. "What is it this time?"

"Not sure, but Kane's asking if we might be available to head to Mexico City."

Niner grinned. "Last time we were there, it was a lot of fun. I'm in."

"I think we have different definitions of fun." Dawson turned to the others. "So, anybody else?"

Atlas held up his beer. "You know what the answer is. Anything for those two."

Spock agreed. "Count me in. You know I'll never leave those two hanging."

"That's what I figured," Dawson said, sending a reply to Kane. "Say goodbye to Belize, gentlemen. We're heading back to Mexico City."

Niner drained his drink. "Is somebody going to warn them?"

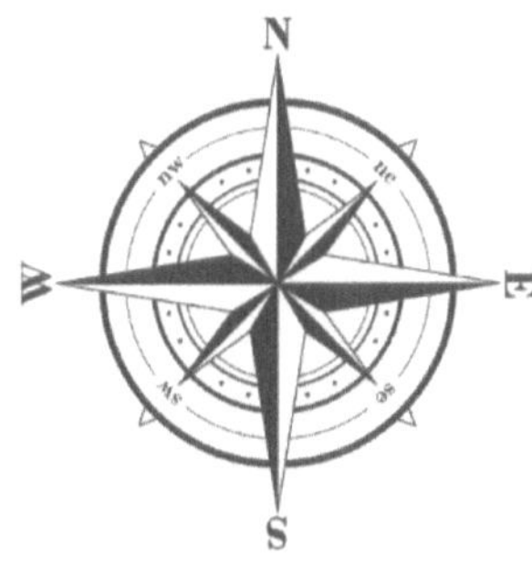

Approaching Mexico City

Acton flinched, his eyes fluttering open as he searched for the source that had disturbed him. He found the flight attendant smiling down at him.

"Sorry to startle you, Professor, but you wanted to be woken up fifteen minutes before we landed."

He nodded, pressing the button on his seat, raising it from the fully reclined bed it had become. The young woman took away the sheet and blanket.

"Can I get you anything?"

"Coffee. Tea for the two Brits."

"Already done."

"Thank you."

The young woman retreated to her galley. Acton reached over and gave Laura a gentle shake. "Wakey, wakey, babe."

She moaned. "Are we there yet?"

"Fifteen minutes out."

She bolted upright. "Drat! I didn't think I'd sleep that long." She raised her seat and rolled up her sheet and blanket, tossing them onto the seat across the aisle along with her pillow. "There's just something about the drone of the aircraft, the vibration. It makes me sleep like the dead."

Acton glanced over at Reading, sprawled out in his own seat, his portable CPAP strapped to his face. "Yep. He looks so calm and gentle like that, doesn't he?"

Reading's hand slowly rose, his middle finger extending. "I'm awake, you bastard," he grumbled.

Acton laughed. "I hope *we* woke you."

Reading raised his seat and turned off his CPAP before removing the mask. "Why would you hope that?"

"Because it means you were asleep."

Reading grunted as he rid himself of his coverings.

The flight attendant reemerged with their morning pick-me-ups. Everyone prepared their drinks as she served their pre-ordered breakfast, a bagel and cream cheese for Acton, a lightly buttered toasted bagel for Laura, and buttered whole wheat toast with jam for Reading.

"Twelve minutes," the young woman reminded them as she headed back down the aisle.

Everybody ate and drank in silence, phones and tablets gripped in their free hands as they caught up on messages.

"I have an email here from Michelle," said Reading. "The Mexicans have confirmed Kruger is dead. Still no confirmation of who he actually is, but once we get his DNA into the system, we might get lucky. Maybe even find a match to prints from an old crime before he got good at it."

"Hopefully. But do we really care about that? He's just a middleman," replied Acton.

"He's a murderer."

Acton conceded the point. "You're right. And I don't mean he didn't deserve justice, nor that his identity is unimportant. I just mean with respect to our immediate purposes, we need to find out who hired him."

Laura held up her tablet, playing a video of the chaos at the airport they were heading toward. "I'm guessing it's this guy."

Acton leaned over and watched the footage for the first time. "Huh. Looks like a priest to me."

Reading, viewing it on his own tablet, agreed. "Definitely. It's too bad the quality of the video is shite. There's no way we're getting a face from that."

"True," said Laura. "But there might be other camera angles. If we're lucky, Tommy, or perhaps Langley, will get a better image." She wagged her phone. "I've got a message here from Cameron. They'll be landing two hours after us."

"Two hours?" Reading raised an eyebrow. "Weren't they closer than we were?"

"It's not the flight time, it was getting from the dig site to the airport. And they had to do that at night. They just got in the air."

Acton grinned. "Are they on the Lima Express, or did you get them a charter?"

"Charter, thank God. Mary was able to get a plane for them, but only because it took them so long to get to the airport."

Acton finished off his bagel and wiped his mouth and hands, bringing up a message from Kane. He smiled.

Friends are on the way. Unofficially.

"Looks like we might be getting some help from Bravo Team after all."

Laura smiled. "Really? Who?"

"I don't know. Kane says, 'Friends are on the way. Unofficially.'"

Reading grunted. "That's good, but without weapons, they might not be very useful."

Laura shrugged. "All I know is I feel safer with them around. But something tells me Mexico City isn't where the danger is."

Acton agreed. "We'll take a look here and confirm what we all know."

"Which is?" asked Reading.

Acton held up his phone. "That video shows what we assume is a priest taking something from around Kruger's neck. It has to be the Grail."

"And you don't think the priest is based in Mexico City?"

"No, I don't."

"You might be right. I have a message here from Detective Shakespeare confirming the identity of the murder victim last night and all of his local contact information. But more importantly, I have a message from Mario with his full personnel file. He's originally from Rio."

Laura leaned forward. "Oh?"

"And get this. The church he last worked at there? It translates to 'The Church of the Holy Grail.'"

Acton raised an eyebrow. "There's no way that's a coincidence."

"Why not? I would think there'd be a lot of churches around the world called that, or some variation thereof."

"No. The Holy Grail isn't Christian cannon." Acton opened a new message to Giasson. "We need to know the history of that church."

"Why?"

"Because of the name. Somebody named it that. We need to know when, who—"

"And why," added Laura. "It might give us an idea of how far back this goes."

"How far back what goes?" asked Reading.

"This conspiracy."

Reading regarded her. "Conspiracy?"

"Yes. A priest from Brazil, from a church named after the Holy Grail, is in New York City working with one of the top art thieves in the world, who arrives the same day the Holy Grail is found, yet no one is supposed to know it even exists. That same priest is murdered—likely so he can't talk and reveal the destination of the Grail, and then another priest shows up at the massacre scene in Mexico City, probably because that's where the handover was supposed to happen. Remember, we were never supposed to find Kruger."

"I'm willing to bet that priest is from the same church," said Acton.

Laura wagged her phone. "Professor Google says it was established in 1858 by Father Lucas Santos, under that name—'Church of the Holy Grail.'"

"Then I think we've just proved that this conspiracy is generational." Acton slumped back in his chair as the landing gear lowered. "Father Santos must have somehow found out about the Grail and became obsessed with it, but for some reason had to leave New York. He made sure someone was always in New York City just in case it was found." He sent the message to Mario. "We need a complete history on this Father Santos." He faced Laura. "And contact Mary. We're going to need emergency visas for Brazil. Mexico City is just a pit stop."

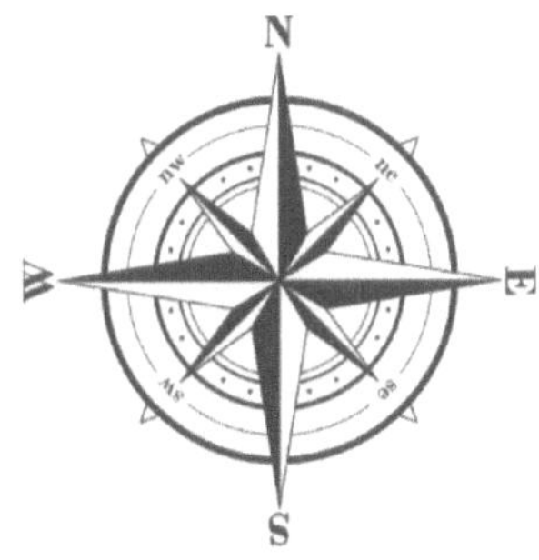

The Vatican

"Why wasn't I informed?"

Giasson skimmed through the history of the Church of the Holy Grail as Father Esposito demanded an explanation as to why he was kept out of the loop regarding what had been happening in New York City. The church had been founded in 1858 by Father Lucas Santos, a bit of an eccentric sent to Brazil, apparently under protest. According to the records, he had at first refused his transfer, insisting he remain in New York City to tend to a matter of great importance to the Church, though he had refused to say what that matter was. Once threatened with defrocking, he finally agreed, leaving New York City, never to return.

He had established a church in one of the poorest neighborhoods of Rio. According to the reports, there had been no problems with Father Santos for the remainder of his career, nor his oddly named church since.

Giasson looked up from the report to find Esposito staring at him impatiently. "Why was he allowed to name the church this?"

"What?"

"I said, why was he allowed to name it the Church of the Holy Grail?"

"I have no idea. Maybe he thought it would appeal to the locals, and the powers that be agreed. Does it really matter? I want to know why I wasn't kept informed about what was happening."

Giasson leaned back. "Because I didn't know if I could trust you."

Esposito's eyebrows shot up. "What? What do you mean?"

"Hardly anybody knew about the site yet something was stolen. We had a leak somewhere. I didn't know where it was, and until I determined that, nobody could be trusted."

"You trusted the professors."

"Yes." He didn't provide an explanation as to why, despite Esposito's glare demanding one. "What do you make of all this?"

Esposito's shoulders slumped and he sighed heavily, apparently giving up the fight. "I'm not sure. I've read the files and the decoded journals. It's absolutely fascinating, even if it is a hoax."

"Do you believe it to be so?"

Another sigh. "I'm not certain. Clearly, somebody believes it isn't if they're willing to kill for a cup made of wood. But I have to admit, if this is a hoax, it's incredibly elaborate, and I can't see the point. As far as we can tell, that room was sealed by this Templar shortly after his final journal entry, which was dated 1832. There's no evidence anybody's been in there since until yesterday. If this were a hoax, you'd want it to be discovered so you could sit back and laugh at everyone you'd fooled."

"So, what you're saying is you think it could be real?"

"I don't know. Wouldn't it be wonderful if it was?"

"Would it?"

"Of course it would! It would be proof that Jesus was real, that His power was real."

"Shouldn't faith be enough?"

"It's enough for men like you and me, but for the masses who doubt, for the masses who don't believe, the Cup of Christ would be a powerful tool to convince the nonbeliever."

"I see it more as a dangerous artifact, whether real or not."

Esposito sat back, folding his arms. "You being in security, I can see that. I prefer to have a little more faith in humanity."

Giasson regarded the man. "Despite all the evidence to the contrary we don't deserve such consideration."

Esposito chuckled. "I suppose you're right. If we assume this cup is indeed *the* cup, what are we going to do about it?"

Giasson had asked himself the same question. It was now evidence in a murder investigation in New York City and a massacre in Mexico City. If the professors were correct, it was headed to Brazil, and he had no doubt it would soon be in the Church of the Holy Grail. He knew enough from his own experience that the idea of a belief, a mission handed down generation to generation for almost 200 years, was absolutely plausible. After all, he was the head of security in an institution begun 2000 years ago, handed down from believer to believer, now encompassing over one billion followers.

"If it's real, we have no choice but to recover it. And if it isn't, then it's a matter for the authorities."

Esposito pointed out the obvious. "But we have no way of knowing until we have it."

"You're right, which means we have to get it first."

"We can't let the Brazilians recover it. God only knows what would happen to it then. That country is so corrupt, there's no telling what they might do with it if they knew what it was."

Giasson regarded Esposito. "They might be corrupt, but they're not stupid. If they're sent in to recover a cup at the Church of the Holy Grail, somebody will put two and two together before they're even through the door."

"How will you stop them?"

"By not telling them."

"What?"

"There's nothing to tell them. This priest they believe took the cup in Mexico City, as far as we know, didn't do anything wrong except take a wood carving. Hardly a major crime. Even the Mexican police are saying he's only wanted for questioning as a person of interest."

"So then, what are we going to do?"

"For the moment, the professors and their security detail are going in to investigate."

"Is that wise?"

"No. But you've dealt with them. Do you honestly think there's anything I could say that would stop them?"

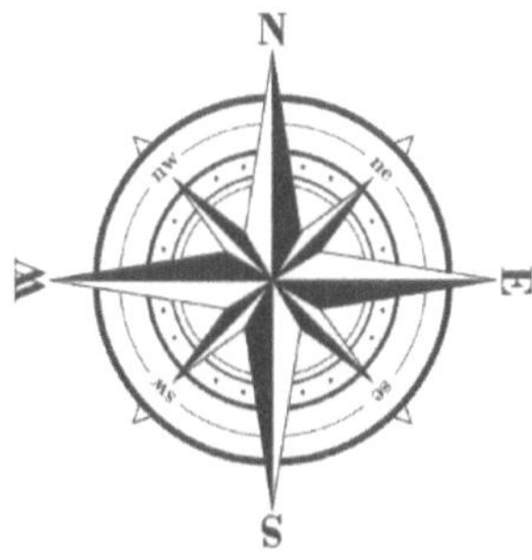

Mexico City International Airport

Mexico City, Mexico

Command Sergeant Major Dawson hailed retired Colonel Cameron Leather as the head of the professors' security detail descended the steps of the private charter. Dawson shook the man's hand. "Good to see you again, Colonel."

"You too, Sergeant Major. I was pleased to hear that you and your team would be joining us on this detail."

"We're not a team. We're just four friends on vacation who decided to briefly check out Mexico City, then, apparently, Rio."

Leather frowned as the ground crew scrambled to refuel the jet. "Those two do like to get around." He lowered his voice. "What do you think? Do you think it's real?"

Dawson shook his head. "Not for a moment. But someone certainly does. And the professors are right. If it is real, it can't be allowed to get into the wrong hands."

Leather grunted. "But whose are the wrong hands? And more importantly, whose are the right hands?"

Niner held up both of his, examining them. "I know for sure these aren't the right hands."

"Definitely. They're too small," rumbled Atlas, holding up his own meaty paws.

"He said hands, not oven mitts."

"Hey, these hands are all I know."

Spock cocked an eyebrow. "Are you about to start singing?"

"What the hell are you talking about?"

Leather chuckled. "Good to see things haven't changed here."

Dawson gave the comedy duo a look. "Sometimes it makes me want to re-muster."

Niner spun toward him. "Coast Guard?"

Atlas smiled broadly. "Space Force?"

Dawson sighed. "Whatever is farthest away from you two."

"Definitely Space Force."

Niner batted a dainty hand at Dawson. "Oh, be nice. You know you'd miss us too much."

Dawson hated to admit it, but Niner was right. These were his brothers, his family, his unit. He couldn't see himself leaving until the day he couldn't do the job. And even then, there were a lot of positions within the Unit, within Delta, that he could still fill—even as his body betrayed him.

He regarded Leather, who had retired and gone private. "Do you ever regret leaving?"

Leather smirked. "Every damn day. But it became too frustrating to be on the sidelines. As much as I felt I could still do the job, I knew I couldn't. Not as well as the younger lads. Me being out in the field to indulge my ego would put their lives at risk, put the mission at risk. Sometimes you have to know when to let go. So I did. But manning a desk just wasn't for me, so instead, I went private. Little did I know the professors' gig would have me seeing almost as much action as I did serving Her Majesty."

Dawson grunted. "Yeah, I've lost track of how many times I've been involved with them. Thank God they're not assholes."

Leather tossed back his head and laughed. "Yes, thank God for that." He became serious. "Just as we landed, I received word that we all have visas for Brazil, courtesy of their mysterious travel agent. What's our plan once we get on the ground? We're not exactly equipped to head into gangland."

Dawson smirked. "Don't worry about that. A little birdie tells me we're going to be met by a mobile armory. My bigger concern is that the professors are an hour ahead of us, and you know them. There's no way in hell they're going to wait for us."

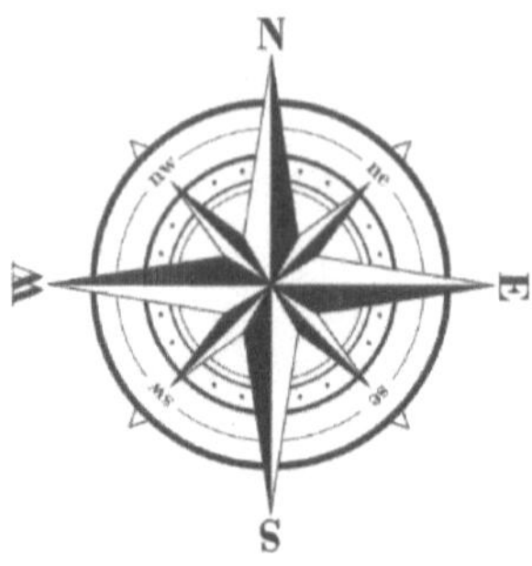

Unknown Location

AD 1652

"Is that what I think it is?"

Marcus turned to see what had caught Simon's attention and couldn't help but gasp. It was a ship, sails filled with the wind, passing the little island they had called home for so long he had lost count of the years. Everyone they had ever known, everyone they had ever loved, had died long ago, centuries ago.

It had been a decent, lonely life. They had landed in Greenland, finding only an abandoned colony. David had been attacked by a massive white creature that tore his head off the first week they had arrived. There was no saving him, regardless of the powers contained within the cup. While the expedition explored the area, searching for evidence of what had happened to the colonists, he and Simon had secretly removed all of their possessions, hiding them where they wouldn't be found.

When the expedition leader announced they were sailing to the second, larger colony, he and Simon had gone out alone the night before and never returned. The ship remained for several days, the crew searching for them before finally giving up.

And then they were alone, in a land harsher than the desert he had spent much of his adult life in.

Yet they had tools, remnants of structures, and the wildlife along the shoreline was bountiful. He assumed the cup would save them from the ravishes of starvation should it be required, yet who wanted to experience hunger when they didn't need to? And besides, fishing and hunting occupied their minds, gave them something physical to do other than simply exploring what had been left behind.

It was during those explorations that a map had been found that showed land to the southwest, and a decision had been made to build a boat and find this land where it might be warmer, where they might grow some crops. It had taken years, but they had built their vessel to sail southwest and found this unknown land. They had spotted strange people on the shore, so they kept their distance, instead settling upon an island—uninhabited but teeming with wildlife, and trees they could build from.

It had become their home for centuries.

"Should we hail them?"

Marcus rejected the idea, receding from the shore, pulling his sergeant with him. "No, we're not ready."

"Ready for what? To see the first people other than ourselves for three hundred years?"

Marcus frowned at the desperate loneliness in his friend's voice. Eternal life—what a horrible curse. He thought back on the Bible verses he had memorized so long ago, describing the Last Supper and what Jesus had said about the very cup they had sworn an oath to protect mankind from. All they had been doing for so long was to that aim. Jeremy was dead. David was dead. They couldn't rely on eternal life to protect the Grail.

He gestured toward their project—something they had been working on for centuries. It was designed to protect the cup should something go wrong. A series of tunnels, of traps, anything they could think of that would prevent someone from finding and abusing the power left on this earth by their Lord. "We have to finish this first. And once we have, then we can venture out into this new world, but not before."

Simon sighed. "So, we *will* venture out into it?"

"We will, and the cup will be protected here. You and I both know it's only a matter of time before we die. It was pure luck I saved your life last year when that tree fell on you during the storm. When I found you, you were on your final breath of life. If I had come upon you only moments later, you would have been dead and I would have been alone. It's the exact reason we began building. We're not immortal. God will eventually take us from this place, and men cannot be trusted with the power our Lord never intended to be used."

Simon sighed again. "Very well, then let's get this work done, because I grow weary of the same old jokes and stories."

Marcus smiled at his friend. "But at least you're not shoveling shit."

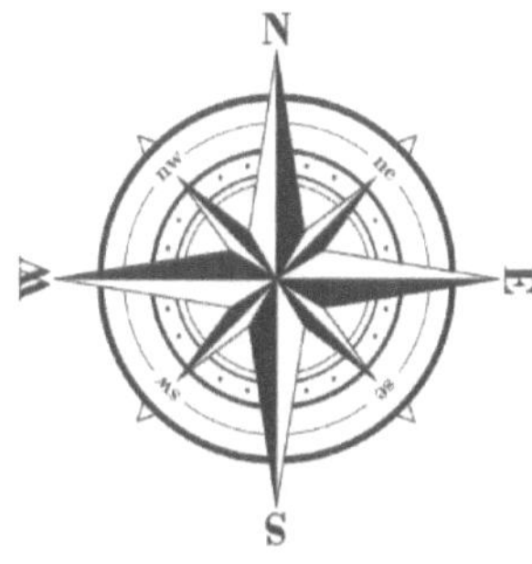

Rio de Janeiro–Galeão International Airport

Rio de Janeiro, Brazil

Present Day

Acton descended the steps and followed Laura and Reading into the private terminal. He loved Rio though hadn't been here in a while. They entered the air-conditioned terminal, and he grinned at his friends. "This brings back memories."

Reading grunted but said nothing, his expression grim. Acton had no doubt his friend was thinking of the young native woman who had taken a shine to him, and he to her. He had taken her death hard, despite only knowing her for a few days.

Acton patted him on the shoulder. "Remember the good times, not the bad."

Reading gave a curt nod, but again said nothing.

They cleared customs—a casual procedure for the well-heeled—and found a young man grinning like an idiot, holding a sign that read "ACTION."

Laura groaned. "I hope that's not foreshadowing."

"I wager it is," said Reading.

The young man lowered the sign. "Professor Action, Professor Palmer?"

Laura smiled at the young man. "Hello. I'm Professor Palmer. This is my husband, Professor *Acton*, and our friend, Hugh Reading." She wisely left Reading's title out of the introductions. It would merely scare the young man.

"Can I get your bags?"

Reading dismissed the offer, all of them dragging carry-ons. "No need. Let's just get a move on."

The man bowed. "Absolutely. Follow me."

They were led out of the terminal and directed to a large Lincoln Navigator that had seen far better days. The badges were torn off, likely intentionally, and it was riddled with dents and scrapes. They loaded their bags in the back then piled inside. As soon as the door closed, the eager young man became all business as he pulled from the curb.

"Sorry for the act. The authorities like to think all chauffeurs are morons. Best to keep up the show and not attract attention. I'm Paulo. Mary hired me to get you safely to this church and, more importantly, safely back to the airport."

Reading, sitting in the passenger seat, regarded the man as he secured his seatbelt. "Are you expecting trouble?"

"Absolutely. I'm guessing you have no idea where this church is situated?"

"I understand it's a poor district," said Laura.

"Oh, it's poor all right. But more importantly, it's one of the zones controlled by the gangs. The police almost never go in. We'll be let in, but if someone takes an interest in us, we might not be let out. We just have to keep a low profile, and you do everything I say, no hesitation."

"No problem," replied Acton.

"What's your background?" Reading asked.

"Brazilian Special Forces. Eight years." Paulo flashed a toothy smile in the rearview mirror. "I'm on vacation."

Acton smirked. "Where have I heard that before?"

"Don't worry, I'll get you in, I'll get you out. I've already checked it out. We'll park right in front of the church, go inside, you can talk to this priest you want to talk to, then we'll leave. Get back in our ride without hesitation and then leave the no-go zone."

"How long do we have?" Laura asked.

"It's ten minutes in the zone to get to the church, ten minutes to get out. I highly recommend you keep your business inside as short as possible. The longer we're parked outside, the more attention we'll draw, even in this ride."

"It looks like it's seen better days," commented Reading, running his hand across the dash, abused by something.

"That's on purpose. She's in perfect running order. This is just made to look unattractive." Paulo reached forward and patted the dash. "But you're still beautiful to me, aren't you?" he said, as if talking to a pet.

Laura smiled. "You talk to your car?"

"You don't?"

Laura rolled her eyes. "Men."

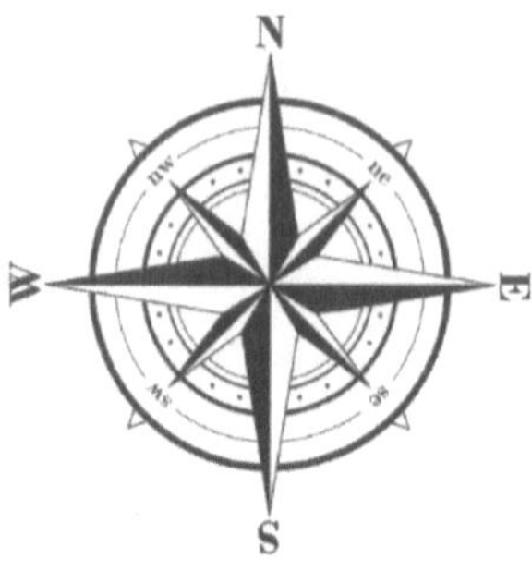

Leroux/White Residence

Fairfax Towers, Falls Church, Virginia

Sherrie, naked as the day she was born, sat cross-legged on their bed, as engrossed as Leroux was in what had been sent to them by Tommy. She put down her tablet. "This can't be real, right?"

Leroux shrugged. "I have no idea. Someone certainly thinks it is. At least twenty people are already dead because of it."

She flicked her wrist. "Forget about that. Of course people are dead. It's the Holy Grail. It's eternal life. People will kill for that, governments will kill for that, just for the possibility. Can you imagine though if it was real? An army that could never die, ER rooms that could instantly heal anybody that came in."

"You're forgetting there's only one cup."

"Yes, but you're assuming you have to drink from the cup." She waved her tablet. "Remember the journal entry that mentions the first time they saw it at work? Somebody put water in the cup, then poured it over the neck wound, and it healed them. There was no physical contact with the cup. So, what if all you need to do is pass the liquid *through* the cup, and then it's blessed, or whatever? It has its healing qualities. You could produce an unlimited amount. Hell, everyone could have a bottle of it in their home. Anything happens, just pour it on the wound, take a drink for whatever ails you. It would change everything."

Leroux regarded his girlfriend. "Judging by the excitement in your voice, I get the distinct impression you think this is real."

Again, she waved the tablet. "This is just too detailed. I mean, why do this?"

"It could just be a work of fiction."

"Found in Templar code, with a Templar under the streets of New York City, in a chamber sealed off for almost two hundred years? Do you really think so?"

His shoulders sagged. "I have no idea. You know I'm not very religious, but I still believe there's something. Did Jesus exist? I think so. I can't think of anyone from that era that's still spoken of who hasn't been shown to have existed. You have over two billion people who believe he did. And the only reason I can think of why is that you've got a dude going town to town, performing miracles. That kind of sticks with you. A guy going town to town giving a speech then leaving might get spoken of for a day or two, maybe even a week. But a guy brings your neighbor back from the dead? You talk about that for the rest of your life. You tell everybody you know, everybody you encounter."

Sherrie smiled. "It is a nice way to think of it. And it makes sense, doesn't it?"

He grinned. "I said it."

She playfully slapped him. "Haha." She held up the tablet. "But back to this. I just don't see the purpose of such an elaborate hoax."

Leroux pursed his lips. She was right. It made little sense. None of it made sense. But as he had concluded earlier, was it his job to dismiss the beliefs of the majority of the country he served? If Jesus was real, and the Last Supper occurred, then he drank from a cup. Jesus wasn't a king in the traditional sense, so wouldn't have been drinking from something bejeweled, as portrayed in Arthurian legend, but instead would have drunk from a plain wooden cup. If the cup were real, and if Jesus somehow blessed it, and the power of it was discovered accidentally or not, it was reasonable to believe the Templars somehow got their hands on it, as described in the journals.

If the cup did indeed work, then everything in the journals could have occurred as described, and the man found in the sarcophagus could indeed have been almost 600 years old when he died.

But what had him concerned was the possibility Sherrie's theory was correct. Healing armies and healing the masses wasn't practical with a cup that had to be drunk from to experience its effects. But if all that was required was for water to flow through it, the equation changed exponentially, and that could prove incredibly dangerous.

What if the Chinese got their hands on it and restricted its use to their leaders and their armies, every soldier sent into battle with a flask? If they get shot, all they had to do was drink from it, and they were good to fight again minutes later.

It was too big a risk to have just out there. He cursed as he picked up his phone.

"Who are you calling?"

"The Chief. He has to be brought up to speed."

"What changed your mind?"

"You. That idea you have is absolutely terrifying."

She smirked. "I always wanted to be a writer. Maybe I missed my calling."

He chuckled as he tapped on Morrison's entry in his contacts list. "Who knows? Maybe that'll be your second career."

"I like the sound of that. Maybe I'll write about this."

He laughed. "No one would believe you."

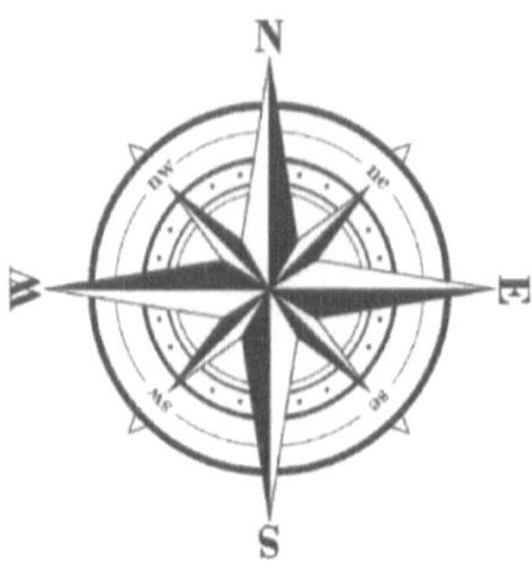

Approaching Rio de Janeiro, Brazil

Dawson looked up from his tablet, a secure message having just arrived from the colonel. "Well, ladies, looks like things have changed a bit."

Spock cocked an eyebrow. "Ladies?"

"We've just been activated and seconded to Langley. It looks like somebody's taking this seriously."

The idle chitchat between his team and Leather's came to an abrupt halt with the implications.

Spock was the first to state the obvious. "Somebody thinks this is real."

"Or at least could be real."

Leather rose from his seat and approached Dawson, standing in the aisle and gripping a headrest as they descended into Rio. "I've been reading those journals. They're incredibly detailed. If it's a hoax, a lot of work went into them."

Dawson agreed. Five hundred years of entries. Sometimes daily, sometimes separated by weeks or months, but hundreds of pages nonetheless, all in Templar code. The very idea that the Holy Grail was real and that it was out there in the hands of those willing to kill for it was more terrifying than anything he had faced in his entire career. The power of God in your hand, making you invincible. How do you fight an enemy like that? How do you reason with anybody? Who in their right mind would give up that kind of power? And then, even if you did succeed and retrieved the Grail, what then? Would he and the others resist its powers? If they could, who would they hand it over to? Could the government be trusted with such a thing, or should it go to the Church?

Niner leaned in. "Penny for your thoughts."

"Just thinking about what the consequences might be if this is actually real."

Spock rose and began pacing. "Obviously, somebody in Washington is thinking the same thing. This is no different than chasing a horcrux or UFO. It has to be fiction. It has to be fake." He dropped back in his seat. "But I swear, when my wife died, a few nights later she visited me in a dream, but I know it wasn't a dream. It was real." His voice cracked. "We were able to say we loved each other one last time, and to say goodbye. I know that was real. And if that was real, then this can be real."

No one said anything. Atlas reached out and gave his friend's shoulder a squeeze and a shake.

Spock wiped his eyes dry on the back of his hand. "Sorry."

Dawson smiled. "Never apologize for something like that. And you're right. There are too many stories just like that out there. Thousands of years of belief. We can't ignore that just because modern society has told us our faith is non-scientific, is just a fantasy, that religion is for weak people with weak minds seeking an explanation for things they don't understand or the false comfort that after they die, there is something there for them.

"So, we're going to take this seriously, irrespective of whether the Grail is the Cup of Christ, or it's just some dude's cup that he drank from every night that went missing one day. We have a mission now. This is no longer about going in and helping out the professors. Our government has now activated us to retrieve the cup."

Niner folded his arms. "And the professors?"

"We protect them as we would any other civilian."

"Weapons?" asked Atlas. "We're not exactly equipped here."

"I have no doubt Langley will arrange a supply rendezvous once we've cleared the airport. They've got weapons caches in almost every city in the world. We won't be going in with six-shooters and wood-stove parts for body armor."

Niner whistled the tune from the classic Clint Eastwood spaghetti western. "That would be cool."

Atlas scoffed. "Your girlish frame wouldn't be able to handle the weight."

"I've got muscles."

"Riiight."

Spock gestured toward Atlas. "You could always just stand behind him. You could probably strap three or four on him."

Niner stared into the distance wistfully. "Then we could call you the Black Panther."

Atlas cocked an eyebrow. "Huh?"

"Like the tank from World War Two."

"Oh."

Leather cut off the frivolity. "Anything in that message regarding my men?"

"No. As far as the American government is concerned, you're all civilians. However, don't forget, we have Kane's private rendezvous as well, so you guys can stock up as much as you want, but you probably won't have the protection of the American government should something go wrong."

Leather glanced at his team. "Nothing we're not used to, hey, lads?"

"Sounds like half the missions I was on when I served," replied one of the men.

Leather lowered the timbre of his voice. "'If you're caught, you'll be disavowed.'"

The others snickered and the seatbelt light gently gonged, indicating they were close to landing.

Dawson tightened his seatbelt. "Then let's make sure we don't get caught."

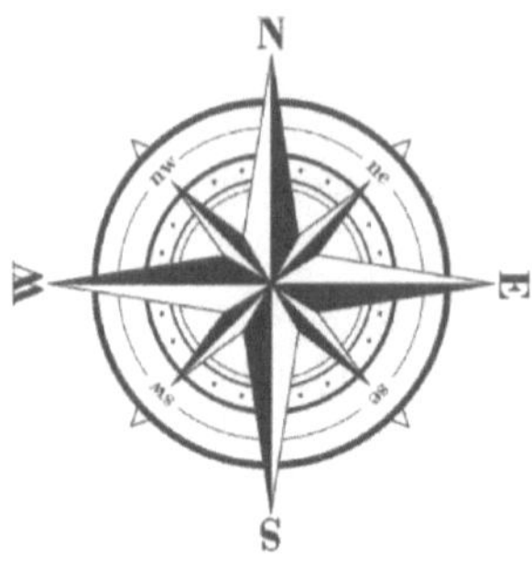

New York City, New York

AD 1832

"Forgive me, Father, for I have sinned. You wouldn't believe me if I told you when my last confession was."

Father Lucas Santos smirked from his side of the confessional. "My son, I can hardly absolve you of your sins if you begin with a lie. If you tell me when your last confession was, will it be the truth or a falsehood?"

"I would never lie to a priest, Father."

"Then tell me, when was your last confession?"

There was a heavy sigh from the other side of the divider. He could make out an old man's shape but little else. The voice was tired, weak, and he suspected this could be a final confession, at least in this man's mind.

A man who still held back.

"Son, anything you tell me is between you, me, and God. I will never repeat to anyone, not even another priest, what you tell me."

"Very well. It has been over five hundred years since my last confession."

Father Santos frowned. "If you're going to lie to me, there's not much point in this."

"I'm not lying, Father."

"Then how would you explain the fact that you're older than anyone else who's ever existed?"

"Well, Father, if you have read your Bible, you would know that many lived longer than I have."

Santos inhaled deeply and held it. If the Bible were to be interpreted literally, then yes, the man was right. But those were different people. Those were the first people, long dead, a part of history. "Then how would you explain this, since you and I both know that today no one lives that long?"

"Have you heard of the Holy Grail?"

Santos cocked an eyebrow. "Of course. It's a myth. Some say King Arthur found it. Others say the Templars. Most say it's nonsense."

"It's not nonsense, Father. And it was the Templars who ended up with it, though they weren't the first."

"And how would you know this?"

"I am a Templar, the last of my order."

Santos leaned forward, intrigued. There was something about this man's voice, his manner, that told him every word he was hearing was the truth. An impossible truth. "Tell me everything, my son."

And the story laid out before him, over five centuries of heroism and heartbreak, was shocking, yet so intricately woven, so detailed, it had to be the truth. "And where is the Holy Grail now?"

"I swore an oath to never tell, nor will I. This will be my final confession. I'll be dying soon, and when I do, the Grail's location will die with me. It is far too dangerous for any man to possess."

Santos squeezed his eyes shut, struggling to control himself. "You could trust me. I'm a man of the cloth. The Holy Grail should be in the possession of the Church. Don't you agree?"

The man vehemently shook his head, dashing his hopes. "The Church betrayed the Templars, resulting in the destruction of our order. I would never trust it with something of such power."

"Yet you're here, confessing to me."

"You're one man, and I'm here for a single purpose—to confess my sins, to receive absolution, so that I may die in peace and join my brothers in paradise. To once and for all finally join the family I left behind so long ago." The man's head slumped. "To finally end an existence that should never have been. Now, Father, will you forgive me my transgressions?"

Santos stared at the screen, at a loss for words. If the Holy Grail were real, if it were indeed the cup of Christ, it couldn't be left forgotten on some man's shelf. It had to be preserved, protected, worshiped, for it was the ultimate of blood relics.

"Father?"

He flinched. "Yes, yes, of course." He quickly completed the ritual, his hands shaking.

"Thank you, Father."

There was a shuffling from the other side of the divider and he listened for the footfalls to fade before stepping out, staring after the man as he made his way down the aisle toward the doors leading outside.

And he made a decision.

The Holy Grail didn't belong to this man. It belonged to the Church, established in Christ's name by St. Peter so long ago. Faith was waning. All it would take would be for the world to witness one miracle as a result of the Holy Grail, and faith would be restored, those dabbling in other religions sure to cast off their false gods and worship the one true God.

He hurried after the old man, the old man who claimed to be the last Templar, determined to recover that which belonged to all mankind, not one lost soul belonging to an order the Church itself had brought down.

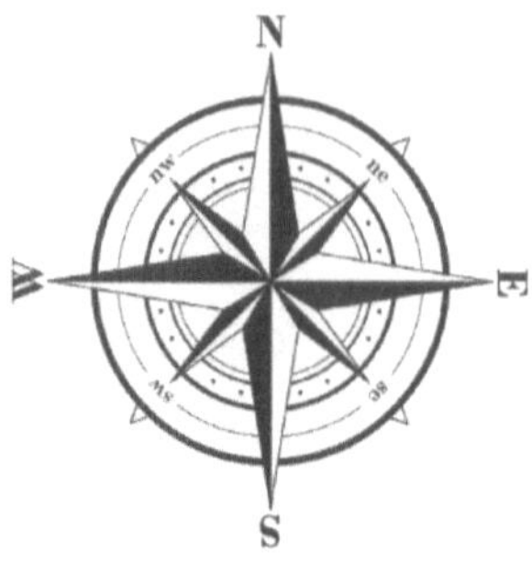

Complexo do Alemão Bairro

Rio de Janeiro, Brazil

Present Day

It was heartbreaking. Acton had been all over the world, in the richest of countries and the poorest, yet he couldn't recall being in a world-famous city with massive neighborhoods of hobbled-together homes entirely controlled by the criminal element. As they drove to the Church of the Holy Grail, the shocking view had him thankful their windows were tinted. He gripped Laura's hand. "I'm not so sure about this."

Reading twisted in his seat. "*Now* you're not sure? A little late, don't you think?"

"Hey, a man's allowed to change his mind."

Paulo glanced in his rearview mirror at him. "Are we aborting?"

Acton wanted to. It was the prudent thing to do, the safe thing to do, the smart thing to do. Yet it was the Holy Grail. Didn't they have a responsibility to humanity to recover it? He turned to Laura, who was of no help.

"It's up to you."

He gave her a look. "Gee, thanks." Whatever decision he made, she would support him. She always did. But he also knew what she wanted. She wanted to go in. She was crazier than he was sometimes. "No, let's keep going. We're almost there."

Paulo pointed ahead. "You're right about that."

Everyone leaned forward to see a large, freshly painted white church that appeared in good repair from the outside.

"It looks like someone has no problem filling the collection plate," commented Reading.

Acton had to agree. There was definitely some money here. Paulo pulled up in front, turning around then backing in, no doubt so they could make a quicker escape should it become necessary.

Reading gestured toward worshippers streaming through the front doors. "Odd time for a service, isn't it?"

Acton checked his watch. "Yeah, that's kind of strange."

Reading muttered a curse. "Maybe we should wait. There are too many people."

Paulo dismissed the idea. "No, the longer we're here, the more attention we'll attract. We need to be in and out fast." He faced the back seat. "Now that we're here, I still haven't heard a plan."

Acton held up the Glock supplied by Paulo. "My intention was to go in, find this priest…what did Mario say his name was?"

"Oliveira," replied Laura.

"Right. Take the cup from Father Oliveira, and leave."

Reading groaned. "That's the daftest plan I've ever heard."

"Perhaps, but it's simple."

Laura agreed. "He's right. We go in, find him, confront him, use our weapons if necessary to intimidate him, get the Grail, and get the hell out."

Paulo cocked an eyebrow. "You're going to hold a weapon on a priest?"

"I'm going to tie him up too. Remember, this priest is probably responsible for over twenty deaths." She jabbed a finger at the doors of the church, still swinging from the last parishioner to enter. "Something's going on in there. Something that's been going on for over a hundred-and-fifty years. What you see when you go through those doors may be unlike anything you've ever seen at a church."

Reading pursed his lips. "While I reluctantly agree that Jim's plan of 'just damning the torpedoes' is probably the best way to deal with this, I don't think that applies anymore. We're going to be walking in on God knows how many people. We can't exactly pull a gun on their priest and expect to get away with it."

Laura sighed. "You're right. We need to find another way in."

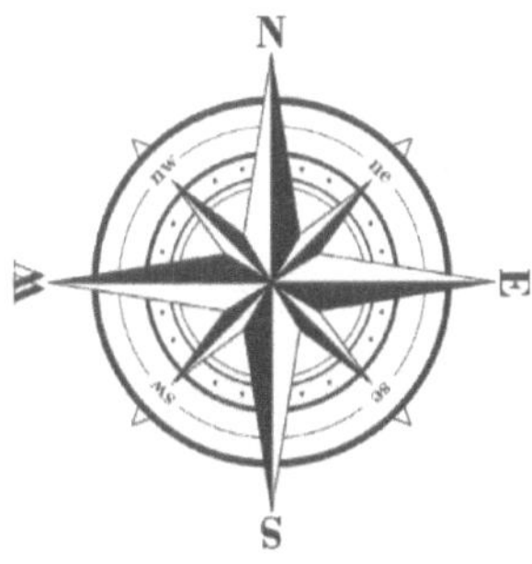

Operations Center 2, CIA Headquarters

Langley, Virginia

As far as everyone but Leroux and Tong were concerned, this was a sanctioned mission with a classified objective. Nothing out of the ordinary. Only a handful of people in the entire country knew what was really going on. Delta wasn't being sent in to recover something of interest to the American government. They were being sent in to recover the Holy Grail, the Cup of Christ, something that might change the course of history.

Especially if Sherrie's theory was right.

The implications were staggering, and part of him prayed this wasn't a fool's errand—that they were indeed attempting to recover the real deal. If merely passing water through the cup transferred the healing powers, it could eventually put an end to all illness on the planet. And so much suffering.

Yet the rational part of him thought it was all bullshit. Even if it were the cup that Jesus drank from during the Last Supper, he simply couldn't believe that it had any power. The Templar find had to be an elaborate hoax. To what end, he had no idea. But despite believing there was something after death, some greater power out there, he couldn't bring himself to accept the possibility that his beliefs could actually be true.

It was curious. Believing something on faith, then, when provided proof, refusing to accept it. It made him think of the current state of his country. Despite proof, despite irrefutable proof to the contrary, when placed in front of the eyes of those who believed the lies, they refused to accept the truth because they had faith in the person perpetrating the fraud.

Faith trumping fact.

And here he was, facing something similar, proof of his faith denied because sophisticated society told him spirituality was hokum.

He exhaled loudly as he stared at the satellite feed. Kane was out of Qatar, that mission over, but now, once again, they were dealing with the troublesome professors. Yet if it weren't for them, they wouldn't know about this potentially earth-shattering discovery.

"Do we know what they're after?" asked Child, spinning in his chair behind him.

"Classified," snapped Tong, not looking up from her terminal. "You read the briefing notes. You should know by now that if they say they're after a classified item, then that means you don't need to know what it is."

Child killed his spin. "Do *you* know?"

Leroux stepped in. "There's to be no discussion of what the item is. It's classified. That's all you need to know. Who knows what, is irrelevant. *You* know nothing."

Child's cheeks flushed. "Sorry, sir. It's just that, well…" He stopped, and Leroux turned in his chair to face him.

"It's just that what?"

"Well, Templars in New York. A priest murdered. A priest at the massacre scene. And now we're heading to a church in Brazil called the Church of the Holy Grail…"

Leroux's eyes flared when Tong saved him. "My God, Randy, don't tell me you think the American government is actually sending in a Delta unit to recover the Holy Grail."

Child's cheeks flushed again. "Well, you know, if you piece together everything…"

Tong groaned. "For the love of God, pull your head out of those damn comic books and get in the real world for once."

The devastation on Child's face, along with the snickers in the room, was enough to tell Leroux that Tong had succeeded in preserving the secrecy of the mission. He rose. "Listen, I know it's fun to speculate, especially when the professors are involved. We've dealt with some weird shit over the years, especially when it comes to them. But in this case, as per the briefing notes, Washington believes this church is a front for a terrorist organization. And with over twenty people dead, including one on American soil, we already know these people are vicious. They've taken something that Washington wants, so we're going to make sure we get it back. That's the mission. Whether the item is data, an alien from

Roswell, or the Holy Grail from Indiana Jones, it doesn't matter. It's an item that needs to be recovered, and our job is to make sure Bravo Team succeeds. As to why the professors are involved, we can only speculate. But you know them. They always do the right thing or what they think is the right thing. We have to assume they stumbled upon something, informed the proper people, and you know how long it takes Washington to take action. My guess is the professors felt they couldn't risk letting the perpetrator get away, so they gave pursuit themselves until we could get involved."

Tong cleared her throat. "Speaking of."

Leroux turned to see Tong staring at the main display.

"They've just arrived," she said.

He faced the screen. "All right, people. Game faces on. There's nothing we can do but observe until Delta can get in position. Status on Bravo Team?"

"They've landed, along with Leather's team. They've already cleared customs. Both teams have separated and should be supplied shortly."

"Best case for them to reach the professors?"

Tong frowned. "Twenty minutes."

Leroux cursed as the professors parked. "Twenty minutes might as well be twenty hours if this goes south."

Three people exited the SUV and headed toward the back of the church.

"Wait a minute. Where's Reading?"

Tong worked her terminal, zooming in from above on the SUV. "Looks like there's some movement in the passenger seat. He must have stayed behind. He's had some recent heart trouble, so that may be why."

The passenger door opened, confirming their theory. Reading stepped out and closed the door.

"Is he going after them?" Child asked.

Reading answered the question by rounding the bumper and climbing into the driver's seat. He was prepping for a quick getaway.

Smart, but it also meant he expected trouble.

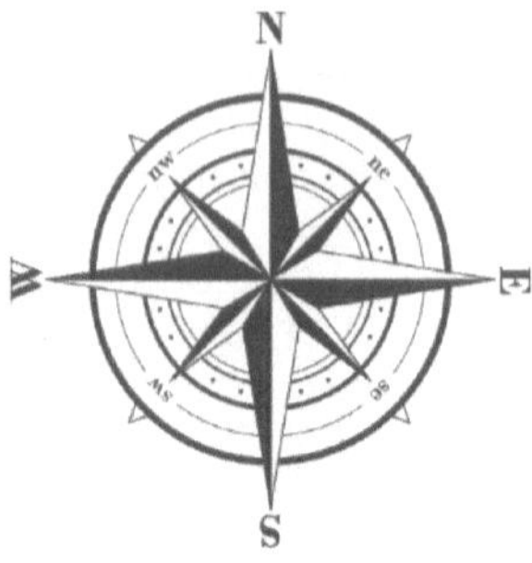

Complexo do Alemão Bairro

Rio de Janeiro, Brazil

Reading climbed behind the wheel and locked the doors, testing the central lock button. He had a sickening sense something was about to go wrong. He wanted to be with his friends, to help protect them, but Acton was right. If the shit hit the fan, the best place for him was here, ready to whisk them away.

Paulo had already programmed the exit route into the GPS. All he had to do was guide them out, saving them what could be precious seconds if they were beating a hasty retreat. Still, he felt like an invalid. A few years ago, he would have been at their side, running along with them, returning fire, saving lives. How quickly things had turned.

"This isn't who I was meant to be," he muttered to himself. Yet here he was, relegated to getaway driver.

He sighed, remembering a piece of advice he had given his son when he was frustrated during his training. "Forget today, forget tomorrow.

Look three months out, and it'll all be done. You'll be on the force, on the streets, doing the job you signed up to do."

It was advice he had to take now. Looking three months back, he recognized he was in much better condition today than he was then. He was a hell of a lot better than after his heart attack when he had been as weak as a baby.

"You're getting old." He grunted. "You're not getting old. You *are* old."

But three months from now, how much better would he feel? He smirked, thinking about someone he had recently met—someone he actually liked. There was something about her, something irresistible. She was cute in her own way, a hard worker, funny, and completely different from him. He wondered why he was always attracted to women he had nothing in common with.

He thought back to Kinti—a young indigenous woman he had fallen hard for in just a couple of days, not that far north of here. The only thing they had in common was that they breathed the same air. They didn't even speak the same language, yet for those few days, it had worked.

And now here he was, again interested in someone he had nothing in common with. Perhaps it was doomed to failure, though it didn't matter. He had no intention of pursuing it, at least not before he was sure he would be alive for a few more years.

He sighed again. It sucked.

My entire life is on hold while I wait to see if I die. What the hell kind of life is that?

He inhaled sharply and held it. If he survived the damn day, maybe it was time to grab on to what was left of life and stop worrying about what if, and instead embrace what could be.

He checked his watch. They had been gone for three minutes, and he hadn't heard gunfire.

Maybe things might go smoothly for once.

Acton tried the handle on the back door of the church and found it unlocked. He slowly pulled the door open, cringing as the rusted hinges creaked. Paulo reached forward and grabbed the door, swinging it open all the way with a single loud chirp.

Acton grimaced, though perhaps the young man was right. One sharp, familiar sound might draw less attention than one long one.

Paulo led the way, his weapon drawn, followed by Laura. Acton brought up the rear, casting an eye over the area to see if anyone had spotted them. There was no one obvious, but for all he knew, there could be a hundred eyes on them through cracks in curtains, the slats of blinds, or holes in the ramshackle residences lining the back of the church.

He jerked the door closed, again grimacing, then blinked rapidly, adjusting to the relative darkness inside. Somewhere nearby, someone was speaking, and the gathered responded. It was all in Portuguese, a language of which he knew little.

Paulo turned. "He's conducting mass," he whispered.

"Let's take advantage. Let's clear these rooms, make sure there's nobody in them, then start searching." Acton indicated the far end of the hall. "Paulo, you start there. We'll start at the other end."

Paulo headed off, and Acton and Laura quickly made their way to the far end of the hall. He pushed aside the first door and Laura stepped in, her weapon drawn.

"Clear," she whispered. They moved on, Paulo doing the same at the other end. Within minutes, they had confirmed they were alone, the mass continuing with the congregation responding. Paulo rejoined them and Acton indicated the far end where the mass was underway.

"You cover us, we'll search."

"It would go faster if all three of us searched."

Acton dismissed the idea. "No, you don't know what we're looking for. You just cover our sixes."

Paulo reluctantly agreed and took up position. Acton pointed at the room at the far end, the first one they had cleared. "You start there," he said to Laura. "You know what to look for."

She disappeared into the room and Acton took the next one. It appeared to be a storage room filled with everything the church might need—from candles to Bibles, robes to communion wafers. There was nothing obvious on the shelves, yet there could be hidden compartments. He quickly surveyed the shelves then began pressing on the walls, tapping for any unusual sounds, checking the floorboards. There was nothing suspicious here, and they didn't have enough time for a proper search.

Assuming this was indeed the destination of the priest from Mexico City, then he wouldn't have had much time to hide the Grail, though they did have a head start. It was frustrating, though he couldn't let that get to him. They could still get lucky—complacency could be at play here.

He moved on to the next room. Laura was still searching hers. He didn't bother asking her how it was going. If she found it, she would tell him. He opened the door and found a kitchen, small but well-stocked. There was no way he had time to search this properly. Any of the scores of containers could have been opened and the cup put inside, yet he had to assume that with the church named after the relic, some reverence would be shown.

He continued searching and spotted a door, likely leading to a pantry. He opened it and reached around, flicking on a light, revealing shelves lined with goods and a small cot lying on the floor. A young boy bolted upright, rubbing his eyes. He opened them, stared at Acton, then screamed.

Father Rafael Oliveira continued through the motions, delivering the mass as he had thousands upon thousands of times before, yet he was on autopilot, his mouth moving mechanically. He couldn't believe it. He had the Grail, almost 200 years after Father Santos heard the confession of the immortal Templar. They had been searching for it for so long, and now he was the one who had retrieved it. He had been blessed to be the head of the church whose mission, since its founding, was to recover the Holy Grail—the Cup of Christ. He was heartbroken so many had died, though the good that would come from it was unimaginable—proof of the power of God, proof that not only did Jesus exist, but that He was indeed the Son of God, with all the power that entailed.

This discovery could unite the world under the one true God, under the Holy Trinity, perhaps even bringing an end to the wars between the major religions. Christianity was the one true religion, and the Roman Catholic Church its one true governor. After all, it had been established by an apostle of Christ at His request.

And I tell you that you are Peter, and on this rock I will build my church, and the gates of Hades will not overcome it.

That didn't mean Jesus was standing in Rome, pointing at a rock where the Vatican currently stood. He meant Saint Peter, whose name, Petros, meant 'rock' in Greek—Saint Peter was the rock who built the Church. The flock now numbered over a billion strong, and it would soon become billions after the power of the Grail was proven to the entire world.

Preparations were already underway to provide this truth. The faithful who knew were hard at work while he tended to his flock, the gathered congregation lined up for communion. If only he could truly bless them with the cup now concealed under his robes. But that was for tonight. If there was a message to be delivered, those true believers who had been waiting, like he had, needed to bear witness to what was to come.

The world needed to bear witness.

"The blood of Christ," he said, and after drinking, the old woman, in desperate need of an unaffordable hip replacement, shuffled away. She was one of the millions that could benefit from the power of the Grail.

The practiced words repeated, one of those in the know now up. "Tonight is the night, my brother."

The man's eyes flared with understanding, and he made the sign of the cross, moving on. The procession continued, his message delivered to those in the know. The energy in the air was palpable as more returned to their pews, aware that the Grail had been found.

Someone screamed—a child.

He spun toward the door leading to the rear of the church. Who could it be? He wasn't sure, though it sounded like the young boy under their care, who had apparently slept in. Oliveira had been so distracted, he hadn't noticed the young altar boy's absence. The boy shouted something, something Oliveira couldn't hear.

"Perhaps the boy had a nightmare," he said to those gathered. He headed to the door and opened it, gasping at the sight of three people. One appeared Brazilian, while the other two were as white as snow.

They were here for him.

They were here for the Grail.

"Intruders!" His flock rose, those in the know rushing forward. He stabbed a finger at the fleeing invaders. "They must not be allowed to leave!"

Scores of parishioners funneled into the narrow hallway as Oliveira stepped aside. They had to be here for the Grail. The substantial wealth the church had was contained in secret accounts, the result of an endowment left to them well over a century ago by a parishioner of Father Santos. That parishioner had been convinced to leave his vast wealth in order to aid in the holy relic's recovery. Everyone in this neighborhood was aware there was nothing worth stealing here except food, which was freely handed out to those in need.

And these were white people, probably Americans. There was only one reason for them to be here. He clasped the wooden cup under his vestments. They couldn't be allowed to have it. This couldn't be kept from the world.

Anger gripped him, mixed with fear. He was so close to achieving their goals. These people couldn't be allowed to interfere.

Forgive me, Lord, but it's for the greater good.

He drew a deep breath and shouted words he thought he would never utter. "Kill them if you have to, but they must not get away!"

Acton held out his hands, attempting to calm the boy who had scrambled off his mattress and pressed into the corner of the room. "Hey, hey, it's okay. I'm not here to hurt you."

The boy grabbed a tin can from the shelf and whipped it at him. Acton blocked it with his forearm, wincing as he stepped back a couple of paces. "Hey, kid, I'm not here to hurt you."

The young boy grabbed another can, and Acton ducked just in time as it smashed against the front of a metal stove with a loud clang.

Laura appeared in the doorway. "What's going on?"

"It's just a young boy. I guess I scared him."

Paulo rushed in. "We've gotta get out of here now."

"But we haven't finished searching."

Another can flew past Acton's head. He quickly closed the door, leaving the child inside. He pounded on the door, shouting something at the top of his lungs before falling silent.

Laura cocked her head, listening. "Do you hear that?"

Acton paused. "Hear what? I don't hear anything."

Her expression turned grim. "Exactly."

"Oh, shit. The mass has stopped. They must have heard the boy."

"Let's get the hell out of here now," urged Paulo, leading the way.

"What about the Grail?" Laura called over her shoulder as the door at the far end of the hallway opened, a priest staring at them in shock, an angry mob behind him.

"We can't do both right now," replied Acton as they turned down the short hallway that led to the back door. Paulo brought up the rear, knocking over several shelves to slow their pursuers as Laura threw open the door to the outside.

Acton cleared the back porch steps in one stride as a shout echoed from inside. "What is it?" he asked a worried Paulo as he rounded the corner.

"I think the priest just told them to kill us!"

"Hugh! Start the car!" Laura yelled ahead of them.

Acton cleared the side of the church just as Laura yanked open the back door of their ride.

"Come on, come on, come on!" Reading shouted from the driver's seat as the front doors of the church burst open.

Laura dove inside, followed by Acton, while Paulo hopped into the passenger seat. Reading slammed on the gas before the doors fully closed, making a sharp left as the navigation system instructed. Gunfire erupted behind them, and the rear window took several rounds, causing everyone to duck.

"It's bullet resistant," Paulo assured them. "So are the side panels. We should be safe from stray bullets."

Acton glanced over his shoulder at the rear window. "But how many hits can this thing take?"

Laura gasped. "Look!"

Worshippers were sprinting after them, shouting with fists raised. Some carried weapons, and cars were already pouring onto the road with people on foot jumping inside to join the chase. At least half a dozen vehicles were now in pursuit, maybe more.

Reading made a sharp right turn, momentarily cutting off the mob before flooring it. "Seconds are going to count," he said. "Every cellphone at that church is now lighting up, telling people to look for us." The engine roared, pressing everyone into the back of their seats. "What the bloody hell happened back there?"

"There was a kid asleep in a pantry," Acton explained. "He screamed when he saw me. Otherwise, everything was going fine until then."

"Any sign of the Grail?"

Acton shook his head. "No."

Laura confirmed her lack of success. "Nothing. But I did find something interesting."

"What's that?" Reading asked, cranking the wheel as they rounded another corner, gunfire still rattling behind them.

"There seemed to be a lot of stuff in his office involving the Christ the Redeemer statue."

Reading stole a glance at her in the rearview mirror. "What's that, the big statue of Jesus?" He jerked his chin toward the distant silhouette.

"Yes."

"Wouldn't that be natural?" Reading swerved left again.

"It would be, though there were old plans and photos of the construction—things I wouldn't have expected." She tapped her pocket. "I took photos, just in case."

"What are you thinking?" asked Acton.

She shrugged. "I have no idea. But if this has been going on for over a century, we have to expect the unexpected."

Bullets pinged off the passenger side of the car as Paulo spoke into his phone in Portuguese.

"How much longer?"

"Eight minutes," reported Reading.

Acton rose from his instinctive crouch and cursed at the sight behind them. There were too many to count, and more people were gathering on the streets as they passed. "The word's gotten out. Everyone in this bairro is after us."

More gunfire thumped into both sides of the vehicle. "Bloody hell!" Reading ducked as someone stepped into the street ahead of them, wielding an AK-47 and opening fire. He floored the gas pedal, silencing the shooter with a loud thud as the front bumper struck him. Acton glanced back to see the body rolling on the ground behind them. Someone immediately picked up the weapon and raised it as Reading guided the car around another bend.

"We're not going to make it." Laura turned toward Acton. "There's just too many of them. Why the hell are they doing this?"

Paulo ended his call. "The priest, probably. He likely contacted the local gang that controls this area. They've put the word out about us. The gangs like to cooperate with the church because they think it'll get their sins forgiven, and they'll get into Heaven despite the evil they do."

Suddenly, something streaked past them and slammed into the side of a building ahead, exploding with a large blast, strewing stone and debris across the road.

"What the hell was that?" cried Laura.

"RPG!" Paulo replied grimly, holding up his phone. "I just called some friends. They said there's no way they're coming in to get us, but if we make it out of the bairro, they'll be waiting for us."

"How far?" Reading asked, still following the directions on the navigation system.

"Seven minutes," replied Paulo. "You're heading for them right now."

Reading's phone rang, and he handed it over his shoulder to Acton, who answered it. "Hello?"

"Professor Acton, this is Chris Leroux," came the voice on the other end. "Listen to me carefully. In fifty meters, turn left, or you're going to die."

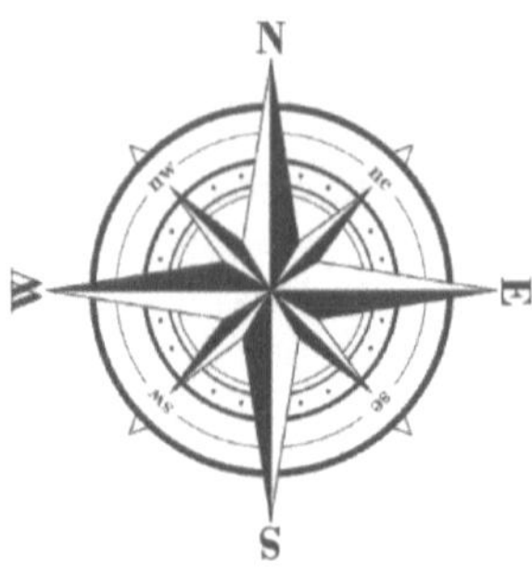

Rio de Janeiro, Brazil

Dawson's trained eye swept the abandoned warehouse they now found themselves in. His team was in an SUV driven by Mateus Costa, a local asset provided by the CIA. He brought them to a halt and gestured toward a large box van.

"Gentlemen, I present to you, Hell on Wheels."

All four doors of the SUV opened and they approached the rear of the van, the back rolling up to reveal a serious-looking local. "Welcome, gentlemen. I'm the Armorer. Take whatever you want. Courtesy of the American taxpayer." The accent was heavy, southern. He might look local, but he was all American.

Dawson hopped into the back, whistling appreciatively at the rows of weapons and ammo. "Body armor first, gentlemen."

Their host jerked a thumb toward the back. "In the rear. Look for your number. The Pentagon sent your sizes ahead."

The others climbed aboard, the van rocking heavily when Atlas pulled himself up. Niner eyed him. "Careful, dude. You're liable to tip us over."

"Somehow, I doubt that," rumbled the big man.

Dawson found his body armor, labeled 01. He tossed the others their vests then quickly donned his own. He immediately felt more comfortable, despite knowing body armor was anything but foolproof, though it always improved the odds dramatically. He wasn't sure who they would go up against today—if anybody, but the worst-case scenario would likely be gang members, probably untrained, with little experience firing their weapons at someone. "Comms?"

"Just there, on your right," responded the Armorer, pointing.

Dawson retrieved one of the sets and hooked himself up, inserting the communications piece deep into his ear canal.

"It's already tuned to Langley. They're expecting your call."

Dawson activated the comms as the others jacked in and began arming themselves. "Control, Bravo Zero-One. Come in, over."

The voice on the other end responded immediately, one Dawson recognized. "Bravo Zero-One, Control Actual. We read you. What's your status, over?"

"Gearing up now. What's the status on our subjects?"

"They're being pursued by at least fifty hostiles, and that number is growing as word spreads."

Dawson cursed as he strapped weapons to his body, handed to him by an already-armed Spock. "What are the locals doing about it?"

"They're refusing to go in, but they're assembling at the perimeter of the no-go zone. If the professors can reach it, they've been guaranteed protection."

"How far out are they?"

"At least five minutes. Their route's been cut off, so we've had to detour them. The computer is now saying six minutes, but that assumes nothing gets in their way again. Whoever is behind this church appears to have an in with the local gangs."

Dawson, now fully equipped, jumped out of the rear of the mobile armory. "Half the congregation are probably gang members." He turned to Costa as he climbed into the passenger seat. "ETA to the rendezvous point?"

Costa hopped behind the wheel and fired up the engine. "Less than ten minutes, depending on traffic."

Dawson glanced behind him to confirm his entire team was inside, then slapped the dash. "Let's get the hell out of here and into the fight. If the Brazilians won't go in, we will."

Costa shifted the vehicle into gear and hammered on the gas. "I hope you're joking. You'd have to have a death wish to go in there without some serious backup."

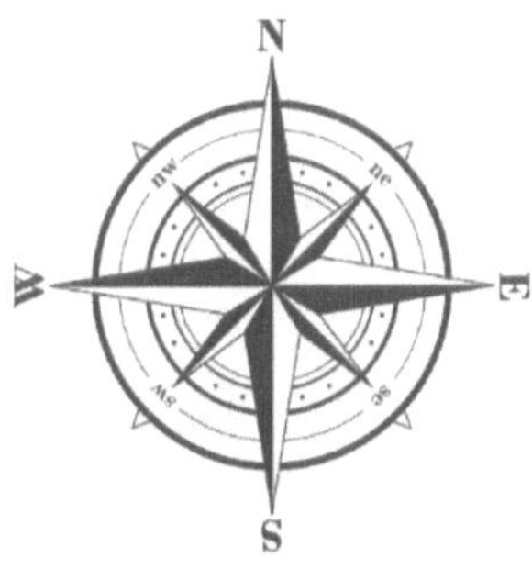

Complexo do Alemão Bairro

Rio de Janeiro, Brazil

"Take your next right."

Everyone held on as Reading cranked the wheel, executing Tong's instructions as she guided them out of the mayhem, having taken over from Leroux. The streets and sidewalks were swarming with people. Those who were just curious onlookers rushed back inside as those in pursuit came within sight, but too many stayed on the street. Acton had already counted at least half a dozen dropping from stray bullets, those behind them firing indiscriminately in the hopes they might get lucky.

Paulo cursed as they narrowly avoided a young boy running across the street. He glanced at Reading. "That was close."

Reading didn't respond, continuing to grip the steering wheel. Acton leaned over and frowned. His friend appeared pale, and his chest was rising and falling rapidly. "How are you feeling, Hugh?"

Reading said nothing, instead following the next instruction from Tong, sending them careening around another corner.

"Remember to breathe."

Reading inhaled sharply, his chest expanding before it dropped.

"That's it. Keep filling those lungs. Try to bring your heart rate down a bit."

Their friend clearly wasn't feeling well, otherwise, he would be protesting the instructions.

Paulo turned to Acton, lowering his voice, though there was no way Reading wouldn't hear them. "Is he all right?"

Acton tapped his chest over his heart and Paulo frowned. There was no way to switch drivers, certainly no easy way, and certainly no quick way. Their only option would be to stop, have Reading and Paulo switch seats, then get underway again. But the pursuers were right behind them.

Reading was in trouble, which meant so were they.

He cursed to himself. They never should have let him come with them. Despite that obvious fact, there was also the fact Reading would never have let them go without him. He was the policeman, the protector. It was all he knew. And Acton was well aware that Reading thought of Laura as a daughter, just like they thought of Tommy and Mai as their adult children. If they were heading into danger, there was no way in hell he would let them go alone, no matter how bad he felt.

But there was no point dwelling on what might have been. They were already up the creek, and it was full of shit.

Laura grabbed a bottle of water, unscrewed the cap, then reached around, pressing it to Reading's lips. "Drink as much as you can."

He thirstily downed most of the bottle, a good portion of it running down his chin and onto his shirt. He pulled his head away. "I'm good."

"Feeling any better?"

He nodded. "A little."

"Next right. You're clear for fifty meters," came Tong's voice through the phone speaker.

Reading made the turn, and Acton noted a little more color in his cheeks as the man continued to control his breathing. "How much longer do we have before we're out of this mess?" asked Reading.

"At least three minutes."

"Three? I thought we were three minutes away three minutes ago!" exclaimed Laura.

"They keep cutting off routes. We're trying to find you an alternate path while keeping you ahead of the closures. Next left."

Reading cranked the wheel, the rear tires chirping as they skidded across the pavement. Gunfire rattled behind them, several more thumps causing them all to flinch. Acton examined the rear window, now a mess of impacts. "That's not gonna hold much longer."

Paulo agreed. "If we don't get]out of this soon, we're done."

Laura slammed her palm against her door. "I don't understand why the hell the police won't help us!"

"Because we were dumb enough to come in here when we knew better. They shouldn't have to put their lives at risk because of our stupidity."

"Amen to that," grumbled Reading, flooring it as they barreled down the street, sending locals scrambling out of the way. It was evident these people weren't innocent—they were attempting to slow them or even stop them. But Reading was wise to that now, no longer taking precautions, allowing them to open a gap with those behind them now that Leroux's team was providing clear routes.

We might just get out of this.

Tong cursed, and Acton closed his eyes. "What?"

"You're about to be cut off."

A dump truck pulled out ahead of them, blocking the road, half a dozen gunmen in the back. Reading spun the wheel, sending them left, but at the far end of the road they could see it blocked by two pickup trucks and at least a dozen gunmen. He hammered on the brakes, bringing them to a shuddering halt. "What the hell do we do now?"

"I think we have to surrender," said Laura.

Paulo vehemently disagreed. "Absolutely not. They'll skin us alive." He held up his weapon. "We're going to have to fight our way out. But count your shots. Make sure you save the last bullet for yourself. You do not want to be captured by these people." He jerked his chin toward Laura. "Especially you."

Acton wrapped a protective arm around his wife. "What happens if this thing rams those trucks ahead? Will the airbags deploy? Will the fuel be cut off?"

"No. I've had this thing customized, so none of those safety features work."

Tires squealed and brakes screeched behind them as their pursuers caught up. Bullets thudded against the skin of the car, one piercing the rear window and embedding itself in the roof liner.

"If we're doing this, we have to do it now," said Reading.

"I know I'd certainly rather go out fighting." Acton turned to Laura. "What do you think?"

"Fighting. Let's do it."

Reading removed his foot from the brake and hammered on the gas. Paulo pointed to the pickup truck on the right. "Its rear end is blocking the sidewalk. Try to hit that one. The back end will be lighter. We should be able to spin it around and out of our way."

Reading adjusted their direction slightly as they gained speed. Those at the roadblock opened fire and everyone took cover, Reading crouching behind the steering wheel. "Everybody hang on! Three! Two! Oh shit!"

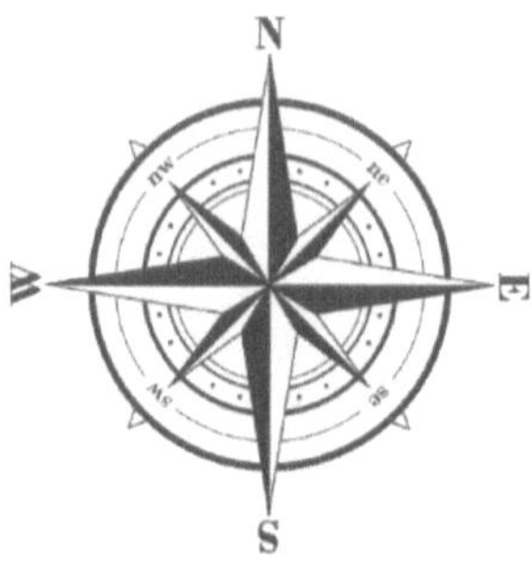

En Route to Complexo do Alemão Bairro

Rio de Janeiro, Brazil

Dawson held his tablet firmly in one hand while his other gripped the handhold as their local asset, Costa, expertly guided them toward the professors. He was monitoring the situation through his comms, and it was clear they weren't getting out. Not without help.

"Three! Two! Oh shit!"

Everyone on comms stopped what they were doing. There was a loud crashing noise as Reading rammed one of the trucks blocking them. Laura screamed, and Acton grunted before the phone went dead.

"Control, Zero-One. What the hell just happened?"

There was a brief pause before Leroux replied. "There was some sort of barrier behind the truck. Not sure what, but it stopped them cold."

"Status on the hostiles?"

"They're closing in now. They're completely surrounded. There's no way they're making it out of this."

"Try to reestablish communications. We need to know if they're still alive."

"Attempting to do so now."

Dawson pointed at the map on the tablet, showing the location of their friends to Costa. "Can you get us there?"

Costa glanced over. "Yeah. Are you sure you want to go in?"

"No choice."

"Then let's do this."

"ETA?"

Costa shook his head. "Too long."

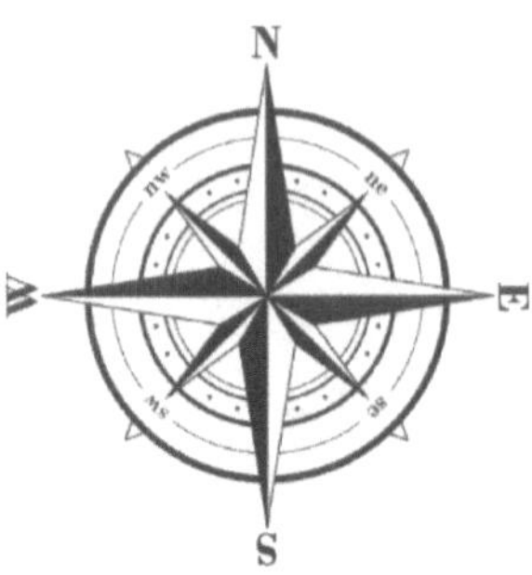

Complexo do Alemão Bairro

Rio de Janeiro, Brazil

Acton pushed up off the floor, straightening in his seat, still dazed from the abrupt impact. "Is everyone all right?" he asked, his voice strained.

Laura moaned beside him. "I think so. Hugh, you good?"

"I think I wish he hadn't disabled the airbags," Reading groaned, rubbing his chest where the steering wheel had bruised him.

"Paulo, you still with us?" Acton leaned over and cursed at the blood running down the man's forehead. He reached forward and gave him a shake. "Paulo!" Still no reply. He quickly positioned his fingers on the man's neck, checking for a pulse. "He's still alive, but he's out cold."

Gunfire thudded against the reinforced skin of the SUV, reminding everyone of their situation.

"We're not going to last long like this. Can this thing drive?"

Reading attempted to restart the engine, but it was futile. The crumpled engine compartment had succeeded where the disabled safety features hadn't, leaving them dead in the water. "We're not going anywhere."

Everyone ducked as bullets pinged off the windows, the weakest points now vulnerable after the relentless barrage. Acton poked his head up just enough to see at least a dozen gunmen surrounding them, all firing freely with their assault rifles and assorted submachine guns. "Maybe they'll run out of ammo."

Reading snorted. "Not with our luck." He extended a hand toward Acton, his expression serious. "It's been an honor."

Acton's chest tightened as he shook his friend's hand firmly. "Likewise. You've been such a good friend to us." He smirked. "Sorry we got you killed."

Reading laughed. "Always knew you would."

Laura reached forward, hugging Reading around the neck. "I hope you know how much we love you, you sweet man," she whispered, her voice trembling.

Reading's voice cracked as he replied. "And I love you."

Acton wrapped his arm around Laura, holding her tight as the gunfire continued to intensify. They held on to each other, both reaching out to grab Reading's hand, the three friends united in their final moments, accepting their fate.

The windows finally gave way, bullets spraying over their heads. Acton repositioned slightly so he could look into Laura's eyes. "I love you with all my heart."

Tears filled her eyes. "I love you too. I'm so glad I met you. I just…"

"I know. Me too." He pressed his lips against hers, closing his eyes as the gunfire grew louder, those who would have them dead, closing in.

Please, God. If anyone has to suffer, let it be me.

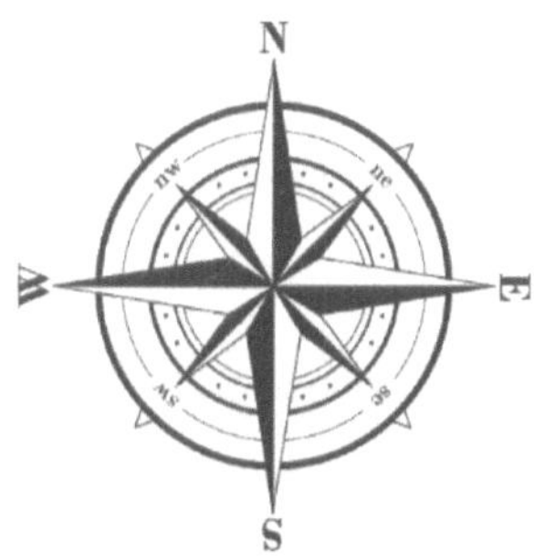

London, England

"Oh, you daft bastard!' Spencer Reading collapsed into his chair as Liverpool scored in extra time, sealing the deal. One-nil, a heartbreaker. The entire pub, subdued, was disappointed, filled with fans definitely not of the Liverpool persuasion. He drained his pint then rose. "All right, that's it for me. I've got work in the morning."

Goodbyes were exchanged, and he stepped out into the chill of a misty late afternoon. He pulled up his collar and headed for his flat, not far from here. His phone vibrated in his pocket and he fished it out, his eyebrows rising. It was his father. He didn't want to talk to him right now—at least not until he reached home. Yet his father always took his calls, no matter where he was or what he was doing. And it was rare for the man to call him. He at least owed him the courtesy of telling him he would call him back.

He swiped his thumb. "Hey, Pops, can I call you back?"

"Oh, thank God I got through!"

Loud bursts of static and high-pitched noises overwhelmed his father's voice. "Pops, I can barely hear you. I think we've got a bad connection. Let me hang up and try calling you back."

"No, no, don't hang up!"

More sounds. Spencer's heart leaped. "Were those gunshots?"

"Yes! Listen, son. I know I don't say it enough—maybe I never said it at all—but I'm proud of you. Unbelievably proud of the man you've become. And I just wish…" His father's voice faded.

"You just wish what? What's going on?"

"I'm not going to make it, boy. I'm so sorry. Just know that I love you. And I'm proud of you."

Conflicting emotions overwhelmed Spencer, fear and terror overriding everything. He looked around for someone who could help him, but what could anyone do? His father was obviously under attack and thought he was going to die.

So, he did the only thing he could think of.

He said goodbye while he still could.

"I love you, Dad. I hope you know I always did, even when we weren't getting along."

"I know, son. Don't you worry about that. We're good now. I'm going to let you go. I don't want you to hear…"

"No, Dad! Don't hang up!"

"Goodbye, son. I love you."

The call went dead and Spencer stood, all strength leaving him, his shoulders heaving as he sobbed.

"Spence, what's wrong?"

He turned to see his friends from the pub.

"My pops is dead!"

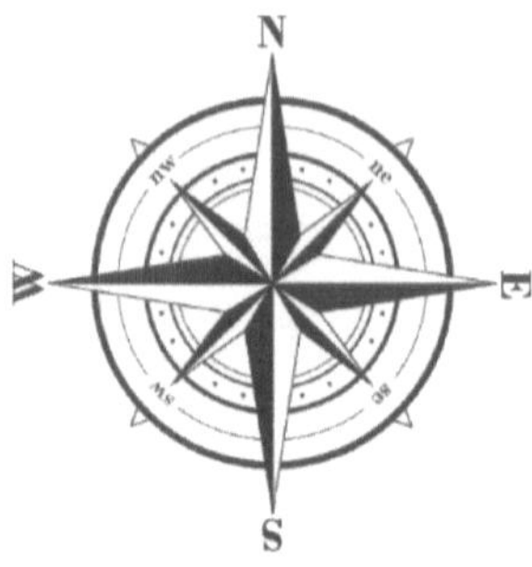

Approaching Complexo do Alemão Bairro

Rio de Janeiro, Brazil

"Next right," said Costa as they rapidly slowed, having reached the outskirts of the bairro two minutes ago. The professors had almost made it, and Dawson just prayed they were still alive. He tapped the roof.

"I assume this thing is up-armored."

"You assume correctly."

"Good." Dawson examined the map. "Looks like they're less than fifty meters up. Stop at the entrance to that street. We'll get out, you back in. We'll use you as cover, take out the hostiles, recover our people, then get the hell out of Dodge."

"You got it. Here we go!"

Dawson activated his comms as Costa brought them to a halt, angling to the left before slapping it into reverse. "Control, Zero-One. We're about to engage. Status on our people, over."

"Copy that, Zero-One. Status unknown. Unable to reestablish communications, over."

"Copy that." Dawson threw open his door and stepped out, as did the others, M4s at the ready. He peered up the road. Two pickups were blocking it just ahead. The SUV the professors and Reading were in was just on the left, the rear end of the pickup they had failed to push out of the way crumpled around a large concrete barrier. They never stood a chance. A matching block on the other side of the road confirmed this position was chosen specifically for that reason, and it had Dawson wondering if blocks like this had been placed all around the area for just such an occasion.

They continued to advance as Costa expertly guided them into the field of battle. So far, their targets hadn't taken notice, everyone pouring lead on the SUV. The windows were shot out, anything happening now purely for fun—they could move in and end this at any moment.

Somebody shouted from overhead. Dawson glanced up to see a local pointing at them, warning the gang members. He cursed, tempted to put a bullet in the moron's head, but instead squeezed the trigger, taking out the first target in his arc. The other MP4s opened up as he advanced, using the bumper as cover, with Spock and Niner on the hood, firing over the roof. Atlas opened up from the driver-side bumper. Within moments, a dozen hostiles were down, but more continued to pour into the area, their attention now focused on the new arrivals.

Dawson sprinted forward as the last of the hostiles on this side of the roadblock fell. Atlas joined him as Niner and Spock continued to cover them. Dawson reached the first pickup truck on the left, slamming into its door. He checked to make sure no one was inside and continued to pick off targets as they entered the battlefield.

Now to find out if this was all for nothing.

"Is anyone alive in there?"

Reading shoved his phone in his pocket, having spotted it on the floor only moments before. He had spoken to his son, he had told the boy what he needed to hear—what needed to be said—and he was at peace with where things had been left. With his hand now free, he clasped it over those of his friends and squeezed his eyes shut as the gunfire continued. They were toying with them, hoping to inflict as much terror as they could.

And as much as he hated to admit it, it was working.

He couldn't recall being so scared in his life. But at least all the worry, all the stress, all the loneliness and disappointment, would soon be over. He was ready to die. He was prepared for it. His only regret was that he had failed in protecting his friends, far too young, especially Laura, to die here today. But at least they would die together, no one person surviving, grieving the loss of their partner.

Something hit his shoulder, and he cried out.

"Are you okay?" asked Acton, concerned.

"I'll live," he replied through gritted teeth. "At least until I'm dead."

More weapons joined the fray, and he was tempted to roll his eyes. How many more guns were needed?

Just get it over with already.

"Something's changed," said Laura.

Reading opened his eyes to see her poking her head up. "Get down!" he hissed. She ducked back, but she was right. The gunfire immediately surrounding them had changed, rapidly dwindling.

"Those are M4s," said Acton. "I wasn't hearing them before."

Within moments, things had calmed down dramatically. Reading pulled back slightly and drew his sidearm. "This might be the only chance we get."

Laura agreed, drawing her own weapon, Acton doing the same.

Reading jerked his chin toward Paulo, still out cold. "We can't leave him."

"We're not going to," said Acton. "We get out, I get him. You two cover me."

"Is anybody alive in there?"

Reading almost cried out in relief, as both Acton and Laura did. It was Dawson.

"Four alive! One incapacitated!" shouted Acton.

"And one wounded!" added Reading. Acton eyed him and Reading slapped the shoulder that had taken a round.

"I thought you said you were okay."

"I didn't say that. I said I would live."

Footsteps rapidly approached as gunfire continued, though from farther up the street.

"Let's get you out of there!" shouted Dawson.

Acton grabbed the door handle and pushed. It didn't budge. He twisted around and used both feet to kick against it. It gave way with a creak. He scrambled out with Laura as Reading shoved against the doorframe with his wounded shoulder, grimacing in pain. Somebody on the other side grabbed the handle and yanked it mercifully open. It was Atlas.

"You okay, Agent?"

"Shoulder wound. I'll live." Reading jerked a thumb over his shoulder at Paulo. "He's out cold. Head wound."

Atlas pointed toward an SUV on the other side of the pickup trucks. "Get in. We'll patch you up as soon as we're clear."

Reading climbed out and stumbled around the rear of their ride, squeezing off a few rounds toward the hostiles. Atlas used his massive frame as a human shield as the gunfire began picking up again as more arrived. Acton already had Paulo out the door, and Atlas tossed Acton his M4.

"Cover our sixes!" the big man ordered.

Atlas grabbed Paulo and slung him over his shoulder, racing toward the SUV. Acton opened fire, rapid single shots erupting from the assault rifle as Laura helped Reading. He climbed up on the rear bumper of the pickup truck then down the other side, damning the concrete block clearly bolted into the ground—an explanation as to why they had come to such an unceremonious halt finally revealed.

Tires chirped on pavement ahead, and Reading cursed. They were about to be surrounded again. The new arrival stopped, four doors opening, the occupants stepping out, assault rifles raised and taking aim toward them.

"Friendlies on your six!" shouted a familiar voice as Leather and his men advanced, joining the firefight and evening the odds dramatically.

Reading climbed into the back seat, shuffling all the way over to the side, Acton and Laura immediately behind him. Atlas dumped Paulo into the passenger seat and slammed the door shut.

"Let's get the hell out of here!" the big man shouted, and the driver complied, pressing on the gas as the Bravo Team members jumped on the running boards, continuing to fire. They passed Leather's position, and Reading turned to see the members of his friends' security team pile back in their ride and rapidly back up. The driver made a sharp left and accelerated quickly, the gunfire fading behind them, their pursuers blocked by the same barricade that had brought their own escape to a sudden halt.

Somebody tapped on his window, and Reading reached over and pressed the button to lower it. It was Dawson. "How's everyone doing in there?"

Reading tapped his shoulder. "I took a round."

"We'll get that looked at in a couple of minutes. Professors?"

"We're both good," replied Acton. "I'm worried about Paulo, though. He's still unconscious."

"There are paramedics waiting. He'll be looked at soon enough."

"Sixty seconds!" shouted the driver as he careened around another corner. "There they are!"

Reading leaned over, peering between the seats and breathing a sigh of relief at the sight of flashing red and blue lights ahead, a large police presence marking the end of their ordeal. He closed his eyes and thanked a God he wasn't sure he believed in.

It was over.

But, unfortunately, that wasn't true. They had failed to recover the Holy Grail, and he had no doubt his friends intended to continue attempting to recover it.

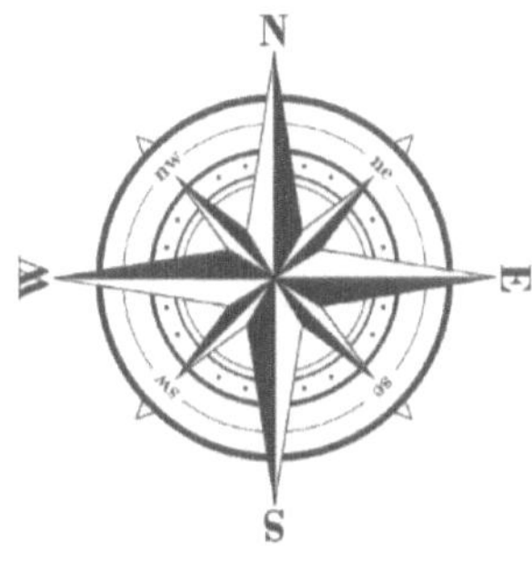

Operations Center 2, CIA Headquarters

Langley, Virginia

Leroux tore his headset off and tossed it on his station as the confirmation came in from Dawson that everyone had cleared the no-go zone. Child spun in his chair, hands extended high into the air.

"Holy shit, I think that's the most intense twenty minutes I've ever experienced!"

Tong flashed a grin at him, no insults today. "You're telling me!"

"That's more exciting than sex!" shouted Therrien, who switched to a teacher's voice. "Randy, sex is when two people who love each other press their private parts together—"

Child delivered double birds to the room with a spin.

Everyone laughed, the tension slowly releasing. Tong raised a hand, pressing her headset tighter against her ear. "Something's wrong!"

The room fell silent. Leroux grabbed his headset, fitting it in place.

"Attempting to resuscitate him now." It was Dawson, his voice subdued.

Leroux clapped his hand over the mic and turned to Tong. "Who is it? What's going on?"

"Agent Reading." She sniffed. "He had a heart attack."

Leroux dropped into his chair, elbows on his knees, head hanging low. "Oh God," he sighed as he prayed for a man he mostly knew from the other end of the phone. "Zero-One, Control Actual, status?"

"Nothing yet. They're using the paddles on him. Third try. The Doc says he's been having heart troubles." There was a heavy sigh. "It doesn't look like he's going to make it."

Leroux abruptly sat upright, tossing his head back. Everyone had made it. They had all made it to the line—and now this? He glared up at the heavens.

Why the hell would you do that? Why would you let him live, then kill him?

It was a question that had to wait, but might be moot—in all the confusion, he had forgotten why this was happening. "Did they recover the item?" It was a Hail Mary. If they had, they could use it to save the man.

"Negative."

Leroux's shoulders slumped. God wasn't on their side today.

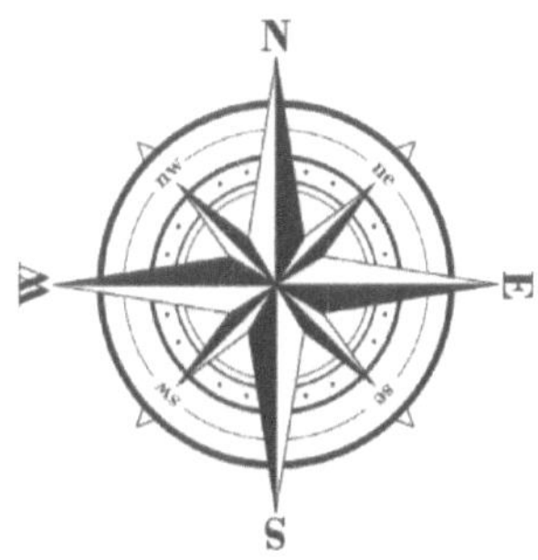

Outside Complexo do Alemão Bairro

Rio de Janeiro, Brazil

Laura wept openly as Acton held her, his own tears flowing freely for the friend that had held on, that had kept them alive, that had the presence of mind to have them share honorable goodbyes, that had provided the comforting words his son needed to hear, and had managed to escape with them, not delaying them.

Yet at the moment they were safe, his heart, put through so much, finally gave out.

Laura had noticed first and screamed. Dawson had hauled open the door, pulling Reading out as the driver shouted in Portuguese for help. EMTs rushed over with a gurney, and in less than a minute, Reading's chest was bare, and paddles were attempting to shock his heart back into rhythm.

One jolt.

Two jolts.

Three jolts.

Electricity fired into his heart, his body jerking with each attempt. The paramedics stared at the monitor and shook their heads, saying something in Portuguese.

"Oh God, James."

Acton squeezed his wife tighter as the paddles were repositioned. The machine indicated it was charged once again. This was likely it. If this didn't bring their friend back, nothing would.

Please, God, he's the finest man I know. Don't take him from us. He still has so much to live for.

He thought of everything his friend had been through since they knew him—losing his job, losing his partner, his heart attack, of how many times he had saved their lives, how he had patched things up with his estranged son, how alone he had been, how hard he had taken Kinti's death.

Acton sighed. "I was thinking of setting him up with—" The paddles zapped again. Reading jerked—and then there was a beep, followed by another, and another. The paramedic fell back on his haunches, a smile spreading as cheers erupted.

"He's back!" exclaimed their driver.

Laura cried out in relief as Reading's eyes fluttered open.

"What the bloody hell happened?" he groaned.

Acton stepped closer as Laura took Reading's hand. "You were dead."

Reading groaned again. "Really?"

Acton patted his friend's leg. "Yeah. Fun, isn't it?"

"Not exactly the words I'd choose." He rubbed his chest. "What the hell did they do to me?"

"Zap, zap!" grinned Acton. "Actually, zap, zap, zap, zap! Four times."

"Bloody hell."

"Is he going to live?" asked Acton, turning to the paramedic.

The young man packed up the paddles. "We'll take him to the hospital right now. The doctors will be able to say with more certainty." The paramedic grabbed one end of the stretcher as his partner gripped the other. Portuguese replaced English as they rushed Reading into the back of the ambulance.

"We'll see you at the hospital," called Laura, and Reading raised a single thumb.

"Call Spencer," he said.

"We will."

They watched in silence as the ambulance pulled away, their friend visible through the window.

Leather joined them. "That was too close."

Acton grunted. "You're telling me."

"We've been asked to leave."

Acton cocked an eyebrow. "Excuse me?"

"My team has been asked to leave. They revoked our visas."

"Why?" asked Laura, wiping her face dry.

"Oh, something about illegally possessing weapons. They're not pressing charges because of the situation, but they want us out of Brazil ASAP."

Laura sighed. "I suppose that's better than jail."

Leather smirked. "I suppose."

"Call Mary, have her arrange a flight for you. Take our jet and have her send another one."

"You two are staying?"

Acton exchanged a look with Laura, and it was clear she was on the same page as him. "Until we retrieve the Grail, we're not going anywhere."

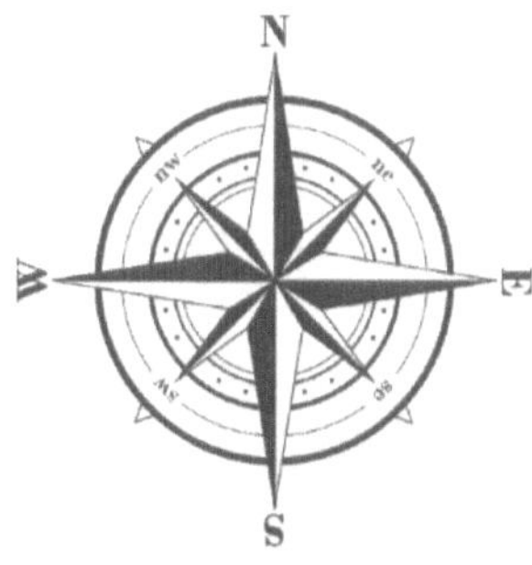

Complexo do Alemão Bairro

Rio de Janeiro, Brazil

Father Rafael Oliveira climbed into the back seat of the church's SUV. "Let's go. Don't draw any attention."

"Yes, Father," replied his driver, Pedro, as he gently pulled them away from the curb. Two other cars, one ahead and one behind, escorted them to their final destination. No one in the bairro would dare touch him, but he couldn't take any chances. He gripped the cup through his robes and closed his eyes, struggling to block out the gunfire rattling through the only neighborhood he had ever known.

The blood relic he now possessed could end so much misery, so much suffering, but that was only part of his purpose. The true purpose was uniting the world under the one true God and His Son, to end the nonsense of multiple religions battling for supremacy, to unite humanity in peace under God. The Grail, and the proof of the Lord's existence that it provided, could end all wars.

And when those wars were a thing of the past, the money wasted on them could help the poor, the destitute, the infirm. That alone would save far more lives than the cup could on its own. It would be reserved for the most desperate, the most deserving. But the source of its power would resonate far beyond the wood-carved piece of dinnerware crafted 2,000 years ago.

He had already taken a drink from the cup and felt fantastic—better than he had in years, and he couldn't wait to share it with his flock, and the world.

Thank you, Lord, for your divine gift, and thank you for finding me worthy of wielding this power on your behalf.

He sighed contentedly. He had always loved serving his flock. There were no kinder people than the poor. Their outreach programs throughout the neighborhood meant he knew everyone—every man, woman, and child—most by name. How many could say they knew their entire neighborhood and didn't fear any of them?

Even the gang members, who had no choice but to be who they were, respected him. Most lived in peace, as long as the authorities stayed out and the various gangs stuck to their territories. It gave them purpose, and while he wished they were all gainfully employed in regular jobs, that simply wasn't an option in his bairro.

But now that he had the Grail, a task handed down to him over many generations—a task he never dreamed would be fulfilled by anyone, let alone him—he could change things for the better. People would pay millions to be healed by the Cup of Christ, and with that power in his hands, he could raise up the bairro to become one of the wealthiest in the city—not to mention the healthiest.

He wasn't certain of the logistics. He had never given them any thought. He had simply assumed the cup was real but would never be found. It had been missing for almost 200 years, and he had assumed it wouldn't be found for another 200, if not 2,000.

He gripped the cup again. Here it was, the Cup of Christ, the Holy Grail, around his neck, its power fueling him. The euphoria he had felt from the moment he drank from it was unquenchable. He felt more human than human, almost godlike.

It was intoxicating.

An explosion to their left, out of sight, jolted him from his reverie. "Turn up the volume, would you?"

"Yes, Father." Pedro leaned over and increased the volume, Chopin playing over the speakers, drowning out the horrors from several streets over.

Oliveira leaned against the window, peering ahead and smiling at the sight of the towering Christ the Redeemer statue. His church had been largely responsible for the fundraising a century ago. This was where one journey would end, and another would begin. His destiny—the destiny of all those before him, starting with Father Santos—was about to be fulfilled.

And the long road to peace on Earth would start tonight.

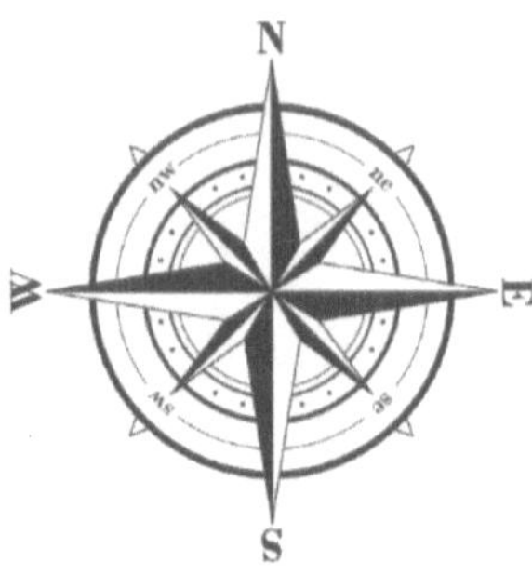

Spencer Reading Residence

London, England

The doorbell buzzed and Spencer Reading bolted to his feet. His best friend, Johnny, waved him off.

"I'll get it."

Spencer dropped back onto the couch, his tears still flowing. His father was dead, and it sounded like he had been in a firefight. His friends had practically carried him home and remained with him the entire time, no one quite sure what to say. They were all his age. You weren't supposed to lose a parent this young. His father was always older than most dads, having met his mother later in life, but not that much older. And it wasn't like he had died of natural causes.

He had been shot and killed.

Spencer didn't even know where his father was. Was he in London? Paris? Rome? He had no idea.

The door opened, and he leaped to his feet again at the sight of his father's partner, Michelle Humphrey. She rushed forward and embraced him, holding him like his mother should be, though that hateful witch had just said "good" when he told her the news. He knew they didn't like each other. His mother had always conspired to turn him against his father and had succeeded for far too long. But his father wasn't the monster she made him out to be. There was no excuse for callousness like that. His father never said anything bad about his mother. He simply refrained from speaking of her, which was fine by Spencer. He didn't want to get in the middle of their feud. But for her to say "good," that was unforgivable.

"Where did he die?"

Humphrey maneuvered him back onto the couch. "I'm going to be honest with you. I don't know much yet. All I know is that the last I heard, he was in Rio."

"Rio? You mean like Brazil?"

"Exactly."

"What was he doing there?"

"Official Interpol business on behalf of the Vatican. That's about all I can say."

"The Vatican?" A pit formed in Spencer's stomach. "It's those damn professors, isn't it? Those friends of his from America."

"Yes, they're there."

Spencer slammed a fist on the arm of the couch. "I knew they'd get him killed one day!"

"Well, if what you described is true, they're likely all dead. I've been trying to reach them but haven't had any success."

"Can't you track the phone? Do something? You're Interpol!"

"Interpol isn't what most people think it is. It's not like the movies. We're a paperwork agency. We coordinate investigations around the world between different law enforcement organizations. We don't have big control centers like the CIA or equipment and personnel like the FBI. But trust me when I say, we are doing everything we can."

His phone rang and he grabbed it off the coffee table, seeing an unknown caller. He took the call. "Hello?"

"Hello, is this Spencer?" It was a woman's voice.

"Yes, it is."

"This is Laura Palmer."

He tensed at the gall of one of those responsible for his father's death to call him. It enraged him. "What do you want?" His hatred was evident.

"I just want to let you know that your father's going to be all right, but he had a heart attack."

Spencer's jaw dropped. The roller coaster of emotions kicked into high gear again. "What? He's alive?" He placed the phone on speaker, and Humphrey leaned in.

"This is Agent Michelle Humphrey, Interpol. I'm Hugh's partner. Who is this?"

"Professor Laura Palmer."

"Am I to understand Hugh is alive?"

"Yes. He had a heart attack, but he's fine. The doctors expect him to recover, but it will take some time."

Spencer's friends held their tongues as disbelief washed over him. "When he called me, I heard gunfire. I thought he was killed in a shootout."

"He almost was. We all almost were, but help arrived in time. Your father saved our lives—all our lives. If it weren't for him—" Laura's voice cracked. "Well, if it weren't for him, we'd be dead."

"Where's Hugh now?" asked Humphrey.

"He's at the National Institute of Cardiology in Rio. I'll text you both all the details. I've contacted my travel agent. She's arranging a flight for you, Spencer. It's a private charter, so bring anyone you want. Michelle, if you want to catch that flight, feel free. Just get the details of everybody to Mary. I'll send you her contact info as well, so she can arrange the visas."

Spencer leaned forward. "Can I talk to him?"

"No, he just got out of surgery. He's sleeping now."

"Surgery? In Brazil?"

"Don't worry. It's a good hospital, and I made sure the best surgeons in the city were working on your father. Trust me, he's getting the best care possible, no matter where he might have been in the world."

Spencer leaned back, relieved, the hatred he felt for the woman gone. Now, he was just grateful for the money she had and what it had done for his father.

"I'm going to let you go, but I'll text you the information in the next few minutes. Get yourselves ready. My guess is you'll be in the air in a couple of hours."

"If you talk to him—" Spencer's shoulders shook as he lost control for a moment. His friend Emily squeezed his hand. He inhaled sharply. "Tell him I love him, and I'll see him soon."

"You can count on it. We'll see you soon. Goodbye."

The call ended, and his friends swarmed him, excited and relieved at the news. His father was alive, but for how much longer, he wasn't sure. Two heart attacks couldn't be good. He might not have that much more time with the man he had hated for so long because of his cruel mother.

He rose.

"All right, I've got to pack a bag. Who's coming?"

Hands shot up all around, and he smiled.

He had amazing friends.

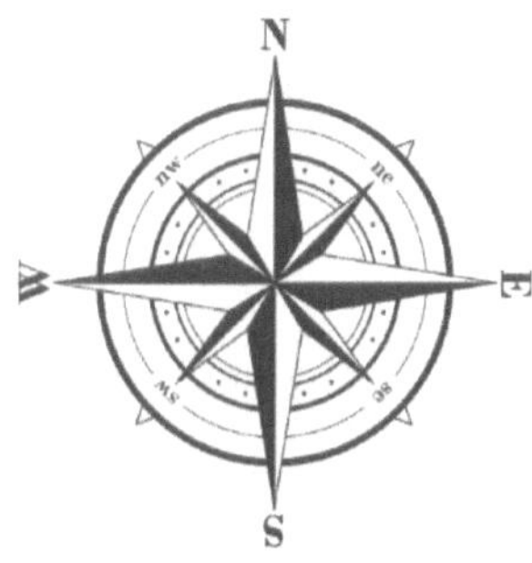

Outside Complexo do Alemão Bairro

Rio de Janeiro, Brazil

"Do you think this means they won't let us hit the beaches?"

Atlas eyeballed Niner. "Are you sure you want to put that little toothpick body of yours on display in two different countries in two days?"

Niner pulled up his shirt sleeve and flexed, displaying an impressive bicep. "Toothpick?"

Atlas flexed, his sleeve straining. "Toothpick."

Dawson chuckled, then noticed the Brazilian scene commander approaching. "Best behavior, boys."

The idle chit-chat stopped as Colonel Martins delivered their fate. "Sergeant Major, I'm here to inform you that my government is extremely displeased that the American military conducted an operation on our sovereign soil without permission."

Dawson opened his mouth to protest that they were merely tourists when the colonel held up a finger, cutting him off.

"However, after speaking with your State Department, we realize this is all a misunderstanding. You believed you were here with our consent, activated after you had already arrived as four men on leave from your unit and on vacation."

Dawson decided it was best to let the man talk.

"Your State Department has informed my government that apparently you are here to retrieve"—he paused—"a classified item that was stolen. Our government has agreed to cooperate in its recovery."

Dawson was about to thank the man when Martins raised his finger again.

"Personally, I think the entire story is bullshit, but like you, I have commanding officers. My government has decided to cooperate and forgive any prior transgressions. Therefore, what's done is done. And besides, if it wasn't for you and your men, we both know those people would be dead."

Dawson said nothing, and Martins smirked.

"You may now speak."

Dawson smiled slightly. "Thank you, Colonel. We apologize for the confusion earlier and appreciate your cooperation and that of your country. Since we're now all on the same team, we still have a mission."

"Can you tell me what the item is that was stolen?"

Dawson decided discretion was the best way forward. "I'm afraid not, sir. It's a matter of national security."

"How did it end up in our bairro?"

Dawson delivered the cover story provided by Langley. "We believe a priest named Father Oliveira, or one of his congregation, inadvertently stole the item. We're leaning toward it being a member of the congregation, of course, probably a petty thief who either didn't or doesn't realize what they have. Three friends of the nation attempted to recover the item, which led to what we witnessed."

"These friends, two claim to be professors. One says he's an Interpol agent. Are they?"

"They are. They're not affiliated with the American government in any way, but they've been useful in the past due to their positions. They happened to be in the area, so a favor was called in because time was of the essence. I'm not privy to all the details. Suffice it to say, they failed. The item is still out there."

"Then how do you propose to find it?"

"I think the best solution is to find Father Oliveira."

"I'm familiar with him. He's rather famous in the bairro. Very well-respected, loved by all. His church helps feed the poor, provides shelter for orphans. They do a lot of good work."

"I have no doubt. And we don't believe he's a bad man, or that he's actually the thief, though we believe he knows who the thief is. Again, we believe they don't realize what they have. Otherwise, they would hand it over willingly. We need to find him so we can speak with him."

Martins frowned. "That could be difficult. We can't go into the bairro, as you saw. It's controlled by the gangs. If they discover we're there for the father, they'll stop at nothing to prevent us from reaching him."

"He has that much of a connection with the gangs?"

"Yes. He's been there for decades. The church has been there for over a century. Everyone in this bairro has worshiped within its walls at one time or another, including the gang members. If you want him, the only way you're going to get to him is to get him to come out voluntarily."

"Easier said than done, I'm sure. Do you have a phone number for him?"

"I can get one for the church, but I don't have one for him. I'm not sure if he would even have a phone."

A lieutenant rushed up and whispered something in Martins' ear, concern growing on the colonel's face.

"Excuse me a moment," said Martins. The two stepped away, a rapid, hushed conversation taking place before the lieutenant was sent away with orders. Martins returned with a frown.

"Problem?" asked Dawson.

"Yes. It appears a large convoy is leaving the bairro. Heavily armed."

Spock cocked an eyebrow. "Is that unusual?"

"Extremely. When the gangs leave the bairro, it's never done publicly. They'll sneak into a neighboring bairro, do whatever business they have, and then return. But this is something different. It appears gang members and ordinary civilians are leaving together."

Dawson tensed. "How many?"

"At least a hundred. Could be more."

"Where are they headed?"

Martins turned and jerked his chin toward the horizon. "They think they're headed for him."

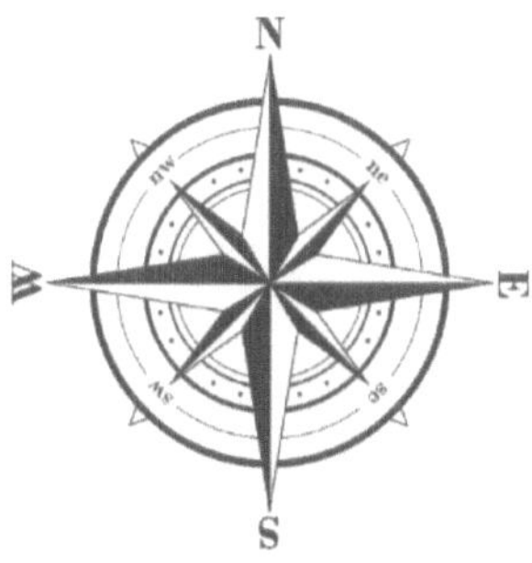

National Institute of Cardiology

Rio de Janeiro, Brazil

Acton peered through the glass, Laura by his side, both relieved to see Reading alive. The doctors had indicated the surgery was a complete success and that he should recover, however, damage had been done. The cause might have been addressed, but it was too late to restore his heart to perfect health. Only time could do that, and even then, it was questionable. He could die today. He could die ten years from now. At the moment, there was no way to know. But he was alive right now, something that, only a few hours ago, couldn't have been said. Their friend had died—his heart stopped for almost two minutes, and apparently, there had been another incident during the ambulance ride.

Reading's eyes opened. He made to sit up when a nurse gently pushed him back onto the bed. Words were exchanged, then Reading turned his head slightly and spotted them. They both waved, Laura particularly excited, bouncing on her toes with a broad smile. Reading gave them a weak thumbs-up, then closed his eyes, his hand collapsing to his side, the poor guy asleep once again.

Acton's phone vibrated and he pulled it out. It was an unknown caller. He took the call. "Hello?"

"Professor Acton, can you speak?" It was Dawson.

"Yes." Acton mouthed who it was to Laura, and she moved closer to the phone so she could hear.

"How's Agent Reading?"

"He's out of surgery and in recovery now. It was a success, but there was damage."

"Understood. We didn't get much time to talk, but there's still a mission that needs to be completed."

Acton shook his head. "Forget about it. I almost lost one of my best friends. Too many died today." He hated saying it. The Grail had to be recovered, but how that could happen without major bloodshed, he had no idea.

"I don't think you understand the situation, Professor. This isn't your mission anymore. This is mine. Washington wants it. They don't want it out there in public. If the Chinese got their hands on it, or the Russians, there's no telling what might happen. I'm recovering the item, unless my government orders me not to."

Acton chewed his cheek for a moment, debating what to say.

"How can we help?" asked Laura, already having reached the conclusion Acton was about to. This was too important. People had died, and more might, but that was the price to protect this type of power. If it was real.

Acton squeezed his wife around her shoulders. "Yes, how can we help?"

"A large convoy, at least a hundred strong, has left the bairro. It appears they're heading toward the Christ the Redeemer statue. Do you think it could be related to the item?"

Laura's head bobbed excitedly. "Yes! When I was in Father Oliveira's office, there were old drawings and pictures, including architectural diagrams of the statue." She grabbed her phone, swiping through her images until she found the one she was searching for. She zoomed in on a particular section and showed it to Acton. He inhaled sharply.

"It looks like there's quite a bit going on underneath that statue. Rooms, staircases, a large area. I'm seeing multiple levels. From my understanding of the statue, except for the first couple of levels, none of that should be there."

"Could it have been part of the original design that was scrapped?" asked Dawson.

"Impossible to say, but I'm willing to bet that's their destination."

"Where are you now?" asked Acton.

"We're at the same location where we extracted, outside the bairro. The authorities here are redeploying to deal with this threat."

"All right. We're going to join you as soon as we can. Just remember, nobody can know, especially the locals, what we're after."

"Professor, *I'm* not even sure what we're after. And sit tight. I'll have a chopper sent to pick you up."

"Understood. We'll see you soon."

The call ended, and Acton stared at their friend, once again sound asleep. He looked down at Laura. "Once more into the fray?"

She smiled and gave him a kiss. "Can't wait."

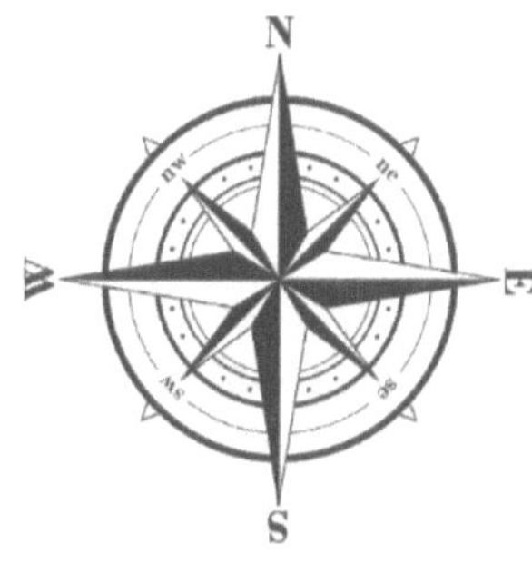

Operations Center 2, CIA Headquarters

Langley, Virginia

"Found them!"

Leroux turned in his chair, looking up at Child, stationed behind him. "Where?"

"The satellite was too low on the horizon to see him leave, but we finally got that cellphone data from the Mexicans. A phone that was in Mexico City during the attack is now in Rio, and it's on the move."

"Show me." Leroux turned toward the main display as Child updated it. A map of Rio appeared, with a red pulsing dot moving across it. "Projected destination?"

"The computer can't be sure, but he's a priest, right? My guess is that big statue of Jesus."

"Like a moth to a flame," Tong muttered.

Leroux folded his arms. "I think it's more than that. Professor Palmer's report said she found photos and diagrams of that statue. And according to Inspector General Giasson, that particular church was heavily involved in the fundraising a century ago for the construction. This conspiracy, whatever it is, has been ongoing since 1832." Leroux scratched his chin. "Could this be part of a larger, long-term plan?"

Tong folded her arms. "Long-term plans are par for the course with cults and secret organizations, especially well-funded ones."

Dawson's last update had indicated the professors thought there were levels underneath the statue unknown to the public. It had his mind spinning. If the architectural diagrams were accurate, what was the purpose of the extra levels? And why would a church determined to recover the Holy Grail need to involve the statue of Christ the Redeemer?

"ETA to the statue?"

"He's going to be there in less than five minutes," said Child.

"And that convoy?"

"The lead elements are only twenty minutes behind him. And ahead of them, over a dozen other cars have already left the bairro and are headed in that direction, all leaving within minutes of the professors being discovered at the church."

Leroux's eyes narrowed. "Then why the convoy? It makes things kind of obvious, doesn't it?"

Tong frowned. "And why isn't Father Oliveira in that same convoy?"

Leroux rubbed his chin. "I'm not sure. Maybe they're related, but only indirectly."

"What do you mean?"

"Let's say he's heading to the statue. Maybe he needs help, or maybe there are certain people he wants there. They all head out around the same time. Word spreads, and now everybody knows something's up. They all get together and go en masse. Maybe the Father doesn't even know they're coming."

Child spun in his chair. "I guess the real question is, are they coming to protect what he has, or take it from him?"

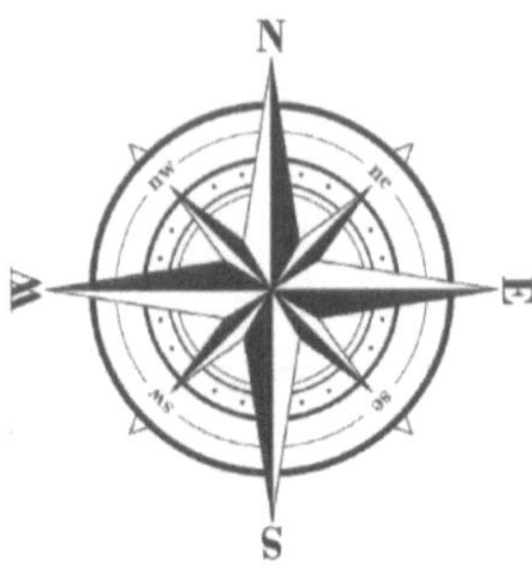

En route to Mount Corcovado

Rio de Janeiro, Brazil

Dawson had been true to his word. A helicopter had arrived for them less than ten minutes after their conversation. Acton sat strapped in with Laura, and Paulo, still with them, insisting his job wasn't over until they were on a plane out of the country, spoke with the crew.

He joined them as the massive statue grew through the cockpit window. "This is turning into something big."

"What did you find out?" asked Laura.

"There's a large convoy—at least fifty vehicles—that left the bairro and appears to be heading for Cristo. Sorry, the statue. Cristo is what we call it around here. Reports indicate many are armed, but many are civilians as well, so we can't just engage them without risking innocent lives or hostages."

Acton frowned. "Is this normal?"

"No. This never happens. Small raids of three or four cars, maybe, but always gang members. This is a mix. It's huge—hundreds of people.

It can't be a coincidence that this happened at the same time you went in. Don't you think it's time you told me what's really going on?"

Acton shook his head. "Sorry. Classified."

"Yet you two know."

Laura smiled sympathetically, but stuck to the cover. "Only because we discovered it. Otherwise, they would never have told us. I'm sure you know how it works—'need to know' and all that."

Paulo grunted. "Yeah, I'm familiar with the concept. Remember, Brazilian Special Forces. Fine. You're not gonna tell me, that's all right, but tell me this—is this something that could get a group like this not only working together but riled up?"

Acton sighed heavily. "Absolutely. That's why we're trying to recover it—to prevent just this type of thing."

"Two minutes!" the pilot shouted from the front in English for their benefit.

"Acknowledged!" replied Paulo. "When we get there, you two are with me. I'll reunite you with the American team, but I stick with you no matter what until I get you on a plane out of here. Understood?"

They both nodded.

"Good. Now, try not to get yourselves killed." He flashed a grin. "It doesn't look good on my résumé."

"Sixty seconds!" the pilot announced.

Acton directed his attention out the window. The 98-foot-tall statue loomed ahead atop its 26-foot pedestal, flashing red and blue lights surrounding the base and below Mount Corcovado indicating a growing police presence.

Laura pointed. "Look!"

Acton leaned over to see a serpentine trail of headlights approaching. "That has to be them. They look close."

Paulo checked for himself. "They are. There's a roadblock set up, but it's not well-manned. It's going to take time for the authorities to respond."

Two helicopters blasted past, swooping down toward the arriving mix of what Acton assumed were gang members and worshippers, though their chopper appeared to be bypassing all that. The helicopter landed atop Mount Corcovado, placing them 100 yards away from the base of the statue.

"Let's go!" ordered a crewmember, opening the door.

Paulo jumped out, helping both Acton and Laura down. They cleared the rotors, and the helicopter lifted off moments later.

"Professors!"

Acton turned to see Dawson hailing them. They jogged over to join him. "What's the situation?"

"Langley has confirmed that Father Oliveira and half a dozen people entered the doorway over there." Dawson indicated the base of the statue. "They've been in there for at least half an hour. Other people have been trickling in. Last count we have is twenty-seven. We have no way of knowing if anyone was in there earlier."

"Are they armed?"

"Some were, yes, and they could have a cache inside. My bigger concern is what's coming." He pointed down the hill at the still approaching convoy. "A lot of them are armed. If they get here, this is going to turn into a shit show fast."

"Then I suggest we get this over with as quickly as possible."

"Agreed. What is it you propose we do?"

"Go in, retrieve the item, get out, leave the country. What are your ROEs?"

Dawson lowered his voice. "The Brazilians don't want us shooting anything. My orders from DC are to minimize civilian casualties as much as possible, however, we are to retrieve the item at all costs."

The rules of engagement were pretty much what Acton had figured. "Are we waiting on anything?"

"No. We're ready to go." Dawson gestured toward the back of a nearby truck. "Body armor is over there, plus weapons. I had them set aside stuff you're familiar with."

They headed for the truck and found Niner and Atlas waiting there for them.

Niner grinned. "Hello, gorgeous."

Acton knew full well the man wasn't talking to him. "Hey, sweet cheeks," he replied. "Still short?"

Atlas swatted the relatively diminutive Niner. "Burn!"

Niner rubbed his chest where Atlas had hit him. "Hey, I've got a girlfriend now."

"You certainly don't act like it."

"What's that saying? What happens in Rio stays in Rio?"

"Wrong city, dude."

Niner shrugged. "Oh well." He handed Laura a vest. "Just your size, darlin'."

She took it with a smile. "Thank you."

Niner helped her with it as Acton and Paulo suited up. Acton strapped a Glock to his thigh and grabbed an MP5, inspecting the weapon.

Paulo eyed him and Laura as she did the same. "Why do I think you two have done this before?"

Acton shrugged. "No idea." He held up the submachine gun. "Which end do I point at the bad guy?"

Paulo rolled his eyes. "Why do I get the feeling I've been set up?"

Dawson joined them. "Ready?"

Laura replied. "Yes."

"Good. The Brazilians have given us point. I guess they don't want to accidentally shoot a priest. They want that bad juju on us if it happens."

"Good," replied Acton. "It gives us the opportunity to retrieve the item without anybody seeing. Remember, we get our hands on it, and we get the hell out right away. We don't care about anything else. Agreed?"

"Agreed." Dawson raised a hand then indicated the door. "Let's go!"

Dawson led the way with Spock, followed by Atlas and Niner. Acton put himself ahead of Laura, with Paulo bringing up the rear. A dozen Brazilians spread out as they approached the door. Dawson reached it first and grabbed the handle.

And Acton had to wonder what the hell they were about to walk in on.

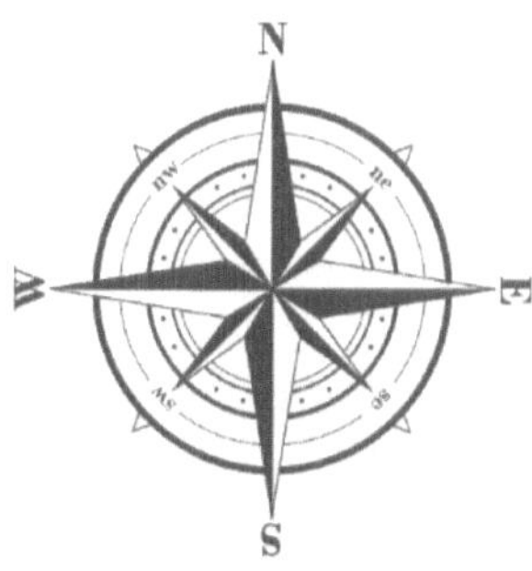

Under the Christ the Redeemer Statue, Mount Corcovado

Rio de Janeiro, Brazil

Father Oliveira's heart had pounded with excitement, with fear, with joy, with trepidation, when they had arrived. The culmination of over 150 years of planning was about to happen. At times, he pictured that it might be him to fulfill this duty, passed down since the days of Father Santos, their founder. But if honest with himself, he had always assumed it was a fantasy. He didn't believe in the Holy Grail—not the one from legend—but he did accept the premise that a cup was used by Jesus at the Last Supper, an event he absolutely believed occurred. After all, it was in the Bible, and the Bible was history, not fiction.

When brought into the fold, he had read the writings of Father Santos, about how he had discovered the Grail's existence, of how he had lost the strange man who had claimed to be a Templar over 500 years old in the crowds of New York City, and it had enthralled him. Then today—here, now—he was about to share with the world the miraculous power of our Lord Jesus Christ.

He descended the steps, the stairwell he was now in known to few. The lower levels of the base of the statue, funded so long ago by his church's efforts, had been built in secret, the plans destroyed, showing only the two levels the public were officially aware of.

A wooden door lay at the foot of the steps. He had been here before, but rarely, only when work needed doing as part of their continual state of readiness for this very day. It had been years since he had last been here. He smiled at the others, all as nervous as he was, all as excited. "Trust in God, my children."

He reached forward and gripped the heavy bar sealing the door. It wouldn't budge. He readjusted his grip, using both hands, and jerked up. The rusted metal gave way, and he winced in pain as the back of his right hand scraped against an exposed nail. One of his men rushed forward and pulled the door aside, a heavy mustiness wafting out.

"Let's get to work. We have little time." His flock surged forward, flashlights illuminating the dusty scene as he slowly entered, enjoying the moment. Candles were rapidly lit, an electrical panel to his left turned on, its circuits barely used since it was installed. Sheets covering the pews and altar were removed by the several dozen of the true believers already here, waiting at the top of the steps when he had arrived.

Oliveira yanked free the sheet covering his pulpit then dusted himself off, making certain he was worthy of this momentous event. Several of his people quickly set up video cameras, one of them giving a thumbs-up, indicating the link to the outside world had been established. A laptop screen showed a countdown, and he inhaled deeply, slowly surveying the room. It was a church, secretly built over a century ago, with one purpose—to be used only when the Holy Grail was recovered.

The plan had changed since he had taken over, modern technology giving them a different way to spread the word. Now they had the Internet—the World Wide Web, social media—and tonight, it would be leveraged, making certain as many people as possible witnessed what was about to occur. The moment he had recovered the Grail and landed safely in Rio, the process had started. Posts had gone up all over the web, spreading word of a blessed event, an event that would change the future of mankind, and now it was time.

"How many people?" he asked one of his team.

They checked the laptop. "Over one-hundred-thousand."

He frowned. "It's not enough. Let them know why we're really here."

"Yes, Father." Keys were tapped, the mouse clicked, and a smile spread. "Just as you suspected, Father. Now that they know it has to do with proof of the Holy Grail, and they've been told to share it with everyone, things are growing fast."

"Good, good."

A young woman in a long white robe approached, flanked by her mother and father. He smiled at her, the brave volunteer chosen long ago for her purity.

"Are you ready, my child?"

She bowed. "Yes, Father." She hesitated. "Will it hurt?"

He placed a comforting hand on her shoulder. "Yes, my child, but only for a moment." He gripped the Grail around his neck. "Once you are healed by the power of our Lord Jesus Christ, you will feel no pain, and will be one with God."

Niner stepped back, the detonator gripped in his hand. "Fire in the hole!" He pressed the button, and the small charge blew apart the lock behind the cabinet hiding the secret entrance located by Laura using the detailed diagrams she had taken photos of. The door swung open, revealing a dimly lit stairwell leading down.

So far, they hadn't encountered any resistance clearing the first two levels. Langley had reported at least several dozen people inside. They had been seen going in, and no one had come out. They had to be below.

The distant thuds of gunfire had Dawson frowning. He turned to Paulo. "Check it out."

The Brazilian Special Forces operator raced up the stairs to see what was happening outside. Brazilian security had stayed on the main level under orders to provide assistance only if requested. No one wanted worshippers from one of the most violent bairros to be massacred by the police. It could turn a tinderbox into a raging inferno.

Dawson strained his ears, listening for any sounds below. He heard nothing. Just where was all the resistance they had expected?

Paulo returned. "They're attacking the roadblock."

Dawson cursed. "Okay. We don't have much time."

Acton's phone vibrated in his pocket and he fished it out. "Hello?" He frowned.

"What?"

"It's Tommy. He says we have a problem."

Father Oliveira smiled broadly at the cameras. He felt comfortable behind them, his sermons always recorded and posted on social media. It was how he had developed the following being built upon today. Over two million people were now tuned in, enough to begin.

"Thank you, my children, for joining us here today. You'll notice I'm not in my usual church, for today is a special day, a momentous day, a day that will go down in history as the day the world changed." He removed the Grail from around his neck and held it up for the cameras. "I'm sure you're wondering what this is. This, my friends, my children, is the Holy Grail. Not the one of Arthurian legend, not the one from Hollywood, but the actual cup that our Lord Jesus Christ drank from at the Last Supper, as recorded in the Bible. Now, I know many of you are thinking that this is fake, that I'm lying, that it can't be true. But tonight, before the end of this broadcast, you *will* believe."

The young woman was led by her parents toward the altar, one of the cameras following her.

"This is Maria. She is pure of body, mind, and soul. She has volunteered to experience the power of our Lord. What you are about to witness will shock you, horrify you, and then, with the power of the Grail, you will witness a miracle. A miracle that we will repeat over and over until everyone on the face of God's creation has borne witness. Tonight, we change the world!"

Maria climbed onto the altar and lay on her back, her father securing her hands to ties at one end, her mother, her feet at the other. Oliveira picked up the knife chosen long ago for this occasion, plain and unadorned, just as the Grail had been described in Father Santos' journals. He stepped over to the altar and placed the Grail back around his neck.

He caressed Maria's cheek. "Are you ready, my child?" He could see the fear in her eyes, and didn't blame her. It was a terrifying thing. Yet all she needed was faith. "Trust in God, my child. Trust in our Lord Jesus Christ."

She nodded unconvincingly, and he raised the knife, gripping it with both hands over his head.

"And now, my children, prepare to witness the power of the Grail."

Gunfire rattled at the door, and he spun toward the sound.

"We're under attack!" someone shouted.

Oliveira jerked his chin toward Pedro, who rushed to a stack of duffel bags nearby. He unzipped one of them and began handing out weapons. His flock spread out, hiding among the pews, prepared to die should it become necessary.

No one could be allowed to interfere with God's work.

Dawson jerked back as an AK-47 rattled below them. As soon as they had begun their descent, they had been engaged. This would take far too long, and Tommy Granger had just made them aware of a live webcast being witnessed by millions around the world, the audience growing exponentially. Apparently, a young woman was about to be sacrificed to prove the power of the Grail.

Their mission was the cup, but he wasn't about to allow a young woman to die because of religious zealotry. Their weapons would take too long, so he had sent Paulo up to plead for the ordnance the Brazilians hadn't wanted them to have.

Paulo returned, holding up a bag triumphantly. "Flashbangs and grenades."

Dawson smiled. "Good. What's the status outside?"

"They're about to break through. Our people are outnumbered. They just can't hold it."

"Reinforcements?"

"They aren't coming soon enough to stop them from getting here."

Dawson cursed. "That's an upstairs problem. Let's just get the item." He held out his hand. "Grenades. Two."

Paulo fished two from the bag. Dawson took the first and handed it to Atlas, then pulled the pin on the second. "On three."

Atlas pulled his pin. "On three."

Dawson counted then the grenades were tossed down the stairwell and everyone stepped away from the door. The massive blasts were deafening in the close quarters, their Sonic Defender earplugs protecting them. He peered down the stairwell and smiled.

The gunfire had stopped.

The deafening explosion blasted debris through the door, wounding several of Oliveira's followers. Members rushed forward to pull the wounded out of the way as the others repositioned, preparing to repel the invaders. There was little time. It would all stop the moment the miracle was performed, he was certain of it.

He stared at the camera. "The forces of evil are at our gates, attempting to stop the power of our Lord, but they will not succeed. You will all bear witness to the miracle of the power of God. You will all forever remember this moment, the moment that united all of mankind under the one true God and His Son."

He gripped the hilt of the knife tightly, wincing as he glanced at the back of his hand. The gash from when he opened the door was bleeding slightly, but he didn't have time to worry about what could be dealt with by a bandage. Now was the time for the power of the Holy Grail to be revealed.

He raised the knife high above Maria, then plunged it into her stomach, her ear-piercing scream echoing through the underground church.

Acton cringed at the blood-curdling cry of agony, the woman Tommy had said was tied to an altar evidently sacrificed. They were too late. Dawson led the team down the stairs and yanked open the door at the bottom, a hail of bullets greeting him. But this time, they didn't engage. They didn't know who was inside. Were they all guilty, or had some been tricked into being there?

There was no way to know, and no time to negotiate. Once the mob from below arrived, they would tear everyone and everything apart to retrieve the Grail for themselves.

Dawson's team tossed in two flashbangs, the result both blinding and deafening. The cries inside told them it had worked, and Bravo Team rushed in. Acton descended the steps with Laura right behind him, their

MP5s raised. Gunfire echoed as the worshippers put up a fight, but Bravo Team's submachine guns rattled in rapid, controlled bursts.

Acton peered into the room and gasped at the sight of worshippers still praying in the pews, arms raised in the air. Father Oliveira stood at an altar, holding the Grail high above his head before pouring its contents over the bloody wound on the young woman's stomach.

"Behold the power of our Lord!" Oliveira shouted.

The gunfire dwindled and stopped, those fighting now transfixed by what was happening. Acton couldn't help himself. He stepped forward, Laura on his heels, both overwhelmed with a sense of religious fervor. Something incredible was happening—something historical that he couldn't miss.

The danger was forgotten.

Oliveira stared as the blood washed away, and he smiled, overcome with the moment. Then frowned. The wound didn't close. His eyes widened with confusion. Maria was still bleeding. He glanced at the cut on his own hand and gasped with realization. He had drunk from the cup, several times. His wound should have healed. He grabbed the carafe of holy water and refilled the cup, pouring it over his own hand.

Nothing.

Something was wrong. This was the Holy Grail. It had the power of the Lord within it. Why wasn't it working, why wasn't it healing not only his minor wound, but this poor girl's grave one?

"What have I done?"

He had killed her. He had thrust the knife into her. But it was all because of what he had been taught, what Father Santos had written so many years ago.

Something he now realized was all at best a misunderstanding.

Or at worst, a lie.

He stared at Maria, his eyes filling with tears as she writhed in agony. "I'm so sorry, my child."

Acton rushed forward, taking advantage of the confusion. He grabbed the cup, still in Oliveira's hand. They wrestled briefly, but the man had lost his desire to fight, and Acton soon ripped it from Oliveira's grip.

"It doesn't work!" Oliveira sobbed. "Oh God, it doesn't work. Why, Lord? Why doesn't it work?"

Acton stared at the Grail, then at the young woman who was still bleeding heavily. A man and woman rushed forward, pleading with God to save her as they untied her. Niner moved in with a med kit, working to stop the bleeding as Dawson and the others disarmed the stunned worshippers.

Acton stared at the cup, then at Laura. "I don't understand. This has to be it, right?"

"Maybe you have to drink from it, not pour from it."

Acton filled the cup with the contents of a pitcher on the pulpit, and downed it, standing still, waiting to feel something—anything, tuning out the noise surrounding him, listening, reaching out with all his senses, seeking anything that might suggest a change.

But there was nothing.

There was none of the euphoria described in the journals, none of the sense of wellbeing, none of the relief from the aches and pains that burdened him constantly.

"Well?"

He shook his head, more disappointed than he could recall ever being. "Nothing."

Dawson ran over. "Is that it?"

Acton wasn't sure what to say. It was what they were seeking, but it wasn't what they thought it was. There was no time to explain. "Yes."

"Good. We need to get the hell out of here. Now."

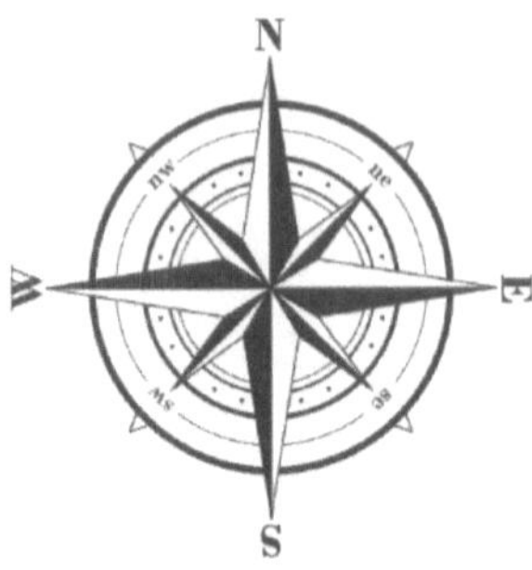

Operations Center 2, CIA Headquarters

Langley, Virginia

Leroux cursed as the roadblock collapsed. The police, outnumbered, fell back as a large pickup truck smashed through the barricade and began racing up the mountain, more following. Attack helicopters swept in, opening fire on the lead vehicles, bringing them to a halt. Cars and trucks were abandoned as people began streaming up the hill on foot, rushing toward what they believed was the Holy Grail. The helicopters held their fire, unwilling to shoot at the mix of gang members and believers scrambling up the mountain.

They had no idea what was happening inside. The last thing seen on the feed Tommy had made them aware of was the priest pouring the holy water on the woman's wound he had inflicted. It was insanity. Yet Leroux had been in awe. He had seen what was believed to be the Holy Grail, and it had changed him. But he had to know. Had it worked? Was she alive? Was she healed? Was it real?

The comms squawked overhead, and he adjusted his headset. He couldn't make out what was being said on the other end. "Zero-One, Control Actual. Do you read, over?"

It was still choppy, but he could make out the reply. "This is Zero-One, exiting now."

"Copy that. Did you get it? Did you retrieve the item?"

"Affirmative."

Smiles were exchanged between Leroux and Tong. They had the Grail. They had accomplished their mission. But what did it mean? Was it a good thing that the American government now controlled the power of God? He couldn't believe that it was. And should it be controlled? What if Sherrie's theory was right? What if they could cure all that ailed mankind? Should that be controlled? Did anyone have the right to possess that?

"Control Actual, be advised. It's a fake. It was never real."

Leroux's jaw dropped as he collapsed into his chair, the disappointment overwhelming him, and he battled the urge to cry. For a brief moment, he had believed. He had believed in everything—in God, in Jesus, in the afterlife, in miracles.

Yet it was all a lie. All a hoax.

But why?

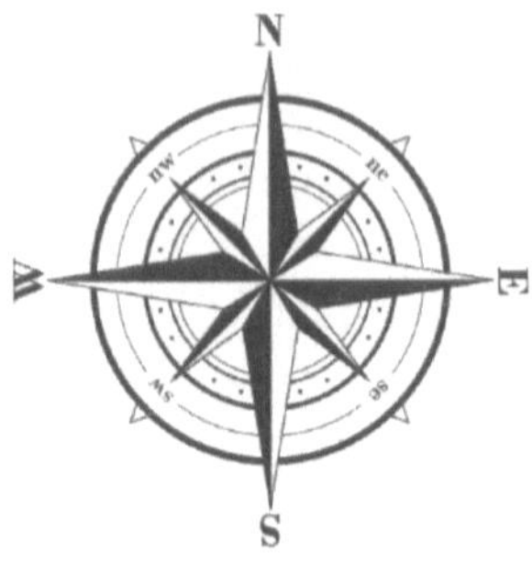

Mount Corcovado

Rio de Janeiro, Brazil

Acton cleared the entrance, finally outside once again. He gripped Laura's hand, and they both stopped in shock at the chaos surrounding them. Helicopters were everywhere, transport and attack, the disturbing sounds of strafing runs farther down the mountain shaking the ground. Who were they firing on? Were they warning shots, or were they killing those in the convoy? His understanding was that there were innocent people mixed in with the gang members.

How many more had to die because of a hoax?

A Brazilian soldier grabbed him by the arm. "Let's go! Let's go!" the soldier shouted, leading them toward a chopper nearby. Acton helped Laura in then climbed in himself. They strapped into the far corner as Bravo Team piled inside, along with Paulo and several others. The moment they were at capacity, they lifted off.

Choppers landed and took off around them as the mountaintop was evacuated. Acton stared out the window, tears flowing from the disappointment. It had all been a lie. He watched those who believed—desperate to believe—swarm the mountain. He wanted to tell them the truth, that it was all fake, all an elaborate hoax, but it was too late.

More would die, and there was nothing anyone could do about it.

It was over. The Grail was a fake, and he and the others had fallen victim to an elaborate hoax perpetrated over 170 years ago, for a reason he couldn't fathom.

And it shook his belief system to the core.

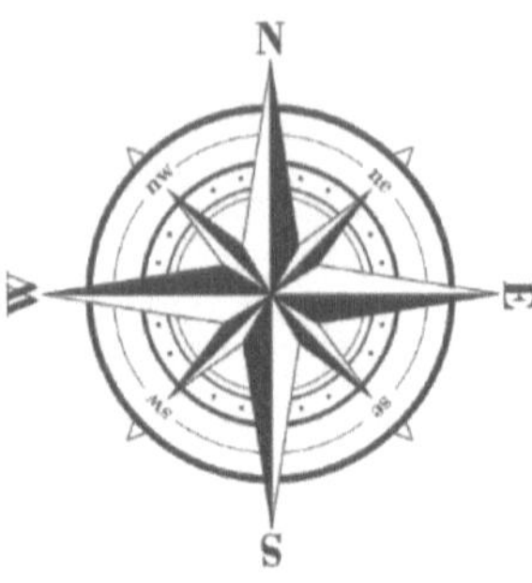

Acton/Palmer Residence, Overlook Village Gated Community

St. Paul, Maryland

Acton smiled at Reading, sitting in a chair designated as his in the family room of their new home. The man looked better—much better. The color had returned to his cheeks, and the doctors had said he should recover, though he would never be his former self. There was permanent damage, but he was out of immediate danger. He had been brought back here under medical supervision, a team here taking over his care, then eventually he would head back to the UK. Spencer had already returned to duty, the reunion touching.

Father Oliveira had disappeared without a trace, likely in hiding in his neighborhood, his parishioners protecting him from the authorities. The cup had disappeared in the confusion of the escape, but with it proven to be a fake, Washington and the Vatican were no longer concerned.

It was all a lie.

"I just don't understand why," his friend said. "It makes no sense to me. You saw that room. That was a hell of a lot of money, a hell of a lot of work."

"Not to mention the journals," said Tommy. "Those were all coded. And the older ones? They were in Latin and French."

"Yee olde-style French," added Acton. "Whoever came up with it must have had one hell of an imagination."

"And a whole lot of time on their hands," added Tommy.

Reading agreed. "And that's what doesn't make sense here. Hoaxes are meant to be discovered so that somebody gets tricked. But if you go to all this trouble, then hide it all away underground where nobody can find it, what's the point? Why do it?"

Acton leaned forward. "Maybe that *was* the point. Maybe he set up the hoax, buried himself alive, and then assumed he would watch from Heaven—"

"Or Hell," muttered Tommy.

"—and have a good laugh whenever it was discovered." Acton sighed. "I don't know." The whole thing was ridiculous. How many had died because of this? Scores. "If there is a Heaven, and whoever perpetrated this is there, I hope God reevaluates the man's status. This was evil." He cursed. "I just wish I didn't feel so stupid right now."

Laura patted his hand. "There's no reason to feel stupid. We were all tricked. We all fell for it. That may very well have been the most elaborate hoax in history."

Reading nodded in agreement. "I can't think of anything that comes close."

Tommy grinned. "The moon landing."

Acton groaned. "Please tell me you're not one of those idiots."

Tommy shrugged. "Hey, it had to be faked. Otherwise, the world can't be flat."

Acton gave the young man the bird, realizing he was being had. He rose, heading for the kitchen to grab himself another beer. He glanced over at the custom-built shelves lining the far wall. dozens of historical artifacts from their travels on prominent display, some more prominently than others. And he smiled at one, tucked at the back of the shelf, perhaps the most worthless and insignificant item they had ever collected.

A plain wooden cup that meant nothing to no one anymore.

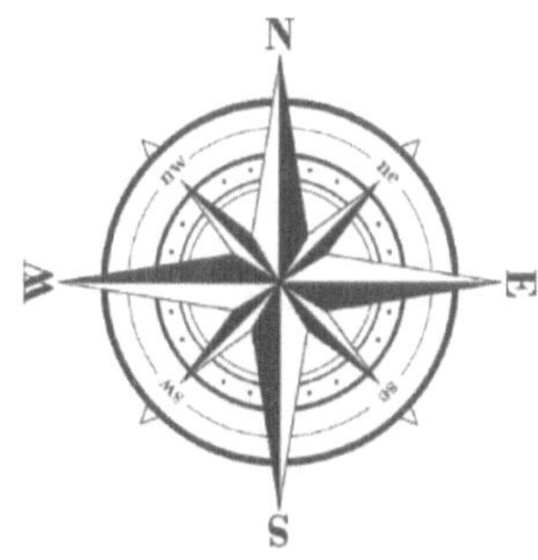

New York City, New York

AD 1832

He stood beside his son's hospital bed, clasping the young boy's hand. The prognosis was terminal, just as with the others. His had been a cursed life. Every child he had sired died before the age of five. This was his third and would be his last. His wife had died in a carriage accident two years ago, leaving him a widower, facing the loss of yet another child—all alone. He envied her, her suffering over, while his had been never-ending.

He had been so lonely, the last to survive. Everyone he had ever cared for was long dead. When the best friend he had ever known died in a cave-in, he had ventured out into society simply for the company. But he had foolishly fallen in love for the first time in his long life. They had been married, and she was aware of his secret. His terrible secret. Whether she believed it was another thing, for there was another terrible secret he had discovered long after the last of them had died.

The cup had no power.

His son's breathing became shallow, then there was a gasp followed by a long sigh. He had seen enough men die to know the last thing he held dear on this Earth was no more.

The nurse stepped forward, taking his son's hand then pressing her fingers against his wrist. She gently placed his arm back on the bedding and turned to him. "I'm so sorry for your loss, sir."

He bowed his head slightly. "Thank you." He drew a deep breath, holding it for a moment before exhaling loudly. "The arrangements have been made already. Someone will be here shortly to collect the body."

"Of course, sir."

He gazed one last time upon the innocent boy's face, so peaceful, no longer racked with agonizing pain. He leaned in and gave him a gentle kiss on the forehead. "Say hello to your mother and sisters, and to my brothers."

He left the room and returned to his far too empty home. He signed some paperwork, leaving it on his desk for his lawyer, said goodbye to his butler as if nothing were amiss, then headed downtown toward the oldest part of New York City. It had been well-established when he had finally ventured out to see what the world had become, and this plan was a long time in the making.

He entered what would now be considered a humble home. Arrangements had already been made with the lawyers to ensure any payments required for its maintenance would continue in perpetuity.

He took the stairs into the basement, then moved aside a cabinet, revealing a secret doorway carved into the stone. He pressed it in three different locations, and there was a click. He swung it aside, revealing a set of stone steps heading deeper underground. He closed the door behind him, the cabinet cleverly sliding back into place to hide the doorway, then descended the steps until he reached a heavy metal door.

He unlocked the several bolts with keys that had hung around his neck since the day this had been installed. And with the echo of the final lock clicking still in his ears, he hauled it open then stepped inside, immediately comforted by what he found—a haven from the modern age above, the insanity of the world created over so many years, a world alien to him, a world he had never felt comfortable in.

A world he was never meant to see.

He closed the door, locking it, then began undressing, donning his uniform one last time. Death was upon him. He could feel it, and prayed the good Lord would grant him one last favor and let him die quickly so he could rejoin his wife, his children, and his friends, to be by their sides for the rest of time.

Man was never meant to live beyond his rightful years, but they had a mission, and he had taken an oath to protect humanity from the powers of what society now called the Holy Grail. Yet, as he had discovered years ago, the cup was never the source of the power—though it certainly had contained it. His theory was that it was the blood of Christ that had the power, and when Jesus had declared the contents of the cup as such, it was only that contained within it that could heal. The cup, made of wood, meant this blessed fluid had permeated into the fibers, and with each use, some of what had been left behind was washed away and ingested by those who used it.

And now, after almost 2000 years of use, nothing was left behind. All that remained was a wooden cup. No matter how much he drank from it, it no longer preserved him. No matter how many times he had his lost children drink from it, it had no effect.

It was over.

It was finished.

The Holy Grail's miraculous powers were no more.

He adjusted his tunic, smoothing out the material before climbing into the stone sarcophagus he had commissioned years ago. He laid down and folded his hands across his chest, the cup gripped tightly in his hands, and closed his eyes, his sworn duty completed. He, along with his brothers, had protected mankind from the power the Holy Grail had once possessed.

And he died, satisfied he had fulfilled his sworn duty.

Lord, this is Sergeant Simon Chastain of the Templar Order. I'm ready for you now.

THE END

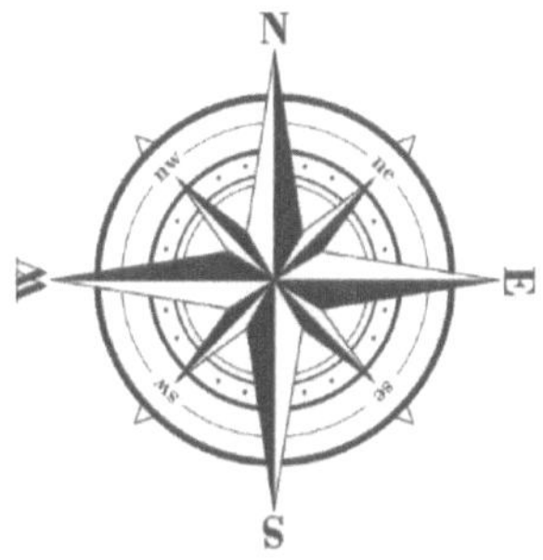

ACKNOWLEDGMENTS

This one was so much fun to write. I love the Templars, and if you've read The Templar Detective novels, you'll of course recognize these characters. I enjoyed giving them a fitting, honorable end. For fans of that series, don't worry, there are a lot of years between when that is set, and when the historical events of this book take place. Detective Shakespeare also shows up, which was fun as well.

I like to take things from my life and inject them into the books. I once again am facing heart failure, something I went through a decade ago and beat. I intend to beat it again, but for shits and giggles, I've chosen to torment poor Reading.

Beginning writers are told to 'write what you know.' This is often misinterpreted, in my opinion, as to write about being an office worker or a homemaker, because that's what you do. While you can do this, most people's lives are as boring as hell. But we've all been through things. We've all lost someone, we've all had tragedies, we've all suffered something. *That* is what I think is meant by 'write what you know.'

I've given characters diabetes, sleep apnea, heart conditions, and more. I take those things from my own life. I put characters through things that I've been through, not only because they're interesting and relatable, but sometimes because it's cathartic.

I remember writing a passage about Red in an ambulance, watching the world he knew through the rear window as he was raced to the hospital. That was me. I was in that ambulance, watching my parents and daughter, my neighbors, my world, disappear through this small window of life. It was heartbreaking, and something I will never forget.

And because I put it on paper, I can relive that whenever I want by simply reading that scene.

As writers, we are blessed to have this outlet to process our feelings, our travails. For those aspiring authors seeking something to write about, look outside your own life, and when you find something, inject your own life experience into the characters you create. They will be all the more compelling to those future readers.

As usual, there are people to thank. My dad for all the research, Brent Richards for some weapons info, and, as always, my late mother who will always be an angel on my shoulder as I write, as well as my family and friends for their continued support, and my fantastic proofreading team!

To those who have not already done so, please visit my website at www.jrobertkennedy.com, then sign up for the Insider's Club to be notified of new book releases. Your email address will never be shared or sold.

Thank you once again for reading.